I0522494

This was supposed to be an adventure, a lark—it wasn't supposed to be dangerous…

A round object entered the tent horizontally, two feet above the ground. Its head was three-quarters of a foot in diameter. It came right over them, followed by its body which was the same, round shape and did not seem to end. It was white with brown blotches.

It was a twenty-five-foot Albino Burmese Python Constrictor.

The monster stuck its long tongue out over the couple, sensing the warm food below. Its head came in several feet, then dropped down under the blissfully dreaming twosome in their double bag, encircling its meal. It began in its death squeeze, squeezing its prey so hard the prey could not breath, only to then swallow them whole.

After the beast went under their sleeping bag, it quickly wrapped itself around it. Its size and strength lifted the bag.

Faint Chance realized something was wrong and tried to jump out, but she could not. Her arms were trapped inside as the beast tightened its first loop and began a second. "*Cameron!*" she yelled.

Cameron opened his eyes abruptly. More of the body was coming in, making its second turn around the couple in the sleeping bag. If it did make a completed second circle around them, there would be no escape. More of its length was quickly coming in, and it continued to tighten its grip. In little time, it would squeeze the last breath of life out of both of them.

A plant exists that could change mankind's evolution, and the key to it resides with an exotic woman in Laos...

When Spenser and Candice Harrington, two research doctors, travel to Laos on a sabbatical, they meet a beautiful and exotic young woman, whom they nickname Faint Chance. They hire her to be their guide while in Laos and offer to sponsor her to come to America. Touched by their kindness and generosity, Faint Chance shares with them a secret—she has the leaves of a special flower that grows only on a cliff near her village in the northern mountains. She tells Spenser and Candice that, if they eat some of this plant before sex, they will create a very special baby. They take her pronouncement with a grain of salt, but they also take the plant and eat it, not wanting to hurt her feelings. Back home in America, Candice gives birth to Devan, who is born with extraordinary gifts. Now firm believers, Spenser and Candice send Spencer's brother, Cameron, to Laos to meet up with Faint Chance and get more of the plant so they research its properties and reproduce it in the lab.

Cameron, a confirmed bachelor, is soon traipsing through the mountain jungles of Laos with the beautiful Faint Chance, thinking his main concern will be not to fall head over heels in love with her while he's there. Little does he know that word of his mission has reached the powerful Japanese Mafia, who see the plant as a way to become immensely wealthy. After all, who wouldn't pay a fortune to guarantee having a gifted child? Soon, Cameron and Faith find themselves embroiled in a life-and-death struggle that will take all of their wit and cunning—and maybe even a little help from the spirits—if they are to have any chance of surviving.

KUDOS for *Mystical Laotian Flower*

In *Mystical Laotian Flower* by Brent Ayscough, Faint Chance is a beautiful Laotian woman, who was orphaned as a child in the jungles of Laos and adopted by the chief of a remote village. Being of mixed blood, half-German and half-Laotian, she is sent away by the chief with some missionaries who come to the village when she is seven. The chief feels that, because she is mixed blood, she needs to learn of her German father's culture and religion. She is taken by the missionaries to the capital city, where she is adopted by another family. But before the child leaves with the missionaries, the chief gives her a special gift. A sacred plant that, if taken under the right conditions, will give her and her future husband a special child, one with unique abilities. Faint Chance grows up in the city and there she works in her adopted father's jewelry store, where she meets two research doctors, Spencer and Candice Harrington. They become very fond of her, and when they offer to sponsor her for immigration to the US, she is touched by their kindness. She gives them some of her special plant, and later in the US, Candice gives birth to a special child, who is very advanced. Being a research doctor, Candice wants to research the plant and make it available to everyone. So she sends her brother-in-law, Cameron, to Laos to retrieve some of the plant. Cameron, an architect and confirmed bachelor, whose only danger in life has been the possibility of getting writer's cramp, soon discovers he is in over his head, both in escaping thugs, who are also after the plant, and falling for Faint Chance. His chances of getting home with his heart—not to mention his life? Faint. Ayscough's character development is excellent, and his scene descriptions vivid. The story is quite fast paced with plenty of action, romance, and suspense. Very well done. ~ *Taylor Jones, The Review Team of Taylor Jones & Regan Murphy*

Mystical Laotian Flower by Brent Ayscough is the story of a sacred plant that grows high in the northern mountains of Lao. This plant, if taken just prior to the conception of a child, with certain prayers, and with a black mushroom that only grows in northern Lao, will give the couple a child with special abilities, including long life and high intelligence, along with superior coordination and muscular development. Sangmouane Saya-sithsena is orphaned at the age of four when her German father and Laotian mother are killed in a car accident near a remote village in northern Lao. She is rescued from the accident scene and adopted by the village chief, a great shaman. But when she is seven, a missionary couple come to the village. The chief forbids the missionaries from preaching their religion in the village, but he does allow them to take the young girl with them to the capital city of Lao, because he believes that she does not really belong in the village. Before leaving, she receives a special gift from the chief, the leave of the sacred plant, and he tells her how to make the magic work. She grows up in the city with another adoptive family, and when grown, goes to work in her father's store, where she meets research doctors on sabbatical, Spencer and Candice Harrington. They develop a strong friendship, and she gives them the plant from the chief so they can make a special baby. When the baby arrives, he is indeed special, and his parents now want to research the plant. If they could reproduce it in pill form, they could patent it and make a fortune. So they send Spencer's broth-er, Cameron, and their Laotian friend, whom they have nickname Faint Chance since her real name is so hard to pronounce, on a mission to northern Lao to retrieve more of the plant for research. But unbeknownst to them, the Japanese Mafia has also learned of the plant and its special properties and have sent two thugs to northern Lao to intercept them. It will take all of their cunning and luck if Cameron and Faint Chance are going to even survive their adventure, let alone get back to the US with the plant. I have always enjoyed Ayscough's work, and this book does not disap-point. His characters are both endearing and realistic, his scene descriptions vivid and detailed, and his plots plausible, as well as fascinating. If you are looking for an adventure, you can't go wrong with *Mystical Laotian Flower*. ~ *Regan Murphy, The Review Team of Taylor Jones & Regan Murphy*

Mystical Laotian Flower

BRENT AYSCOUGH

A Black Opal Books Publication

GENRE: ROMANTIC THRILLER/ACTION-ADVENTURE

This is a work of fiction. Names, places, characters and incidents are either the product of the author's imagination or are used fictitiously, and any resemblance to any actual persons, living or dead, businesses, organizations, events or locales is entirely coincidental. All trademarks, service marks, registered trademarks, and registered service marks are the property of their respective owners and are used herein for identification purposes only. The publisher does not have any control over or assume any responsibility for author or third-party websites or their contents.

MYSTICAL LAOTIAN FLOWER
Copyright © 2018 by Brent Ayscough
Cover Design by Bill Oliver
All cover art copyright © 2018
All Rights Reserved
Print ISBN: 978-1-626948-85-3

First Publication: MARCH 2018

All rights reserved under the International and Pan-American Copyright Conventions. No part of this book may be reproduced or transmitted in any form or by any means, electronic or mechanical, including photocopying, recording, or by any information storage and retrieval system, without permission in writing from the publisher.

WARNING: The unauthorized reproduction or distribution of this copyrighted work is illegal. Criminal copyright infringement, including infringement without monetary gain, is investigated by the FBI and is punishable by up to 5 years in federal prison and a fine of $250,000. Anyone pirating our ebooks will be prosecuted to the fullest extent of the law and may be liable for each individual download resulting therefrom.

ABOUT THE PRINT VERSION: If you purchased a print version of this book without a cover, you should be aware that the book is stolen property. It was reported as "unsold and destroyed" to the publisher, and neither the author nor the publisher has received any payment for this "stripped book."

IF YOU FIND AN EBOOK OR PRINT VERSION OF THIS BOOK BEING SOLD OR SHARED ILLEGALLY, PLEASE REPORT IT TO:
lpn@blackopalbooks.com

Published by Black Opal Books **http://www.blackopalbooks.com**

Mystical Laotian Flower

Chapter 1

The beige Land Rover bounced up and down and from side to side on the narrow, Laotian mountain path. The riders were jostled about as it bounced over the bumps and holes in the desolate road, the condition of which was so poor that their speed had to be often slowed to no more than that of a brisk walk. Huge, tropical green foliage smacked the sides of the vehicle, as nothing wider then an occasional elephant traveled through the vegetation. Occasionally, the vegetation smacked the passengers in the vehicle, bending around the windscreen posts.

A square-faced, healthy-looking German of thirty-five maneuvered the vehicle over the challenging path. In the back was equipment used to prospect for gemstones. Although tied down, the equipment still bounced about, much to the concern of the driver, who was in Laos working for a German company trying to find and develop new areas to mine for native gemstones in the northern mountains where few from the West had been. The area was only recently opened by the government, as it had never been entirely cleared from unexploded bombs that America rained by the thousands during the war and especially on the Ho Chi Min trail. There were still reports of people being blown to bits from inadvertently stumbling onto an unexploded bomb.

Sitting beside Falk was his Laotian wife, a striking

young woman of twenty-four with coal-black hair. On her lap was their daughter, Sangmouane, named after her, a stunning girl of four. Apart from the coal-black hair of her mother, the young girl did not resemble either of her parents with her mixed blood, especially with her striking, emerald green eyes.

Appearing in front of them was a working elephant traveling the same direction with a young Laotian man sitting atop his neck, guiding him with the assistance of a stick. There was no way to go around the elephant, as the foliage was much too dense for the elephant to move enough to one side to allow the Land Rover to pass. Although the Land Rover was moving slowly, the elephant was still slower, and Falk let it be known that he wanted to pass by driving up close to the elephant.

Beep-beep! The German tooted his horn. The young man looked around slowly at the Land Rover and then just turned his head back toward his direction of travel, as there was nothing he could do to allow the vehicle to pass.

The monsoon winds quickly rolled in dark, heavy clouds and, with them, a deluge of rain. The couple did not mind the cooling effect, and they did not stop to erect the canvas top. Their soaked clothes provided refreshing relief from the steamy day.

Finally, the path widened such that Falk could pass. Falk hit the horn again, and the young man steered his elephant to one side of the path without slowing his pace.

Falk seized the opportunity, gunned his motor, and zipped around the big creature, brushing its tail as he did, rubbing the foliage hard on one side. Restrained and frustrated by the slow pace of the elephant, he sped up, faster than he should, given the fact that he was completely unfamiliar with the area.

The rain made the sandy path slicker than it was, and the front wheels of the Land Rover slid around the tight curves as Falk maneuvered.

He was not sure exactly where he was, and only had an

idea of where he was going from an earlier look at a map.

The direction ahead obscured by green foliage, Falk realized he had made a mistake when he came upon a tight turn to the left. He was going too fast. He hit the brakes and turned the wheel smartly to the left.

The Land Rover's front wheels locked in the left turning position, and even though he was going slow, his speed was still too much. The front tires and front end slid over the sharp cliff straight ahead that went down a gorge eight hundred feet to a river below. The rear end of the vehicle went over the cliff in a somersault motion. The Land Rover began its long fall to the bottom of the gorge, the adult passengers helplessly en route to their demise.

But the force of the Land Rover somersaulting over the cliff threw young Sangmouane out of the arms of her mother in the passenger seat, and she landed miraculously in some brush that grew out of the side of the cliff, down from its crest some twenty-five feet from the top. The brush contained unusual purple flowers with bright orange centers.

The brush caught the clothes of the light Sangmouane, stopping her fall. She could go nowhere, helplessly lying there, as her parents continued their fall. The last sound she would hear of her parents was the noise of the Land Rover hitting the bottom of the gorge, crushing itself and everything, and everyone, in it.

ᜒᜄᜒᜄ

Two days later, a native tribal man, dressed in his traditional village outfit, out on a hunt from his village with his teenage son, came to the same cliff and stopped to look down at the frightening sight of the gorge below. The son resembled his father closely. Unlike the locals, they were fair complected with light hair.

Standing at the edge of the eight-hundred-foot gorge, he

instructed his son, "This is where the very special plant grows, the *ton mai piiset*." He pointed down to a colorful plant twenty-five feet below the crest growing out of the vertical side of the cliff.

As they looked on, a huge black bird with red tips on its wings flew menacingly out in front of them a hundred yards away in the middle of the gorge, watching the two. The bird's nest was apparently not far off and, and, although threatened by the humans' presence, it showed no fear.

"I see it, Father!" the young man nearly shouted, pointing toward the brush that also contained the bright purple and orange plant they were looking at growing out of the side of the cliff twenty-five feet below.

"This is the only place left where it grows, in the soils from ages past," the man said to his son. "You must come here to get the *ton mai piiset* for your wedding."

"What's that in the brush?" the son asked, pointing to the cluster of colorful plants where they were looking. Something in light-colored fabric was caught up in the bushes. "It moves!" the young man said excitedly.

"I think it's a child!" the father said. "I'll go down the path to see."

The father went to one side some distance away, where a very narrow, perilous, pathway came up to the cliff's edge. From there it was possible to sidestep down to the area where there was a young child stuck in the brush. All the while the huge bird circled around over the gorge, looking on the child in the brush as a source of food—and possibly the adults as well.

Chapter 2

Three years later, a commotion was heard at the outskirts of the remote, highland village where the chief and his son were from. A white couple in their late fifties had found the village and were walking into it by the pathway through the dense jungle. They had on the European backpacks with aluminum frames, filled with camping equipment and provisions. And Bibles.

A village woman carrying freshly picked vegetables in a hand-woven basket saw them coming and hurried on ahead into the village center to alert the chief. As the couple approached, children playing ran to hide.

The couple could then see the village with its wooden houses and thatched roofs situated on small, rolling hills, elevated several feet on stilts of teak wood.

The white man said to his wife, in Dutch, "Dear, I think we have found a village not on our map."

She looked around with fear. "Do you think they'll harm us?"

"Our fate is in the hands of the Lord," he answered.

Two village hunters formed ahead, and it was clear to the couple that they were reaching a sort of check point. One had a bow and a quiver of arrows, the other a hand crafted machete, and they looked very capable.

The white man smiled and spoke in Laotian. "We're

missionaries and would like to meet with your chief."

There was no response, and the white woman said, "Dear, I don't think they speak Laotian, or perhaps very little of it. No doubt there is some very local dialect. They probably don't understand the term missionaries."

The white man smiled. "We're friends."

There was no response. Then one of them motioned for the couple to follow and went ahead. The other, the one with the machete, fell in behind, keeping a constant vigil.

The couple was led to the house of the chief. Like all the houses, it was raised up on teak stilts about three feet off the irregular ground. The hunter with the bow and arrows went inside to announce the arrival. He came back out and motioned them inside. The two hunters escorted the couple inside and stood behind them as guards to protect their chief. Inside was the chief, sitting on a section of the floor against one side elevated about a foot and a half. He looked quite different from the villagers. He was tall, fair-skinned, with blond hair turning to gray, and blue eyes. He motioned them to sit on a hand-woven mat in front of him on the lower part of the floor. This put him in a position of authority.

Light came through the doorway, two small windows, from small cracks in between the horizontal boards of the walls, and from a few knotholes. There was no glass to be found.

Hoping to communicate, the white man said in Laotian, "Do you speak Laotian?"

The chief said, "Yes."

"Oh, wonderful!" The white man exhaled in relief, turned to his wife, and smiled that he would be able to communicate.

"We are Mr. and Mrs. Oosterlink. We're missionaries from Holland, but we have been living at a Christian mission in Vientiane. We've been backpacking for four days since the last village. We are very pleased to meet you, and may God bless you."

"You have come a long way," the chief told them. "Why have you come? Did you know of my tribe?"

"No, not specifically," Mr. Oosterlink answered. "Your tribe does not appear on our map. We knew only that there were a number of remote tribes in these northern Laotian mountains. Yours is the sort of tribe that we came to encounter that has not had the blessing of coming into contact with the holy scriptures. We have had a very hard journey through these mountains, but it is worth it to bring the word of God as His missionaries to whoever we can find that has not yet been enlightened. We hope you will receive us."

The chief made his decision without hesitation. "I'll not have you spreading your religion or any religion here. There were other missionaries here before, years ago, also from Europe. My tribe will do quite well as is, without importing the miseries and wars of the rest of the world."

"Please allow us to bring His words to those who wish to hear," Mrs. Oosterlink pleaded.

"No, you may not. You must leave. My tribe is quite happy without the religions of other places. We have a simple life here, without the evils of your world. You must leave without attempting to spread your religion. I'll provide you with food and water for your journey out. You may rest, and then you will leave the day after tomorrow."

The missionaries' attention turned to a girl of seven years of age as she wandered into the chief's house. She was so beautiful and graceful that the missionaries could not take their eyes off of her as she approached the chief. She gave a big smile and came next to him, her emerald-green eyes very distinctive.

"Who is this charming girl with such beautiful green eyes?" Mrs. Oosterlink asked the chief. "She does not look like the other children."

"This is my adopted daughter. She was left orphaned when I found her. I was on a hunt with my son some distance from here. I believe she was in a vehicle with her parents that went over the largest cliff in the area and killed them. She was caught in brush growing on the side of the cliff, which kept her from falling to her death. She was near death when I found her and brought her here to the village. That was three years ago."

"What's her name?" Mrs. Oosterlink asked the Chief.

"Sangmouane Sayasithsena."

"What a beautiful child!" Mrs. Oosterlink exclaimed. "Were her parents foreign?"

"The father was a white man, her mother Laotian. Sangmouane remembers that her parents looked for precious stones. She speaks Laotian, our village language, and also some European words. I have given her mother's first and last names rather than her father's so that she would have a Laotian name and not seem strange to the other children. She has learned the village dialect quite well."

"Do you plan to keep her here in the village?" Mrs. Oosterlink asked.

Summarily prohibiting religion was easy for the wise chief, but the future of the young girl was another matter, and his expression changed to one of concern. "I have thought about this often as I have watched her grow. She had western ways in her by the time she came here. I think she hungers for a western education and the things that you have in the cities where she came from. I think it would be better for her to go to the city and get a city education."

"Do you plan to take her to a place where she can get such an education?" Mr. Oosterlink asked then, looking at the beautiful young Sangmouane.

"There is nowhere to take her nearby. There may be some place in the capital city of Vientiane, but I have not been there myself. It would be a long journey. I have no way to take her there, and no one there to take her to."

An idea raced through Mrs. Oosterlink's head, and she laid the groundwork. "We come from a Christian mission in Vientiane. There we learned Laotian. My husband and I decided that to do His work, we needed to go out and reach the needy. We'll go back to the mission when we do our best to bring Christianity to those who have not been touched by His miracles on our journey outside Vientiane." She closed her eyes with a soft "Amen," and her husband echoed it.

She continued. "We can hire transportation after we get to the next village about four days hiking from here. We would be pleased to take this young child to the mission when we leave if you will allow it. The mission sometimes takes in orphans and finds homes for them, and they will do it for us. Would you let us take her there? I can assure you that she will be cared for, and we can do our best to find her a nice home in the city with a good family."

Mrs. Oosterlink turned to her husband and said in Dutch, "Oh, dear, do you think that God led us here to find this young lost soul?"

"It may very well be His will," Mr. Oosterlink said. "It could be that God sent us here for just this purpose, to save this young soul. Even if we save one soul, our work will be worth all effort."

Mrs. Oosterlink raised her hands in prayer and closed her eyes. Mr. Oosterlink joined. "Amen" ended the prayer.

"We will do this, as we believe that we have been instructed to do this as His will." Mr. Oosterlink then worried that he must reveal his intentions in order to be honest before God. "But we would be obliged to attempt to teach her of God and His miracles, as it is our mission in life to do so. May we do that?"

"She has some knowledge of your Christian religion from her European father," the chief said, "so it will not be new to her. I suppose she could do worse, as she has visions of things of her past that give her ideas that she belongs in the city and not here. I will speak with her."

He thought for a while and then decided. "You may take her with you to Vientiane to the mission. But I must first spend time with her. You may go with her the day after tomorrow when you leave. There are some things that she and I must say to each other before she goes. I've loved her as though she was my own."

"Of course," Mrs. Oosterlink said. "She's such a lovely child, and so in need of His words. I know now why God led us to this village. It was to save the soul of this poor child who lost her parents and to return her to Christianity. Praise the Lord."

☙❧

In the late afternoon, atop a hillside overlooking a field of village crops below, the chief and Sangmouane sat alone. He said, "I believe it best for you to return to the outside, and so you will leave with the missionaries tomorrow. They'll take you back to your own people. You will go to school and learn all about the Western people like your natural father. You will learn of their sciences and developments that we do not have here."

Sangmouane had suspected something was wrong when her father brought her there with the strangers still in the village. She burst into tears from her emerald-green eyes.

"It's best. You can return one day when you are older. You'll go to city schools and learn so much."

With her little arms, she reached out to hold on desperately to her father, as the tears flowed from her cheeks. She clung to him as he sat her on his lap.

"Now stop crying, and let me give you something very, very special."

The chief took out a small bag from his satchel. Out came crushed purple and orange colored leaves as he poured the contents onto a piece of cloth.

"This is called *ton mai piiset*."

Sangmouane tried her best to listen past the overbearing sadness of the moment.

"Unlike many people in the place that you will be going, we believe that spirits live in plants and certain things. *Ton mai piiset* has very special spirits that live in it or that are contacted by it which have great powers. When taken at the wedding time with the proper prayers, the spirits can be asked to give your child special abilities that one day will allow him to lead others. It's a very rare plant, and only grows in a very special place in soils of ancient times. It does not grow in new soils. The soils above where it is found have many years of other soils on top, as it is found on a cliffside. It only grows where I found you, and I believe that your karma is tied to it, although I'm not exactly sure how or why. My parents took the plant when they married, and that is why I was able to be the one who speaks to the spirits, as *Great Maw Pii*. I took it with my wife when we were married, and our son was born with those special abilities that will make him a powerful chief one day. Now you can be the next one to have a child with special abilities.

"I love you as my own daughter. I do not want to let you go, but I believe it to be best for you. You are not well suited for the simple life here in the village. In the city, you will get a formal education and also get things that I do not have to give to you. So, it's best."

Tears streamed down Sangmouane's cheeks. "No! I don't want to go!" She clung on to him as though it would keep her there.

"My darling Sangmouane, you can stay here and have little. Or, if you go, you will learn about the world and find an educated husband. I want to keep you, but you are not best suited to be a village girl. And, you can come back one day to visit when you have grown."

Losing Sangmouane brought tears to his own eyes. "Now that you are leaving, I'll not be able to teach you further."

He held her for a time and then said, "This *ton mai piiset* is something I can give you that you cannot get elsewhere, and I want you to have it as my special present. This is the most valuable thing that I have to give." He then put the strangely colored leaves back into the bag and gave it to her.

"Now you must listen carefully and remember what I'm going to teach you. You will marry. Beginning on your wedding night, you and your husband are to take some of these leaves that night. On that night, you must also take some of the black mushroom growing only in the north of Lao. The mushroom will not last like the leaves, and so you must obtain one for the ceremony. If you cannot get one of the black mushrooms when you marry, then take with it northern *Lao-Lao,* as the black mushroom is used in the making of *Lao-Lao* here in the north of Lao. It must be *Lao-Lao* from the north, not from the south.

You must also learn two special prayers that I'm now going to teach you. One summons the spirits, and the other asks for the powers to be given your child. When you do this, the spirits that live in the *ton mai piiset* will be summoned and give your child the special powers. Do you understand?"

"Yes, Father."

"Now I'll teach you the prayers." He took out some white strings spun by hand from his satchel. "First put *baci* strings on your wrists and on your husband." He tied one to each wrist. "You must pray these prayers." He held his hands together in a prayer position and then chanted the first prayer for her.

"That is the prayer to summon the spirits," he told her. "Now, you."

She performed the prayer as he taught her.

"That's correct. You must repeat it for both you and your husband a number of times. Then you must pray this next prayer." He chanted a different prayer for her. "Now, you do it."

Sangmouane chanted the second prayer.

"That's right. You must also repeat this prayer in the ceremony a number of times. Now do both," he told her.

Sangmouane performed them again, chanting the prayers as he taught her.

"Again."

She performed them correctly again, and he smiled in satisfaction. She looked at him through her tear-soaked eyes, knowing that she had done it well and that the occasion was a parting event between them.

He interrupted her thoughts. "You may only take the *baci* strings off three days after the wedding, or longer, and then you must not cut them—you must only untie them."

"I love you, Father."

"I shall always remember my daughter Sangmouane."

As the sun set over the field of crops, the two embraced the moment and each other.

Chapter 3

Fifteen years later in America:

Cameron, why don't you find yourself a nice woman, settle down, and have a nice family? I know someone you might like," asked Sharon, the busybody secretary of the architectural firm they worked for.

Cameron sat at his drafting bench, working on plans for a small shopping center, trying to ignore the question as though he had not heard, hoping he would not get snagged up in her busybody topic.

She refused to accept non-compliance to her magnanimous offer to set him up with who she assumed was a perfect catch, that being her girlfriend, and continued, "I've been married now for six wonderful years and have two wonderful children. You are the only bachelor in the office. I know you'd be much happier once you start a family. Why don't you let me fix you up with my friend Liz?"

Cameron could not successfully ignore her further. "The idea of getting married doesn't scare me, but the thought of children does. These days the women want to work and still have their own career, so both the father and the mother are always running around to daycare centers, making arrangements for the kids to be here or there, at the doctor, at a friend's house, the movies, soccer practice, and doing this or that—your whole life becomes one for the children. And that lasts until they go away to college at eighteen. And, nowadays, they move back in after college rather than pay rent for their own place. If you're lucky, they'll leave home at sixty!"

Sharon laughed.

"Look at what you have to do," Cameron continued. "If you don't pick your kids up from the day care center by five-thirty, you're fined. On the third occasion, if you are ten minutes late, the kids are expelled from the center. How could I stay late and do my architectural work under threats like that? Last night, I was here until nine. How could I ever be a success with an overriding commitment like that?"

Sharon could not argue with those facts but tried to ignore them. "Oh, you don't really mean that. I know you. You love kids just as much as anyone. You just say that."

"Dream on! I'm not going to spend my life chasing around after kids."

The owner of the architectural firm walked into the work area, unknowingly providing rescue. "Cameron, can you come to my office for a minute on some changes to the center that the owners want?"

"Sure," Cameron said, relieved to be out of the interrogation. "Well, back to the grind."

♋♋

"Candice and I will be taking a year-long sabbatical, and leaving in two months," Spencer said to his brother Cameron at dinner. "We're making preparations now and have cleared everything with our employers at the institution. We still have a great deal to do, from handling mail to paying utilities here. We are going off to India first, and then elsewhere in Asia, and do not anticipate returning for an entire year. We have told the attorney to make up wills for us in case anything happens, and we've made you executor."

"An entire year!" Cameron said. "Good Lord! How does one do that? I couldn't even consider it!"

Of the two siblings in the Harrington family, Spencer was the oldest and a research doctor, and Cameron, the younger, an architect. Spencer had married but had no children yet. Cameron had not married. Candice, Spencer's wife, was also a research doctor. They both worked at the same research hospital, but in different wings. There were no children yet to carry on the name of Harrington.

"I'm ready for a sabbatical,' Spencer said.

"Me too," Candice joined in.

Cameron directed his words to his brother, initially. "But you have become such a name in the field of research medicine for lowering cholesterol. You're invited to go all over the world to give lectures to doctors who need continuing education credits to keep up their licenses. And you, Candice—" He looked at her "—your research in genetics…how can either of you possibly go away for a year? And, you have traveled so much already!"

Spencer shrugged. "When I go to give a lecture, I spend a day going, a day coming back, and usually two days there at most. On occasion, I only spend one day. I only get to see the inside of the hotel and the meeting hall where I give the lecture. I'm always taken to a dandy dinner somewhere, but as the captive of a few of the local doctors, I rarely get to do anything else.

"When I'm in the city of the lecture, usually several of the doctors and their wives have a dinner planned for me, or for both of us if Candice goes along. Their conversations are all the same—hospital cut backs, government cut backs, the horrors of Obamacare, cutting back on their ability to earn as much as they used to, ungrateful patients, avoiding malpractice claims, the horrors of continually increasing socialization of medicine, being on call and having to stay nearby the hospital on weekends, how the government makes them be on call for indigents who are many more times likely to sue for malpractice, problems with the raising of their children, how expensive it is to provide higher education for their kids, and so on. Boring."

Candice smiled. "I'm almost always invited to go with him on a free ticket. But I don't get the invitations for lectures like Spencer, as genetics is not the rage like cholesterol. But, I must say, we do get first -class tickets when we're invited. When doctors request another doctor to come and lecture, they never question expenses. For a doctor to question the travel expenses of another would be sacrilegious."

"Aren't you going to miss all that?" Cameron said.

"Well, it was fun for a while," Spencer said. "We got to visit a good number of places. But now it seems more like work. I'm bored with it all. I want to go off and meet people who are not doctors. Candice loves her photography. We want to go into India first, and wander off into places that are not just first-class hotels and tourists spots. We want adventure and to experience something new and different. In Asia, we were only invited for lectures in Sydney, Singapore, and Tokyo. We did go once on a tour organized by a medical organization that we paid for into China, which took us to Hong Kong, Beijing, Macau, and Shanghai. That's the extent of our Asian experience so far. Also," he continued, "I want to go all around India. I hear it gives you a different perspective on life."

"Let me show you how exciting India looks." Candice left the dinner table and went to the bookcase for a picture book. "Here."

Cameron flipped through the pictures. The architecture caught him up. "This is amazing architecture! I'd love to go there for architectural inspiration myself, if there is much of this sort of thing. I might benefit from a trip like this."

"You ought to consider it too," Candice said. "Before long, we'll be old. These containers, our bodies, are frail containers once you're in your forties. Just as a person gets to the age of some value in his calling, he finds out how vulnerable his body is. Cancer is the biggie. But there are heart attacks, diabetes, gout, osteoarthritis, diverticulitis, swollen prostrate, high blood pressure, dementia, and a long list of other maladies that can and will afflict us."

"My God!" Cameron exclaimed. "You make me feel like I have only moments left." He pondered his age and life for a few moments at her comment. Then he came back to the moment. "But isn't going away for a year going to put a pretty big financial dent in things?"

"What better way to invest than in experiencing what to see of the world?" Spencer responded profoundly. "We would much rather do this than to just go buy some eighty grand status car to run around in to impress other doctors."

"Well, you make a good point. And you, Candice, usually make a wonderful meal!"

"Thank you, my sweet brother-in-law. And speaking of cooking, in addition to my photography, I hope to learn real recipes of Asia. There are so many spices and wonders I'll never possibly learn unless I go there. I really have to go."

Spencer looked at his brother. "Now that dad has died, and we have some extra money from the inheritance, the finances will be okay. And, we still have no children, so this is the absolute best time for us. We'll never get to do it once we have a child."

Cameron looked at Spencer. "What'll happen to your research when you're gone for a whole year? Aren't you the guru of lowering cholesterol? The world level of cholesterol may rise without you."

Spencer smiled. "There are plenty of things set in motion to more than occupy a year without me."

"Well, the trip sounds like high adventure!" Cameron said. "I'll help hold down the fort here while you two are gone by looking after the house."

"My genetics research can wait," Candice added. "Humans are millions of years old. Our travels away from the lab won't make a big dent in mankind."

She would later learn that would not be the case.

Chapter 4

There it is!" Spencer shouted and grinned at Candice as they walked through the entry courtyard to the arched opening where tourists got their first glimpse. It stood one hundred yards away from where it was first viewable, the afternoon sun illuminating it with a yellow glow on its magnificent structure. The white marble with its inlaid semiprecious stones glowed in the radiance of the sun's rays. A reflection of it in the water pond in front of it projected a second image of the world's most famous architecture.

"The Taj Mahal! It's even more beautiful than I ever imagined!" But Candice was already getting her camera warmed up with settings and walking forward through the arched opening that separated the entry courtyard from the magnificent structure. She was overwhelmed and began taking pictures from different angles.

Spencer followed her, reading aloud from a small book on the Taj Mahal he bought at the airport in New Delhi. "'It was built as a mausoleum by Shah Jahan in memory of his favorite wife, Mumtaz Mahal. It is entirely inlaid with semiprecious stones. It took seventeen years to build.' Mumtaz must have been some kinda' honey! I wonder what she did so well."

"I'm so glad we came!" Candice said, ignoring his

comment in the presence of the structure before her. "This is truly the most magnificent structure in the world. I wish Cameron, the consummate architect, was here. Can we spend an extra day here in Agra so I can photograph it in the morning light?"

"Why not?" Spencer said. "Maybe we can find out more about this super woman."

"You're hopeless."

୧୬୧୬

Three months later, at a café in Kerala, South India, Spencer and Candice sat outside at a table sipping Indian beer—the only alcoholic beverage the Indians made that was drinkable—people-watching those going by. The day had been hot, and they were recovering from another sight-seeing excursion earlier in the day.

Sitting nearby at another table, also sipping beer, was a light-completed, blond-haired, tall, slender young man in his early twenties. In front of him was a bottle of large-sized Kingfisher beer, the Indian brand. He had the backpacking, rustic look of a traveling college student.

Catching them looking at him, he asked, "Hi. Where are you from?"

Spencer answered, "America. You?"

"Germany." But that was obvious from his accent, as their accent must have been obvious to him. "Have you been in many places in India?"

"Yes," Candice answered. "We've covered a great deal of India. We stayed on a houseboat in Srinagar, Kashmir, for five days and went around the area. From there, we went by car up to Gulmarg and skied the Himalayas. We traveled by steam engine through Rajasthan out to Jaisalmer to see the old trade routes. There we rode on camels and saw the architecture of the past. The same train took us to Agra, where we saw the Taj Mahal. We have also been to the erotic temples of Khajuraho. Oh, yes, not to forget the castles in Aurangabad. We then moved off the main routes and went into the countryside and traveled through many small villages. We went mostly by car, with a driver and guide. We have seen many things, and it has all been fantastic."

"*Das is gut.* How long are you traveling?"

"We are taking a year-long sabbatical. We are both research doctors. How about you?"

"I'm still in school. I am alzo taking off a year to do the travel, *mit freundin.* Are you going elsewhere besides India?"

"We're open to go anywhere," Spencer said. "We've been here nearly six months now. We've just come back from travel into some of the small villages in the central region and here in the southern parts. The poverty gives you a different perspective on life. But the Indian people are wonderful."

"Ya, ze people are *wunderbar.* Where do you go next?"

"We haven't decided. What do you recommend?"

"You should go into Lao."

"Is that the same as Laos?" Spencer asked, not understanding the omission of the "s."

"Ya."

"Tell us about it," Spencer said.

"My girlfriend, who is at za hotel taking a nap just now, and I too are backpacking, und zleeping out often. Lao is more like a frontier than India. Traveling in Lao gives you za feeling dat you are going back in time."

"How long were you there?" Candice asked.

"Two months. We only took a hotel once in a while. The hotels are very cheap, but we are traveling on a student budget." He tilted up the glass, and his beer was emptied.

"Let us buy you a beer while you tell us about it," Spencer offered.

"Ya, sure."

Spencer hailed the waiter and ordered a large beer for

the traveling student, and one for Spencer and Candice to share.

The cold Kingfisher beer arrived. The heavy, cold beer was perfect for the hot, southern Indian sun.

"Very cooling," Candice mused as she drank down the nice, heavy Indian beer, utilizing the Indian expressions of 'cooling' and 'heaty.' "The Indian-made liquor is undrinkable, but their beer is good. What is so interesting about Lao?" she asked the student, as she sipped the cold beer, it making her more talkative.

"Well, there are some interesting remote villages, especially in za highlands. Like centuries past. There is no electricity, no mail, und no contact with the outside. Alzo, you can take a boat trip down za Mekong River, from Ban Houei Sai to Pak Ban und zen to Luang Prabang. If you go be sure und take za boat."

"How does it compare to India?" Spencer asked.

"India is much larger, *und* with many more times za population. Seven million compared to one point three billion. Za population is much denser in India. Crowded is za word. Alzo, Lao does not have beggars like India. Und, there are not zo many tourists. It's much more remote."

"What about photo opportunities?" Candice asked, always involved with her passion for photography.

"There is zo much in India to photograph as it is zo much larger, but Lao is quite a gut photo opportunity. I brought a camera myself. Things are very cheap in Lao, und ze people are very nice. I got gut pictures in both places."

"Maybe we'll do Laos," Spencer said, looking at Candice. "We have pretty much done India."

"You will enjoy," the German said. "*Meine freundin* und I going next to China, und later home. We are traveling as long as our money holds out. We camp outside most of the time."

"That's too adventurous for us," Spencer said. "We stay in hotels."

"But you are working, ya, und we are only students."

"You are more adventurous than we are," Spencer responded. "We envy your adventurous spirit."

Candice nodded in approval, and they toasted the German, who had absolutely no trouble finding an excuse to take another gulp of the good beer. "Well, it has been nice talking to you, but I must get back. It is only now und den dat we have a hotel, und I want to make use of it. Thank you for ze beer."

"Thanks for the information," Spencer told him.

"*Auf Wiedersehen.*"

"Good bye and good luck in your adventure!" Spencer said, and the German was off.

Spencer shook his head. "God, can you imagine back packing in places like this? I thought we were adventurous."

"We are just too old and too used to our luxuries and security, luv," she told him affectionately.

What do you think, luv?" Spencer said, looking at her. "Laos next stop?"

"Let's check into it," she said. "The idea of going to a frontier makes it alluring."

"Besides, I have acquired a beef deficiency here in India," Spencer said.

❧❦❧

Spencer and Candice entered their room in New Delhi. Spencer put down his parcels and looked at the visas for Laos that they had just obtained. They had also been given a packet of advisories to review.

"Boy, getting these visas to go to Lao has been a chore," Spencer said. "Without help from the US Embassy, I don't think we could have gotten them."

"At least I collected a couple of neat cookbooks on curries while we have been waiting this week," Candice said as she organized them on the hotel room table. "I'll send them home rather than lug them around."

"You should see some of these advisories that they gave us at the US Embassy on travel in Laos," Spencer said. "Here, just listen to this." He began to read. "'The Lao People's Democratic Republic, known as Lao PDR, is a landlocked country between Thailand and Vietnam. To the south is Cambodia, and to the north a border with China. Seventy percent of the territory was mountain ranges, highlands, and plateaus. The Mekong River forms a large part of the border with Thailand.

"'Its population is seven million. It has four broad ethno-linguistic families, with Lao-Tai at sixty-seven per cent, followed by Mon-Khmer, Hmong-Lu, Chine-Tibetan, and then forty-nine distinct ethnicities and too hundred ethnic subgroups. It is one of the poorest countries in Southeast Asia. There are only two doctors for every ten thousand people.'"

Spencer then looked up. "Wow! Two doctors for ten thousand. Maybe we should practice medicine in Lao. We would have a near monopoly." His expression changed to one of concern. "Oh, oh. There are medical advisories provided," Spencer continued, flipping through several pages. He read and condensed parts to her. "'Internal parasites, such as worms and unicellular organisms, can enter the body by penetrating unbroken skin, but most are ingested when eating fecal contaminated or undercooked food. Parasites eaten in egg form hatch out and become viable for years. Since not all of the parasites are detected reliably with single stool tests, it is suggested that you undergo de-worming twice a year.'"

"De-worming?" Candice repeated. "How you do that?"

"There's more." Spencer read on. "There is a whole section just on malaria. 'Of the four species of malaria, a unicellular parasite transmitted by the Anopheles mosquito, plasmodium vivax, malaria, and falciparum malaria, which can be fatal within a few days. The malaria mosquito bites mainly during nighttime, starting in the early evening up to the early morning. One can recognize the Anopheles mosquito in its sitting position: its abdomen is tilted upward and its head is bent downward to the surface it is sitting on. The best way to prevent getting malaria is to avoid being bitten,'" he read, skipping about in the materials.

"Hah! Can you imagine being so close to one that you can see how it tilts its head? And avoid being bitten," Candice said. "That's funny."

"It actually tells you." Spencer read on. "'Wear long trousers and sleeves if outside at night; apply repellent; avoid wearing dark clothes and perfume because they attract mosquitoes; use a sleeping net; screen the windows; and bring your children in before dark."

"Hah." Candice said. "Bring your children in before dark. That's rich."

"Suggested treatment for falciparum malaria is quinine six-hundred milligrams every eight hours and Doxycycline two-hundred-fifty milligrams every six hours,'" Spencer continued. "'For vivax malaria, chloroquine tablets, four every eight hours starting dose.'"

"Sounds wonderful!" Candice said. "Can there possibly be something else to watch out for?"

"'Dengue fever, a viral disease transmitted by an Aedes mosquito which bites in the morning. So far there is no treatment for dengue fever because it is a viral disease. Symptomatic treatment is bed rest, two Tylenol every four hours, and three liters of electrolyte fluids daily with bananas, rice, salt, or potato for better absorption. Do not take aspirin, as it increases the risk of hemorrhaging.'"

"Charming," Candice said.

"There's more," Spencer said. "'Japanese encephalitis, a mosquito-borne viral disease by a night-biting mosquito culex is found where pigs are bread, peaking between June and August.'"

"So, it's simple. Don't go out at night to avoid the Anopheles mosquito. Don't go out in the day to avoid the Aedes mosquito. Just don't go out!" Candice concluded. "What else?"

Spencer smiled and read on. "'To avoid hookworms, which penetrate the skin, be sure to wear shoes when outdoors. Before eating lettuce or unpeeled, uncooked fruit, clean it with a brush and soak it in a solution of one teaspoon of iodine to one liter of water for twenty minutes. Wash hands before eating to avoid hepatitis A and B. Every household should have Coca Cola or Pepsi on hand for bacillary dysentery as they contain more electrolytes.'"

"I think I've got the hang of it," Candice said. "Don't go outside ever. Bring iodine to soak fruit and vegetables. Be especially careful of mosquitoes that sit with heads tilted down. Keep your entire body covered."

"Wait. It gets better," Spencer said with a smile. "Avoid certain routes as there are 'insurgents and bandits,' and it identifies the routes. It says to stay clear of areas where a group called the H'mong is active. And there are over two hundred people killed yearly from unexploded bombs that were dropped on the Ho Chi Min trail in Laos during the Vietnam War. More bombs were dropped in Laos than the entire world dropped during World War II. My God!"

"No wonder no one goes to Laos! Anyone interested gets scared off by our own government," Candice said, looking at the papers on the health risks. "It sounds like the government wants to scare everyone off so that they won't find out about all the bombs dropped on the place!"

"Here's one for you." Spencer read on. "Women should not attempt to touch monks. Monks are not allowed to touch women. Hah!" He laughed at the directive, as he knew it would get a reaction from her.

"Now, I call that a tiny bit old fashioned," Candice said. "About two thousand years." Then she asked in a serious tone, "I think we should not venture too far out into Laos, but just stay in the general vicinity of the capital. It all sounds too dangerous to go too far away. What do you think the chances are that we would come into contact with something that would affect our lives?"

Spencer thought about it as they had to make a serious

decision in the face of all the advisories. He applied his medical research background as a cholesterol research doctor, and gave her what he thought was a serious and correct estimation. "There is only a faint chance."

Candice nodded, agreeing. "The government probably puts up these warnings for most third-world places. Anyway, we wanted adventure, and this has got to be it. What the heck, let's go."

"I have a list of hotels here in the capital city Vientiane," Spencer said. "But the embassy said they do not take reservations. Can you imagine?"

Candice grimaced. "This may be more adventurous than we first imagined."

Chapter 5

Welcome to Laos," Spencer said to Candice as the small jet turned off the runway and onto the taxiway toward the small terminal at Vientiane, Laos.

"Laotians say 'Lao,' not 'Laos,'" Candice reminded him.

A little blue taxi with tuk-tuk painted on the back was available outside the small terminal. It appeared to be a combination of a motorcycle and a car. The back was a bed, like a pickup, but covered by a metal roof, the sides open.

"Let's go!" Spencer said, and they crawled in the back.

The little popping motorcar took off toward the center of the city, its little one-hundred-cubic-centimeter engine popping like a coffee percolator on the rough road.

They pulled up in front of the hotel, which, to their delight, was completely surrounded by beautiful flowers. Just inside, the floors, doors, and trim were all in thick teak, and grand.

"Teak comes from here," Spencer said. "And look at these high ceilings. I always have wondered why the US has lost the high ceilings. I only see high ceilings in old movies. Cameron would love all this."

Their room was up a flight of curved, beautifully carved teak stairs to the second floor. From their room, the window looked down on a courtyard of beautiful bougainvilleas, held up by raised rectangular frames of teak, three feet wide and six feet high, forming trellises. The effect was to create cascading bougainvillea branches of different colors, high enough that one could walk underneath them.

Candice was excited. "Tomorrow when there's sun, I'll get some great pictures."

Spencer had the more practical idea, took out scotch from his bags, and made himself a stiff drink.

After settling in, they went down to the front desk and asked the clerk, "How can we find a good tour agency?"

The young man listened intently and then just smiled. It was obvious he did not understand anything Spencer was asking.

"This could get agonizing," Spencer said, turning to Candice with a twisted expression on his mouth, trying to exaggerate his despair.

Aware that the couple at the desk needed something that he was not providing, the young man went to the back. Out came a young woman who had a slightly better command of English. After explaining what he wanted several times, the young woman pointed to several small stacks of brochures, standing up in a holder, that were in English. One was obviously from a travel agency.

"May I use the hotel phone?" he asked, looking at a phone on the edge of the desk. She brought it to him, a phone on a cord, and smiled. He showed her the number on the brochure which she then dialed for him.

Much to Spencer's relief, an English speaking man answered. When Spencer hung up, he said, "Cool! I've hired a private coach for tomorrow."

"Well, we still have the afternoon left," Candice said. "Downtown is close, so why don't we walk down there now and look around—some window shopping? This is the capital, and there's supposed to be a concentration of Laotian goods here, according to a brochure.

❧❦❧

As they walked down the short main street, they passed a tiny appliance store and a few other shops selling very modest things. They both formed an early impression that shopping opportunities were modest. There were no clothing or handicraft stores in the area. The stores were open to the sidewalk, with metal pull-down doors when closed.

"Perhaps we are not in the tourist area?" Spencer suggested to her in the form of a question. "Do you want to continue in this heat?" His shirt was getting moist. There was no breeze whatsoever in the area, and the still heat was taking its toll.

"Let's walk on down to the end of the street there before we turn around," Candice said.

After walking three short blocks farther, in the last block at the end of the street, they came upon a shop that had glass windows and a glass door, looking very much more up-scale than the others. It obviously had air conditioning as the glass front door was closed. The air conditioning was a welcome enticement over the nearly unbearable heat of the afternoon. As they looked more closely, they saw that it was a jewelry store. Not particularly caring what it sold, as they wanted to cool down, they went to absorb the air conditioning.

In the shop was its Indian owner, a dark-skinned Tamil Indian of forty-five. He was dressed in dark slacks, a white shirt, and no tie. The whiteness of his shirt made his extremely dark skin look even darker.

The shop had a square of glass showcase counters in the center, such that one had to walk around the square to see what was for sale. The walls had glass cases displaying gold necklaces and other jewelry items, and the shop had substantial inventory for a Laotian store. They began to look at the jewelry on display so as to justify their using the air conditioning, and, it was something to do.

As their eyes adapted to the interior of the store, they both noticed another person standing in the back section of the inner square. They both turned their attention from the glitter of the jewelry to that other person working there. Capturing their attention was the shopkeeper's assistant, a young woman in her early twenties. They could not help but stare.

Tall for a Laotian, olive-skinned, with long, rich, coal-black hair, she wore a blue *sinh*, the Laotian, tubular skirt, with gold silk embroidery around the bottom, and a plain, blue, western-styled shirt with short sleeves that was the accepted style with the Laotian women. Her olive skin was richly radiant, appearing as though from a summer ad of an US company selling suntan lotion. She wore the suspicion of modest lipstick, and bright blue eye shadow. On just anyone, the eye shadow might have been too much, but on her, it was exotic. But what mystified them were her deep emerald eyes.

As they approached, she smiled politely at them, and gave a *nop*, the bowing of the head with the hands in front in the prayer position. The subservient attitude that was displayed by the *nop* melted any resistance that either of them had to looking at the store's wares as long as she would help them.

Most all of the small shops they had been to in Asia had staff consisting of family. But her olive skin was so much lighter than the Tamil's that it did not seem as if she could be part of his immediate family. They walked around the circle of the small shop, looking at the jewelry in glass cases, the graceful young woman standing in the background, in case they had a question, never closing in so as to make them feel uncomfortable. Two other shoppers entered what was the quiet ambiance of the shop and spoke to the Tamil in English, but with German accents, most likely, from the German Embassy. They did not look like tourists, with dress shirts and ties, but no coats. They engaged the Tamil in conversation about something they wanted.

With the Tamil owner occupied, Spencer went to the glass jewelry case nearest the young woman, hoping to get her to wait on them rather than the owner taking over for her.

"We would like to look at Laotian stones," Spencer said, looking down at the glass case but not pointing to anything specific. "Nothing too fancy."

The Tamil turned away from the Germans, and it looked as if he might take over, which neither Spencer nor Candice wanted.

"Would you care for tea or soda?" he inquired. He was trying to lock them in as customers by offering a drink, something Spencer and Candice had experienced in rug shops in Kashmir, India.

"Thank you, but just cold water would be welcome," Spencer responded.

The Tamil barked off something toward the back of the shop, where another dark-skinned, young man suddenly emerged from seemingly nowhere and presented himself to the store owner as though at military attention. The Tamil gave a command to him, which was apparently to fetch water. He scurried out the front door.

Spencer and Candice pulled out two stools that had been under the glass counter. They looked at the gemstones for sale. The two Germans occupied the Tamil, leaving the emerald-green-eyed beauty to wait on them, and so the timing was good to ask for help.

The young man returned through the front door with two plastic bottles of cold mineral water for them. With the heat outside, the water was a welcome inducement to stay and look at the stones for sale. The Tamil had hooked them in now with the complimentary mineral water, and they were obliged to look at his wares—a good salesman. But they wanted to meet the beautiful young woman.

Looking at her, Spencer said, "We would like to look at Laotian rubies and sapphires." He then looked down at red and blue stones appearing to be just that, but, in reality, he had no idea what he wanted, or what sort of stones came from Lao. He pointed to a large, individual blue sapphire stone mounted in gold to his right, away from the owner, in hopes the girl would continue to wait on them instead of the owner. "Could we please see this?"

By asking her to take something out of the case, he realized he would probably end up buying something just to be polite.

"This one is blue sapphire," she said as though her voice was made of sapphire as well. She had a British accent. "The mount is twenty-two karat gold."

The sapphire was the size of the end of Candice's thumb. Huge.

"It must be far too expensive for us to actually consider," Spencer said, and handed it to Candice, whose eyes opened in amazement.

"Beautiful!" Candice said with gleaming eyes. She stared at it, wondering if she could ever own such a thing.

Spencer looked away and down into the glass case at other stones as Candice examined the sapphire, considering it too expensive, hoping she would not become too attached.

"How can we be assured that these are, in fact real, sapphires and rubies, and not man made?" Spencer asked, referring to the entire lot of stones in front of them, skeptical of cheating merchants.

"Oh yes, sir. These are very real indeed." The young woman looked rather puzzled as to why they questioned that her gems might not be genuine. Looking toward the sapphire stone that so mesmerized Candice, the girl touted her wares. "These sapphires are from the mines at Bokeo, near the Golden Triangle where Lao, Myanmar, and Thailand meet. They are among the finest in the world. See the beautiful color. If you are skeptical, may I show you how to look at sapphires?"

She picked up a piece of white paper from the desk in the center of the glass cases that surrounded it and put it on the counter. She put some loose sapphires on it, and then picked up an artificial one from the desk behind her and placed it near the others.

"Look through the real stones this way," she said as she passed a magnifying glass. "You can see if the stone has been artificially colored. Notice how these are uniform throughout and have no striations. These are genuine and not colored."

"How do we identify a striation?" Spencer asked.

She pointed to the artificial one. "Now look at this one."

Spencer looked through the magnifying glass at the artificial stone. "I can see! Look, Candice. She's right. You can see the lines on this artificial one." He passed her the magnifying glass.

"There is a German company in Lao that has a method of impregnating the stones of lesser color with more color," the young woman added. "They're still pretty, but not as nice. And, of course, much less expensive."

Candice put the large blue sapphire on the white paper so it could be examined with the white background.

"Please look, the sales woman said. "This is not only genuine, but top quality."

Spencer examined the stone with the magnifying lens. "Yes, I see."

Candice looked on and nodded in agreement.

Spencer then said defensively, establishing his right not to purchase it just because he looked at it, "Although we cannot afford it, I would just like to know how much the stone cost in dollars?"

She turned behind her, picked up a calculator from the desk in the center area, and tapped in numbers to arrive at the US equivalent of Laotian currency, as she could tell they were American from their accent. She then announced the price at a fraction of what they expected.

"So cheap," Candice blurted out. She should have known it was imprudent to talk that way in front of a shop clerk, but the price was so little that it never even occurred to her to bargain.

Then it sank in that it wasn't expensive as Spencer had suspected. "Okay, we'll take it!" He took out his traveling wad of cash from his front pocket and counted out the asking price, thinking the price too cheap to haggle over— anyway, there was something wrong about haggling with this super model.

"Thank you, luv," Candice said. She gave him a big kiss on the cheek, which he resisted as out of place in public.

"Do you have a gold chain that will work with it?" Candice asked

The exotic sales girl nodded. "Of course." She then brought over a square tray covered with black, completely full of gold chains of every style, length, and amount of gold content.

Candice picked one, a thin one and of the length she wanted. The sales lady motioned for Candice to lower her head and then clasped it on Candice's neck.

Candice raised her head and then turned around, modeling her new fantastic treasure.

Spencer said to the sales woman with a big smile, "I guess we made her happy!"

"She will always treasure it," she replied, "possibly as one of her favorites." She then put the chain into a fancy box, put in the receipt, wrapped it, and put it into a bag.

Spencer exhaled, tired and hot, wanting to get back to the hotel for a nice shower.

He looked at the sales girl. "Now that we have done our shopping, would you mind if we asked you to recommend us to someplace for dinner? Perhaps you would be good enough to write it down in Lao, so we can hand it to a tuk-tuk driver. We like to ask locals where to go, as they usually know best."

"Is there any particular food that you prefer?" When no one immediately responded, trying to find out if they had some religious or other type of limits on certain types of food, she changed the question. "Is there any particular food that you do not take?" This would cover a variety of food that many did not take, such as Jews and Muslims with pork, vegetarians with meat, some no gluten, some organic only, and many on special diets.

"We have no particular diet," Spencer said. "We would like to sample the local cuisine and like to try most everything. We want to sample Lao food, something like you yourself eat."

"I do not think you would like the places that I sometimes go to as much as the spots that the tourists and embassy staff frequent which cost more than I can afford. Mine are not fancy."

"We would like to go for real Lao food," Candice said, thinking the same as Spencer.

The young woman thought for a solution. "There's a new place that the foreigners go that is supposed to be very good. Embassy staff who come into the store talk about it. It's been open only for a month. I think that would be best for you. I've heard it has a variety of Laotian dishes and Western ones as well."

Spencer and Candice looked at each other and without any words spoken each nodded affirmatively to the other in answer to their unspoken thoughts.

"Would you show us tonight and be our guide? We would be honored and treat you if you would be so kind," Candice asked her. Coming from the wife, the invitation, Candice thought, would be proper. They both were anxious to get someone local to tell them about Lao, and this young woman spoke English. Candice hoped the local would introduce them to real local food. If she would, they would have someone local to talk to, order the food, and to tell them about Vientiane and Lao.

"Oh, I can get the directions for you. You need not take me."

"Actually, we would much prefer to have someone local to talk to, to help us order the food, to tell us about Lao and what to see in the country," Candice said.

"If you are absolutely certain that it would not be a problem for you, I would be delighted to join you."

"I think we are in for a delightful evening," Spencer said. "Should we come for you in a tuk-tuk?"

He realized that was a bold statement after saying it. How was he going to communicate anything to the taxi driver? If her address was not something that the taxi man would know, he would never find her.

"I don't live too far away, but you may not be able to find it easily," she told them. "The tuk-tuk drivers do not speak English. I can come to your hotel. It's easy for me. Let me do that, if you please. Will eight work?"

"That'll be fine," Candice responded and gave the name of the hotel. "What's your name, dear?"

"Sangmouane Sayasithsena."

"I'm afraid that may take some doing for us to pronounce that properly," Spencer said.

Candice realized that Spencer had not introduced them. "I'm Candice Harrington, and this is my husband, Spencer."

Chapter 6

I t's half past seven," Spencer announced to Candice in the hotel room. "I see you are already having a shooter. Since the sun has gone over the yardarm, I'll join you. Why don't we take our drinks down to the courtyard? There are so many beautiful flowers there."

Drinks in hand, they walked down the hotel's teak circular staircase to the lobby and out into the floral courtyard to wait for their new contact as the hot Laotian day cooled.

The hotel featured an interior courtyard through which they walked under trellises of bougainvilleas of many different colors.

"This would be spectacular in the sunlight," Candice said. "I must come down in the sunlight tomorrow and get pictures in the sunlight on these colorful flowers."

Their new restaurant guide arrived as promised. She appeared as a model arriving on a set, as her attractiveness was out of place. She wore a maroon colored *sinh*, the tubular skirt, with ivory colored embroidery, and an ivory, western-styled top, looking much like a regular shirt. She greeted them with the *nop*.

"*Sa-bai-dee*," she said, greeting them in Laotian with a big smile.

They had concluded that this gesture and saying were to be returned on occasions, so they both tried returning it to her, clumsy as they were. She acted pleasantly surprised, as though they had done it correctly.

"I see you have learned some Lao," she said.

"Hardly," Spencer said. "We only know *Sa-bai-dee* for hello, and *kop chai lai* for thank you. Not much of an accomplishment in learning a new language. Shall we go to dinner?"

Outside, they mounted a tuk-tuk. Their guide spoke to the driver, and off they went down the dusty, unpaved street.

The restaurant was very newly decorated in Western decor. The patrons were all Western, apparently embassy staff, speaking a number of languages.

The menu given them was in English, and they decided on several dishes. The prices were dirt cheap. Their guide also ordered sticky rice, or *kiiao tiee-ow*, eaten with the fingers. "We also pick up foods with the sticky rice."

"You must show us," Candice told her. "We want to eat in the same fashion as you."

The restaurant owner, trying to cater to the various government and embassy staff members from foreign countries, came and proudly told them that they had wine available, as though it was something very special to have, and presented a list of imported wines.

"Bring us this one," Spencer said. "I have no idea what I'm ordering. However, it's an import."

"That's a good one," the restaurant owner said and left for the wine.

Spencer looked at their new friend, "How do you pronounce your name again,"

"Sangmouane Sayasithsena." She giggled.

"Impossible!" Spencer said in defense.

Sangmouane said it for them again. "Sangmouane Sayasithsena."

"I don't think we'll ever get it right," Spencer said. "I give up. Is the Indian man in the shop your father?" He changed the topic. He knew that the Tamil proprietor of the

jewelry store could hardly be her father with his dark color-
ing, but the question seemed to be the most diplomatic way
of broaching the subject.

"My real parents are no longer living. He's my adoptive
father, and the second one at that. I'm only half-Laotian.
My real father was *ein Deutscher* in Lao prospecting for
gems, and met my mother, a Laotian. My name is hers.
They were traveling in the north in a remote area looking
for new mines in their motorcar, with me, when their vehicle went off a very high cliff. I was thrown out and survived. I was four."

"That's some story," Spencer said.

"I was caught in the brush on the cliff's side. I lay there
for two days until I was found by my tribal chief, my next
father, out from his village on a hunt. He was from a local
village, and took me there, adopting me. There're still
villages like that in Lao that have almost no visitors and still
live much like there is no rest of the world. The village I
lived in was in the mountains that had almost no contact
with the outside world. There life was, and still may be, like
it has been for centuries—no electricity, no phones, nor
hardly any contact with the rest of Lao. Nothing from the
modern world has come, so far as I know, even to now."

"Have you returned to visit," Candice asked.

"No. I have not been able, but I would love to do so."

"Do you write to the chief now?" Candice asked.

"No. There's no mail there."

"Now, that is remote," Spencer said. "Imagine a place
with no mail! Wow, Candice, just think, no junk mail."

"How did you come to leave the village?" Candice
asked, mesmerized.

"When I was seven, two Christian missionaries came to
the village. When they learned of me, they told the chief
that they would take me to the mission here in Vientiane if
the chief would allow. The chief agreed with them that it
would be best for me to go back to a city, as that's where
my people came from, and that I should continue with a city

education. There was no formal education in the village. One can only learn the ways of the villagers. So the missionaries brought me here to Vientiane, to their Christian mission. The nice people there tried to find Christian parents for me, but they couldn't find any." Her audience was listening intently, so she continued. "My present parents, who had migrated to Lao from India, heard about me. My new mother was unable to have a child, and when they were looking to adopt, they met me and decided to take me. I was so lucky!"

"That's a fascinating story," Candice said. "You look different from the Laotians we have seen so far."

"That's because my natural mother was Laotian and my natural father German."

"Oh yes, of course, I forgot. What languages do you speak?" Candice asked. "You have a British accent."

"My adoptive parents spoke mostly English at home. They learned their English in India. That's perhaps why the Americans all say I have a British accent, as the English spoken there is from England. And I speak Lao, of course. My father and mother here also speak some Tamil and Hindi, which I can also speak. There are French in Lao, and I have learned a little French. There are occasional Germans in the store, and I can speak some conversational German. And I know the village dialect from the village I was in that I told you about, but I have not heard or used it since. It was a very simple language."

"Communication, or the lack of it, is what either allows or keeps most people from getting ahead in the world," Spencer said. "If you did not speak English, we would not have met."

"Yes," she said. "I'm so lucky to have had my English-speaking parents."

"You are very beautiful with your mixed blood," Candice said. "It's no wonder why your Tamil parents chose you."

Sangmouane blushed. "You're too kind." As though to

shift the subject from her, she asked them, "What do you do in America?"

"We are research doctors," Spencer said. "I do research in cholesterol and Candice in genetics."

"That must be very interesting, but I do not know of such things. I feel so honored to meet two medical doctors. Do you have children?"

"No, we do not," Candice admitted.

Sangmouane looked surprised. It was not routine in Asia that people did not have children. "Do you plan to have children?"

"Yes, we do," Spencer said, "When we get back from our trip."

"I think one child would be enough," Candice added, announcing that she still wanted to pursue her career in research medicine and not give it up to be a full-time mother with a big family.

"You'll enjoy this," the restaurant owner said, interrupting their conversation as he approached the table. Following him was a waiter and an additional helper behind, each with a large tray with their food.

Sangmouane explained the Laotian dishes as they ate.

"I hope to learn to make some of these," Candice said. "Do you know how to cook?"

"Oh, yes Sangmouane said. "I can make Lao food. I can also make Indian food, especially south Indian food. Mother taught me."

"We are trying to get to know people on this trip," Spencer said, "and hope to be able to do more than just see monuments and that sort of thing. We'll be here in Vientiane for the week, and then we leave. We did not plan on going off into the unpopulated north because of advisories from our State Department. What's there of interest here in the capital?"

"Well, tomorrow a girl I know is to be married. Would you like to come to a traditional Lao wedding?"

"Absolutely!" Spencer said. "That is just the sort of

thing that we have been hoping to get to do on our trip. We'd love to be able to get to do such a thing."

"Will it cause any problem, bringing us outsiders?" Candice asked.

"Not all at. There will be a lot of people there, and it will be fine that you go."

"What sort of present could we bring?" Candice asked.

"Money in an envelope will work very well," Sangmouane said.

"This is really very nice of you to let us see a slice of the local culture. Thank you so much for inviting us," Spencer said. "I can hire a private, chauffeured car so we won't have to take a tuk-tuk."

"The wedding is at eleven. I will come for you at the hotel at ten. There will be food served following the wedding."

"That sounds perfect!" Candice said. "That is the sort of local things we want to do most, rather than sightseeing. Wow! Are we lucky, or what?"

☙❧

The wedding ceremony was performed with the bride and groom sitting on the floor in front of a wreath, four feet in diameter, laced in flowers. Everyone else surrounded them on the floor. A man who knew the proper chants sang in a mix of chanting and talking, with repetition. By custom, everyone tied pieces of white strings called *baci* strings, onto the wrists of someone near, who could be a stranger or someone familiar, and announced a wish, such as good health.

Sangmouane told her guests, "The person whose wrists get the *baci* strings is not to take them off for three days, and then they must not be cut, only untied. Only in this way can the wish or prayer come true."

On three occasions during the ceremony, everyone in the

room at the same time touched the person in front of them at the same time with the fingertips of one hand, and said a prayer, chanting in unison. Nearly all tied a *baci* string on the bride and groom. Some of the strings had a bill of money rolled up and tied in the string. During part of the ceremony, a shot glass of *Lao-Lao* liquor was passed to the bride and groom, who drank it, the crowd encouraging them with another chant.

"It's over," Sangmouane said. "Now we go outside."

Outside in the courtyard an enormous feast had been set up on tables that had been pushed together. They went around the tables, filling their plates, and then found three chairs together to sit and watch under the partial shade of a tree. A sound system had been set up, and there were singers. The music was a mixture of modern and Laotian, but the words were in Laotian and fairly bad to the Western ear. A man did much of the singing, and then there were two women who sang alternatively. As usual at such events, the volume was too loud.

"When do we give the money present?" Spencer asked. Following the advice of Sangmouane to bring money, Spencer and Candice brought an envelope along from the hotel and passed it to Sangmouane. "Would you address it, please? And, how much money do you think we should give?"

"Your American money goes a long way here," she said sheepishly.

"Well, we could use some sort of advice," Spencer said. "Please tell us what you are giving."

"I'm giving the equivalent of five American dollars."

Spencer was shocked. He realized that this was a very poor country, and the amount spent on wedding gifts here would naturally be much smaller than he was used to giving. Sangmouane had an envelope in her purse, and showed it to them. The envelope was in natural paper, hand painted, and artistic.

"I tell you what," he said. "Here." Spencer handed her a

hundred-dollar bill. "Give them this for the three of us. You keep your kip, and make this part of your gift as well."

"Oh, my! That's a fortune. They'll be delighted." She put the bill into the envelope, wrote on the unpainted side the names of the all three of the donors, and went to a special box for money gifts on a table, and dropped the envelope in it.

Riding back in the chauffeured minivan Spencer hired for the day, Candice told Sangmouane, "That was super. It's exactly the sort of genuinely local thing that we wanted to do most on our trip. We would never have had such an opportunity if it weren't for you."

Arriving at the hotel, Sangmouane said, "I should go to my father now until he closes the shop."

"Please come with us again tonight," Candice asked.

ᜉᜈᜉ

At half-past seven, the phone rang.

"Meestahh Harreentun, sir, your guest is here."

The hotel lounge, although small, had a spectacularly luxurious feel. The floor, tables, and chairs were all made of thick teak, sanded smooth and varnished in a medium tone. The teak-framed windows were arched openings in the stucco walls without glass, and ceiling fans moved the air.

Sangmouane had arrived, too striking to be part of the local scenery. She wore a bright blue *sinh* with beige embroidery along the bottom, and a Western top in plain blue.

"So nice to see you." Spencer complimented.

She greeted them with the *nop*, "*Sa-bai-dee*," followed by her irresistible smile.

"*Sa-bai-dee*," returned Spencer, and then Candice, with the *nop*.

"Let's get a drink here," Spencer said. He looked at the bartender. "Vodka Martini, dry, for me. Ladies?"

"The same," Candice said. "How about you?"

"I'll take the same."

"A female that takes a proper drink!" Spencer joked, admiring her taste of similar to his.

"The wedding was fabulous!" Candice complimented. "I took all sorts of neat pictures."

The martinis arrived. Spencer sampled his and proclaimed, "Ah, a civilized drink!"

"Please don't let us impose on you, and don't hesitate to say no," Candice said. "But I'm going to ask you if it would it be in any way possible for you to take us about as our tour guide tomorrow? We insist on paying you as a tour guide if you could take time off from the jewelry shop for a day."

"I can take off a day," Sangmouane acquiesced. "There is no need for you to pay me any money. I do not take a salary, as I just help out my family. My father will not mind."

"Fantastic!" Spencer said. "Are you so nice to everyone?"

Sangmouane was quiet for a few moments. "I had a feeling come over me when I met you in the store that my karma is somehow connected to you, but I do not know how or why."

"Karma," Spencer said, pondering the Eastern concept. "Well, perhaps it is our karma that we meet." He moved to a more earthly topic. "What do you want to do most with yourself, as you are so young and have so much life ahead of you? Do you plan to marry?"

"Well," she answered, sheepishly, "I hope that maybe I might find someone one day to marry me." Her pensive answer left them quiet as they tried to imagine what options were open to her, and they seemed so few.

Spencer broke the silence. "What would you do if you could do whatever you wanted?" His question was brazenly harsh, as it contemplated the mobility that he had, but she was without.

Sangmouane thought pensively. "If I had my wish, I would travel to the West. America would be my first choice. I've heard so many wonderful things about it. I love Lao, but there are not many opportunities here."

Spencer, influenced by the drink, blurted out, "Do you think that you might ever come to America one day?" After he asked, he realized that coming as a tourist was ridiculous, given the income of Laotians. The embassy material given him about Lao said the average Laotian annual wage was a few hundred dollars per year. The clumsy question increased the distance between them. It was coarse, rude, and indelicate.

She responded with what Spencer and Candice both found to be a very unusual and provocative answer. The seeming impossibility of going to America, the expense, the visa necessary, restrictions put up by America to keep out a flood of people wanting everything from the scourge of welfare to importing terrorists, but still not wanting to believe that there was no chance at all to come, she finally answered, "I would like to think that there is at least faint chance."

Spencer was so taken by the answer he had to pause. "A faint chance," he repeated aloud.

He looked at Candice, and she was silent as she was equally moved. Here was a young woman who was very smart, full of youthful ambition and energy, charming, spoke English, and incredibly beautiful. Her answer represented knowledge of the basic truth and reality that there was no likelihood of her ever coming to America, but, at the same time, she did not absolutely foreclose the possibility. She refused to completely eliminate the chance that she might one day get to go to such a place and make a better future. It seemed the perfect answer, covering all parameters of her so-dismal choices for her future.

"*Faint Chance*! What a lovely answer," Spencer said and then got creative. "Given the fact that your real name, 'Sangmouane Sayasithsena,' is impossible for us to pronounce, would you mind if I give you a nickname? I propose Faint Chance."

"Ubercool!" Candice added. "Agreed! Do you mind?"

"It's a lovely nickname," she politely replied with a warm smile.

"So, we'll call you that, if you don't mind then," Spencer said. "Faint Chance." He said it with the British accent, especially on the "a" in "chance," which he pronounced "ah."

"Faint Chance," Candice repeated.

Their new friend looked about at both of them in a quandary as to what was happening to her.

"Spencer held up his drink. "I propose a toast to the new name, Faint Chance."

Candice held up her glass and clunked it against his, and then Faint Chance, catching on, did the same, accepting the toast. A waiter came around in a white, starched, cotton uniform top with brass buttons.

"Another round," Spencer said, without asking the gals if they wanted another.

At dinner in the hotel restaurant, they ordered their first bottle of wine. The seed of her desire to travel to America having been planted, and Spencer, with a substantial dose of alcohol narrowing his focus, pondered how unfair the world was and how such a charming young woman who spoke English could not go where she wanted, due to the lack of money and mobility to do so.

"You really should come to America one day," he told her.

Suddenly he realized that he already suggested that earlier, and that it was impossible. Her expression changed to somewhat hurt as she felt inadequate, in that she knew she would never have that much money or opportunity. She barely had five dollars for a wedding gift. Spencer realized he was inadvertently rubbing in the fact that he and his wife had so much mobility, whereas Faint Chance had none. An embarrassing feeling of awkwardness and lack of manners overcame him. Wanting to rectify this, and the alcohol reducing his subtleness, he blurted out, "How would your possibility of coming to America be greater than just a faint chance? How would you like to come to America?"

Faint Chance looked puzzled. "How can that be? I would need a sponsor and a fortune in savings."

"What do you think of us sponsoring her," Spencer said, openly looking at Candice.

Candice realized the commitment that was being offered and tried to relay an expression of concern to Spencer without saying anything. She hoped he might realize what they would do if it did not work out. She was a bit upset with Spencer blurting it out without first discussing it with her beforehand. His drinking had emboldened him too much. But the idea of helping Faint Chance did provide a warm feeling of satisfaction.

"Yes, we would love to have you come live with us," Candice added to her husband's offer, thinking she would chastise him later.

"Would you really do that for me?" Faint Chance asked in a state of disbelief.

"We insist! We would love to have you come over and stay with us," Spencer said emphatically to make sure it was not taken as an offer that was to be politely rejected.

"Absolutely," Candice added, confirming, to be polite and to back up her husband's impulsive offer.

Faint Chance's eyes opened in surprise at the prospect. It was something that she never really believed could happen to her. The biggest thing ever, thus far in her life, was happening!

Candice realized that maybe this was too hastily conceived. "But can you leave your parents and the store? We don't want to be the cause of breaking up your family."

"My father knows one day I'll leave him to be married and to go off to raise a family, so my leaving is expected one day. He and mother will be happy for me. They had very little in India, and will understand the meaning of such an opportunity. I can hardly believe it!" Her eyes began to water as emotion overcame her.

Spencer, to try to downplay the event a little so Faint Chance would not cry, said, "It really is not much of a gift. We'll probably have to sign for you and guarantee your support in the United States as your sponsors. It may take some doing to get you a visa and will take some time for the government to provide you with papers." He added this so she would not get the idea that she could just jump on a plane. He did not know what was involved and was worried that he might be raising false hopes of immediate travel to America, aware that a single foreign female could not simply just go get a green card without some considerable obstacles, whatever they might be.

"Oh, I'm aware of that," she responded. "But once in America, how can I live? Is work available?"

"You can live with us as long as you wish," Spencer said. "After you get settled, and get a good job, you can do what you want. And yes, there are many jobs, but first you will have to get a work permit. In the meantime, you can learn to drive, and you can show Candice how to make Laotian cuisine. How does that sound?"

"I have not been so happy since I was adopted by my Indian parents as a little girl from the mission. I'm truly blessed!" She began to cry.

"It's really our pleasure," Candice said, "and really is not much for us to do. We enjoy the feeling of helping someone, and you have taken such good care of us here. We'll enjoy having you at our house."

"I'll go to the US Embassy before we go," Spencer said, "and get the papers for you to start the process. The American government will be asking your Laotian government if you have any criminal background, for proof of birth and citizenship, and that sort of thing. There are restrictions on people coming into the United States, such that there may be some delay in your coming, depending on how quickly the American government acts on the application. Although we are leaving Lao, we will not be finished with our trip in Asia for another month or two, and it will undoubtedly take

time to get your clearance, so, it will work out timewise."
He really did not know what was involved, but he had heard
of such obstacles when people wanted to migrate to the US.

"It all seems too impossible to be true," Faint Chance
said. "I saw a vision in my future when I met you, and it's
coming true."

"How come we don't see such things in the future?"
Spencer said to Candice.

"Good question," Candice responded, "Perhaps if we
stayed slightly more sober."

With that, they all laughed.

Chapter 7

The following morning, the same driver arrived with the tour company's little white van. Faint Chance arrived shortly afterward in a gold-colored silk *sinh* with a brown top.

Her eye makeup was in green, showing off her emerald eyes. The morning sun reflected intensely off her gold *sinh*, and emphasized her natural sway in her hips as she walked from the tuk-tuk to the hotel entrance where Spencer and Candice were ready.

She greeted them with her *nop*, *"Sa-bai-dee."*

"Sa-bai-dee," said Spencer with his version of the *nop*.

"Sa-bai-dee," said Candice, doing the same.

"What suggestions do you have on where to go?" Candice asked.

"I would like you to see silk weaving," Faint Chance said. "You'll love that, and I know a very good place where you can see the making of the materials."

"Perfect! Let's do that," Candice said.

An hour out later, the van pulled up to a building where silk weaving was the business. Faint Chance spoke to the female owner. The owner then became their tour guide as they walked about the open-windowed, silk weaving business, with Faint Chance the interpreter. The windows were openings without glass or screens, and the rain, which came on and off, was kept out only by the overhang of the roof.

Faint Chance translated, "All Laotian females wear the *sinh*. The full name is *paa sinh*, or cloth *sinh*. The material is made here or similar places. Also made here are wall decorations, and other smaller articles. Bedspreads are made at other places, with bigger looms. Come along to the back."

In the back, they learned that not only was the place a silk weaving shop, but a place where the silk was died. A young woman wound raw silk into bundles two feet in diameter on homemade wooden boards with pegs. Standing a few feet away, a dye master was busy making his dyes from berries, tree bark, and by other tricks he had learned. He had no artificial dyes or chemicals. The various dyes were made in buckets in which he put the tree bark, berries or whatever materials he used with water. Then some of the colored water would be put into a can heated underneath with burning wood. Salt was added, and when it was just right, he put in a bundle of silk, and then took it out and beat it on a wooden rail.

The results were stunning, with colors of the freshly dyed silk, bright and beautiful. Other females put the silk on wooden spools, and then on to large wooden bobbins to end up with the weavers-all in a primitive process, as though out of the distant past.

Inside another part of the building again with no glass windows, young women sat weaving at wooden looms, five to six feet high. The patterns were achieved by the weaver pushing a bobbin of a certain color from the point just before two or more rows of silk thread came together from the loom. She knew just how to change colors and when.

So many hours, and even days, would go into a single piece of cloth. The labor simply had almost no value. It was a view into the past as to how fabrics were still being made.

In the front, there was a small store comprised mostly of a few stacks of dazzling silk scarfs. Spencer and Candice bought most all of them for gifts back home—and a few for themselves.

∞

On the next day of their Laotian adventure, still having luck keeping Faint Chance as their tour guide, they engaged her once again. She offered to take them to a teak forest.

The forest was uninhabited. As they arrived, it began to rain. The trees did not provide shelter, as the odd-looking teak trees did not have spread-out branches. The teak leaves, a foot in diameter, grew close in to the trunk of the tall, thin, pole-like trees.

"We don't mind rain," Spencer said as they exited the van.

After a time, Candice realized that there was more to this forest than trees. She began to shoot Faint Chance against the trees, the wet exaggerating her shape. The three of them walked deeper into the forest, with the canopy of the tall trees making it a bit darker.

They came to a clearing in the woods, with the sun coming through. Ahead was a spectacular waterfall, falling down a rock formation sixty feet high, landing in huge, odd-shaped natural, shallow pools. The pools, in turn, drained down the hill in small streams. Crystal clear, without mud or debris, the water had a blue cast, appearing to be devoid of pollution. The sound of the waterfall was loud, adding to the intensity. Red flowers surrounded the waterfall and floating in the water, as though the scene had been made for a photographer. There were no people to be found anywhere.

"Has this ever been photographed?" Candice said. "This is too much! I can't believe something like this exists in nature with no one around. Imagine this, right out here in the middle of nowhere. Perfect!" She went crazy taking pictures.

The rain let up, and rays of sun came through the trees. Faint Chance stood by in her rain-soaked *sinh,* watching Candice taking pictures, also soaked and wiping water off her camera. Candice suddenly realized she was completely missing the mark with dumb "natural" photos. "Faint Chance, you're already soaking. Would you mind terribly getting in the waterfall?"

Her answer was to comply. She took off her shoes and walked right on into the pool just below the waterfall. She realized Candice wanted a show and began a traditional Laotian dance, the only dance she knew.

Then, to the complete surprise of Candice, Faint Chance began to undress. She took off her brown silk western top, and tossed it on a rock. She next took off her black bra. But she did not stop there. She undid her *sinh,* and put it on the rock as well. She then took off her black panties.

"Faint Chance," Candice exclaimed. "What are you doing?"

"You are now my family." She said it as though it explained her conduct.

Standing there, naked, she moved into the falling water, providing contest-quality material for Candice. Her legs were lean and shapely, and her beautiful olive skin was without crease lines anywhere. She danced naked without a trace of inhibition.

Candice switched her digital camera to movie and continued the erotic shoot.

The experience gave Candice a deeply sensual feeling. She interrupted her train of thought and looked at Spencer for his feeling, but he did not seem to notice the request, perhaps because he was consumed by the erotic dance, perhaps because of his own sensual feelings, or perhaps the strong sound of the waterfall. Or all three.

৩৩৩

The next day, Spencer and Candice walked from the hotel to the nearby US Embassy. It was situated behind a stucco wall, eight feet high. The entrance was not on the main street, but down a narrow side street, also with eight feet high walls on either side. The area was kept very clean, and two, uniformed off-duty Laotian policemen stood outside, one at either side of a very large iron gate, twenty feet wide and eight feet high. Across the gate was the familiar gold American Eagle, a warm sight in such a foreign place.

Another man on the inside of the big iron gate approached them and asked through the bars, "Sir, what's your business?"

"We're Americans, and are here to see someone about the immigration of a Laotian to America," Spencer told him.

The man behind the gate told the police outside something in Laotian. They jumped to the task and pushed the big gate open manually. It was on rollers but still took two men to move it. It was then clear to Spencer why the two local policemen were there, as it was no doubt cheaper to hire two of them at Laotian wages than it would have been to put in a motorized gate.

They walked inside the embassy courtyard, and into the building. Inside, there was a wall with a glass top separating the employees from the visitors with a window opening. A lady came forward.

"We need the forms for a Lao citizen to apply for immigration to the United States, and also whatever forms we need as sponsors," Spencer told her.

The lady they talked to went over and spoke to a secretary, who got up and went to a filing cabinet. She collected a series of forms and brought them forward. They were to learn, in talking her, that the process was a long one, and involved more than just simply filling out and submitting some forms.

"Is there anything to expedite the process of immigration?" Spencer asked.

"These forms have to be completed and submitted to the Department of Immigration and Naturalization," the lady told them. "Here is a duplicate copy of each form you will need."

"Thank you," Spencer said. "Can I use your phone for a local call?"

She led him to a phone, and he called the jewelry store. Faint Chance answered.

"Hi. This is Spencer. Can you come by the hotel after work? We have forms for you from the embassy."

"Yes, I can be there at six-thirty."

Leaving the Embassy, Candice said, "Spencer, let's go to the shopping area. I see it there just across the street."

They walked across the street and entered the Vientiane version of a shopping mall, a large cluster of shops in an area without walls. They walked through it once and found many little stalls selling woven silk goods such as *sinhs* and scarves, handicraft, and inexpensive jewelry.

"Spencer, I want to shop for a silk *sinh* for myself," Candice said, "and maybe a few scarfs for gifts. You'll get impatient. Why don't we meet back at the hotel in a couple of hours? I'll take a tuk-tuk. Okay?"

"Sure. I want to look at some of the handicrafts. See you there."

⌘

At the hotel, Candice was inside waiting for Spencer. There was a knock on the door.

"Yes?" Candice said.

"It's me!" Spencer announced.

Candice got up, went to the door, and opened it saying, excitedly, "Spencer! Wait until you see my neat, hand-woven, silk *sinh*!"

Spencer walked in, barely fitting though the door with a sheepish grin, holding an incredibly realistic, carved wooden, elephant's head three feet high, with carved ears as wide as its length, and long tusks. He looked as proud as if he had bagged it as a record trophy on a big game hunt.

"Oh my God!" Candice exclaimed.

"Perfect, eh? And cheap!"

"We'll have to ship that! We're not going to lug that all over Asia for the rest of our trip!" Candice protested. "I'll bet it will cost more to ship than it cost!"

"Minor details," Spencer said. "How can you put a price on love?"

☙❧☙

Faint Chance arrived at their room, and they went right to work filling out the papers for her to migrate to the United States.

"When you get your Laotian background records to prove you have no criminal record, take the package to the US Embassy and leave them there," Spencer said. "If you have any problems, call us collect. Do you have a computer?"

Faint chance looked a bit inadequate. "No, sorry, no computer."

"That's okay, just call us," Candice said. "You can either call collect or use some money that I will give you for expenses."

"Let's have a drink now and toast your coming to America," Spencer said. "Here's to our new guest in America!" he said, raising his glass.

The three of them clanged their glasses together in the toast.

"I've never been happier!" Faint Chance said with a huge smile. She was very excited.

☙❧☙

Later, they sat in a seafood place that Faint Chance introduced them to. It had a full bar, and they were having another round of drinks, having already started in their room.

"May I please be so forward as to ask you a very personal question?" Faint Chance asked. "I would not do this, except that you are leaving, and I have good reason to be so personal on one subject. I hope you will not think it rude, and if so, please do not answer the question and forgive me."

"Of course," Spencer said.

"Ask away," Candice acquiesced.

"Are you ready to make a child at this time?" Faint Chance asked.

Spencer and Candice looked at each other when confronted with this most curious, personal question, without saying anything to each other. Spencer finally spoke. "Well, it has occurred to us that if we are going to have a child, we'd better do so soon."

Candice came into the topic with, "If I do not do so, I'll be too old, and problems become a higher risk with women that are past my age. I suppose this is as good as a time as any. Actually, if we were to start now, the baby would be born well after we got back, and we would have all the benefits of US medicine. It would not ruin our trip, as we would be back before I would get heavy."

"If you're willing to make your baby at this time there is something that I can do for that will make your baby very special."

The couple went silent. They looked at each other, and then at her.

"What on earth can that be?" Candice asked. Her medical curiosity was aroused.

"Yes, what on earth are you referring to?" Spencer asked.

"Remember the chief of the village that I told you about who took me in and adopted me?"

"Yes," Candice said.

"When I was leaving the village with the missionaries, the chief gave me a gift that he would have only given his own child. It's for my wedding one day. The gift is the means to summon special spirits that will give a child special powers, so that the child will have special abilities and will be a great leader one day. It requires special prayers to summon spirits," Faint Chance said. "As you are giving me such a great gift, by inviting me into your family in America, that will change my life, I want to give you for your new child to be a very special gift that the chief gave to me.

She took the little bag out from her purse that the chief had given her years earlier and put it on the table. She produced a small bottle of clear fluid and small white strings, each a foot long. She opened the bag to show them its contents, consisting of dried, purple and orange colored plant leaves that were crushed into small pieces, no doubt from having been cut years earlier. There were also *baci* strings for the wrists, and a bottle of *Lao-Lao* liquor.

"It's a tradition of the tribe I lived with that, on the wedding day of the chief, he and his bride, and only he and his bride, undertake a special ceremony that makes their child very special," Faint Chance explained. "The ceremony summons spirits that live in these leaves, or perhaps they are contacted through the leaves. The spirits are asked to give their child special powers. The child will be born with those special gifts, powers, and abilities to be chief one day, just like the present chief."

"Isn't the tribal Chief always a male?" Candice asked, feeling discrimination. Then she joked, "The men always get the best spots."

"As far as I know," Faint Chance said. "But I believe that if the child to be is a female the child will also be very special."

Curiosity aroused, Spencer asked, "Tell us more." This was exactly the local experience that he had hoped to find by taking the sabbatical and year off from work.

"I want to give you this very special gift. You must swallow it when I say special prayers, and then make your child. Your child will be very special. Of this I am sure."

"Is this like the ceremony of the wedding couple we went to?" Candice asked.

"Oh no!" Faint Chance responded with determination.

Candice, especially after all the advisories of medical health in going to Lao, worried that there could be something unhealthy in the plant. Spores? "But, we've already married for a long time now," she said, making reference to the fact that the ceremony was said to be for a wedding couple, which they were not. She tried to get out of accepting. "Won't it only work at a wedding?" She was hoping that would be an easy way out, looking for some excuse not to have to go through with having to ingest some strange leaves from God knows where.

"This will work even if it is not your wedding night, as the prayers summon spirits for the offspring and are not for the marriage. The chief taught me."

Spencer's research involved testing uncommon substances and their effect in lowering unwanted cholesterol, and therefore he did not dismiss the idea out of hand. "What are those leaves from?"

"They only come from a very special place, some distance from the village where I lived. They come from the spot where the chief found me, and that is the only spot. It's so rare that it has no specific name in Lao or in the dialect of the village other than 'special plant,' or *ton mai piiset* in Lao. The chief referred to it as plant for the *Maw Pii* who is the one that can talk to the spirits. He's the *Great Maw Pii*. So, '*Special plant of the Great Person who can talk to the Spirits*' would be the closest interpretation."

As the doctors looked on with skeptical scientific curiosity, she continued, "The chief gave me these leaves when I left the village with the missionaries. He wanted me to have a child with the abilities of one of his own children since he considered me his own. He said that since I was found by him at the place where the plant grows, that it was my karma to have his gift."

Karma, Candice thought skeptically. She realized that this woman was no scientist and that the whole thing sounded like an old wives' tale.

Trying not to be rude or disrespectful, the two doctors listened on intently. "What's in the bottle?" Spencer asked.

"That is northern *Lao-Lao*, the Laotian liquor. This must be taken at the same time as the *ton mai piiset*, and the spirits can only be contacted if the prayers are used. The northern *Lao-Lao* is made with a special mushroom. It must be from the north."

"Was the chief a special person?" Candice asked.

"Oh my yes!" Faint Chance exclaimed. "The chief was the wisest man in the village, and not just respected for his bloodline. He was a *Great Maw Pii* to the villagers, the one who could talk to the spirits. He solved the problems of the people in the village. Sometimes people from other villages would come to him to speak to the spirits and to solve problems. He was considered, in addition, by many to be a great shaman."

"This *Great Maw Pii* sounds like the equivalent of the Hindi name given Mohandas Karamchand Gandhi, *Mahatma*," Spencer said. "Mahatma had extraordinary abilities, some say supernatural, and so the Indians give him the name, the English translation of which is *Great Soul*. Go on, please. This is really cool!" Excitement was building, and he propped up in his seat, listening intently. "Do you know of him?"

"Of course," Faint Chance said. "My Tamil parents taught me."

"What's involved in the ceremony," Spencer asked, getting back to the present. "When we go back, so we have to slaughter a goat on top of an Aztec pyramid during the full moon to make it work? Or sacrifice a sixteen year-old virgin? But there are no sixteen year old virgins left in America."

Candice smiled, but Faint Chance did not laugh—perhaps she thought he was serious. Spencer realized that whether she understood his jokes or not, this woman was dead serious and giving up her most precious possession, so he would have to try to ignore the effects of the drinks he had and would have to try to be more serious. She had just offered the contents of her tiny hope chest to them. She was too poor to have a dowry, without higher education with which to earn money or perhaps get a work visa to most places, or little else to offer to a suitor, and she was now offering the only thing she had of value. It was indeed a solemn occasion. He must be quiet and go along with it, notwithstanding the amount of booze he drank.

"If you take these plant leaves in the ceremonial way, the spirits will bring you a special child," Faint Chance went on. "I was taught the prayers and can perform them for you when you take the plant. The child will have great wisdom, and be very respected. The child will be a leader to many."

"These were given you when you were seven and left the village. Can they still be good? How do you know that it's not poison?" Candice became skeptically scientific and rather rude to acceptance of the gracious gift.

Faint Chance frowned at Candice's disparaging assessment of her most cherished possession, "The chief said that the leaves are the medium where the special spirits either reside or can be contacted, and he was very wise. The spirits can be contacted by the plant, regardless of its age," Faint Chance said with the utmost sincerity, upset at Candice's skepticism. "Spirits do not die."

Candice noticed from her expression that Faint Chance could sense she was being doubted, and it was terribly rude to treat this royal gift so nonchalantly. This was the most valuable thing this poor creature owned, and Candice was treating it like it was unclean. She decided to break the ice that was forming, and hopefully back out of having to accept this wildly bizarre gift. "Faint Chance, we are deeply touched by this greatest gift you are offering to bestow on us, but we cannot possibly accept anything so valuable. This is for your wedding, and not for you to give away. This is probably your most valuable possession, and you must keep it for yourself. You owe us nothing. We are delighted to sponsor you without remuneration, and we'll be quite content with only your company living with us."

Faint Chance—as she had to insist that those who would take her to the promised land of prosperity and opportunity across the sea that she had only heard of, and would otherwise never know, affecting her life, in order to give them something in return—said, "I can get more. You must accept this. Not to do so would be very rude in Lao," she lied, as she had no way to know if she would ever go back to the tribe, see the chief again, or be able to get more of the plant. But she made it clear that she wanted them to accept her gift. And she did want that.

Both Spencer and Candice paused as they wondered if it really would be rude to decline the special gift. The idea of consuming some strange plant, especially after having read all the medical warnings about Laos before they came, was scary. But she was playing her trump card, accusing them of rudeness should they decline.

"And just how does this ceremony work?" Spencer asked, hoping to reduce his apprehension.

"I have to do it. When you create the child, I will summon the spirits with the special prayers the chief taught me. They'll be summoned, and, if they agree, it will happen."

The drinks they consumed, the lateness of the evening, their intense desire to live and experience local customs, and the wonder of it all, made Spencer and Candice look at each other affirmatively, albeit reluctantly. It was all too irresistible. Here they were on the other side of the world, where so few had been, and offered a chance to make a child with chieftain powers. Who could refuse?

"How about tonight?" Spencer said.

No one answered.

"Have you ever done this yourself?" Candice asked. She realized she was assuming that Faint Chance had a child.

"Oh, my no! The prayers will take some time and are loud to invoke the spirits. We'll need to go to your room to be alone. I have to be there to summon the spirits."

"Okay, let's go do it," Spencer said.

Faint Chance bagged up the exotic plant and off they went.

Chapter 8

Faint Chance set up her things on a teak coffee table in the sitting area of the spacious, teak wood trimmed hotel room. She had with her in her bag, *baci* strings, a bottle of northern *Lao-Lao* liquor, and the colorful purple and orange special plant leaves. She also had a bottle of scented massage oil, something they might use to facilitate or amplify the sex act as may be useful. She turned off the lights and lit the two candles already provided in the room in case of power outage, which was not that all uncommon, especially in the monsoon.

Trying to overcome the effects of too much booze, Spencer and Candice did their best to try to get serious, knowing how much it meant to Faint Chance.

She pointed across the table. "Spencer, you sit here, and Candice, you here."

She took the inside of Spencer's wrist and began a chant. She rubbed the first *baci* string on one of his wrists, pushing downward toward his hand. Then she tied it. The prayer chant changed, with loud moments, as though the loudness might drive something out. "This will cleanse the soul of evil spirits," she said.

"Is this like an exorcism?" Spencer said.

"Hush up, dear," Candice said. "Go along with it."

Faint Chance then repeated the ritual with the other

wrist. She then held both of his wrists and repeated the chant. She rested his arms on the table, turned to Candice, and repeated the ritual on both of her wrists.

"Now take the leaves. You must swallow it with this northern *Lao-Lao* liquor."

Spencer, not one to turn down a drink, gave it a try, swallowing a pinch of his portion of the leaves with the clear, northern *Lao-Lao*. As he took it, Faint Chance began a chant, and as it went down, she made a loud noise, ending in what seemed like an *uuuurrrrr* sound.

"Not all that bad," Spencer said. He tried to ease Candice's consternation. He finished the rest of his portion of leaves in three rounds of *Lao-Lao* sips.

It was Candice's turn. She took a pinch of the plant leaves and downed it with a swig of *Lao-Lao*. She then followed, taking the rest and a big shot of *Lao-Lao* as Faint Chance chanted.

Faint Chance put both Spencer's and Candice's hands together in front of her and put her hands on top. She began a different prayer, chanting a mysterious language.

She took the wrists of both of them, each in one of her hands, and held them tightly. She chanted the prayer again, and this time she closed her eyes. She repeated the chant several times.

She opened her eyes. "The spirits are here. You must now consummate the marriage in the same way as if you were just married and conceive your child. I'll leave you now so you can do that." She left.

Spencer felt a growing intensity of the effects on his senses. He looked at Candice. "It's working."

They went to the bed and began their consummation, and the hallucinations not only continued but became very intense.

At first, he became scared of hallucinations he was beginning to experience. But the visions were not nightmarish, and, in fact, were so wonderful that he pushed his fears aside and relaxed to absorb the spectacle. At first, the background all around went black, and he saw thousands of lights of galaxies and stars as if in space. He seemed to be traveling past them. He ended up on a world somewhere in space and time in a surreal, mystical garden. A loud waterfall emptied into a pond. A tall canopy formed above by tall, lush trees, and green plants with huge leaves were everywhere. The colors were enhanced, intense, and sometimes shifting. There was a breeze, making noise from the leaves that danced about.

Hardly supporting a scientific explanation, Candice experienced nearly the same hallucinations as Spencer when they compared their experiences later. Then things began to change. Figures with only an outline of shape appeared, moving about as though flying. Some had only an outline made of an iridescent color. Some had wings and flew.

A huge, translucent, purple flower appeared directly in front of them. Its leaves turned into variegated colors of purple and orange. Translucent butterflies flew across their field of vison. Streaks of iridescent light of red, green, blue, magenta, and yellow moved horizontally across their field of view. Some lingered, some went by quickly. A small white bud appeared, and then slowly bloomed, larger and larger, with a blue center which turned into a blue eye in the middle, as though looking at them. Small bursts of light came all over their field of view and left quickly. A kaleidoscope of colors appeared and then passed. Flowers of all colors continually appeared and disappeared. A few hummingbirds flew about. Several winged angelic women with flowing gowns and white skin hovered. Small dots of exploding light came and went. A sweet fragrance was detectable. The fear of the event was leaving, and they were enjoying it. They would debate later if there was music.

They both felt their sensations increasing as they neared consummation. There was something more in the plant than hallucinations, as they simultaneously had the wildest, most ferocious, orgasms either had ever experienced, or ever would.

ᘓᘐᘓ

The blissful couple awoke in the morning. Sun illuminated the red bougainvilleas just outside and below the picture window of the second story hotel room unto the courtyard below. The rain had let up. Faint Chance was gone.

"Wow!" Candice said first. "That was the wildest sex I have ever had!"

"Out of this world! That plant could sell as a million fold replacement for Viagra," Spencer said. "You don't anything else to make sex wilder."

"Something made me lose complete contact with my surroundings," Candice said.

The strange feelings now gone, Spencer decided to break the mood that had overcome them. "This was supposed to be for the consummation of our wedding, but that means, of course, that the consummation is sex, not vows of marriage? Or is it?

"I think the wedding is not necessary, only sex," Candice said. "If we were to try to duplicate our wedding night exactly, as in consummating the wedding in a tradition that Faint Chance spoke of, we would have to take a cruise on a big cruise ship, and we'd have to pass out before we consummated anything. Hah! Some Romeo you were that night! But this is something! What an adventure to tell back home!"

"Can we really tell this story to anyone back home?" Spencer said.

ᘓᘐᘓ

In the afternoon following, it rained. Spencer and Candice came by the jewelry store to say goodbye to their provocative, fascinating, and mystifying new friend.

Faint Chance took off and accompanied them to the

small café a few doors away. She and Candice ordered tea, but Spencer ordered beer.

"That was the most fantastic experience I have ever had," Spencer said to Faint Chance.

"The same for me," Candice said. "I don't know if it was the plant, the spirits, you, or a combination. But it was wild beyond anything I have every experienced."

"I only know about contacting the spirits," Faint Chance said. "I have not done it before."

"We leave tomorrow in the morning," Spencer said. "We should have a way to contact you, other than by mail. Do you have any way to get access to a computer?"

"No, sorry. Only big, fancy stores have those."

"Well, you can always call us collect," Candice said, "although I don't actually do that from here. Or, if you do get access to a computer, you can email us or call us on a live chat program. So, I guess this is goodbye for now."

Spencer, the quartermaster of the cash for the trip for he and Candice, said, "Here's something for expenses you might have in getting your papers and things together." He handed her an envelope with one thousand dollars.

"We'll pay for your ticket at our end. We're hoping that everything will work out quickly and we'll see you in a matter of months. We can't thank you enough for showing us about and for everything you have done for us."

They hugged for goodbyes. Tears formed in the emerald eyes of Faint Chance.

"Don't worry about a thing," Candice said. "I'll have your own room set up for you when you come, and everything will be ready. We'll look forward to having you."

"I'm so happy!" Faint Chance said. "I look forward to coming to my new family in America. There will be a new child there soon, a special child."

"Ah, yes, to be sure," Candice said, normally not believing it, but left with doubt after the experience she had with the plant.

❧❧❧

Cameron, having received only a few emails from Spencer and Candice thus far, was quite surprised to turn on his computer and find an email.

Dear Uncle Cameron:
We are finally at a hotel that has computers in the rooms! We are in Penang, Malaysia.
Guess what? You are going to be an uncle! Candice is nearly four months along now, and getting bigger. It's a good thing this didn't happen at the beginning of the trip! We are sampling the marvelous Malay cuisine. This country has some really delicious foods. Wait until we do these at home. My favorite is chilli crab. There are lots of super noodle dishes and curries too.
Malaysia is our last stop, so we got a ton of spices and seasonings. Candice will be cooking up some spectacular meals at home, and you will be invited to try our new recipes.
We will be coming home in three weeks. The trip could not have been much better. We have so much to tell, and Candice has hundreds of pictures. We will notify you of the flight information. We look forward to seeing you, and to coming home.
Spencer and Candice

Uncle? Whoa! Cameron read the message again in disbelief! He was about to be Uncle Cameron. The ultimate revolting concept! A twinge of a muscle spasm went through him as he thought of having to give up his motorcycle if he had a child. He debated trying to find a muscle relaxant or tranquilizer.

Chapter 9

S pencer and Candice looked a little different to Cameron as they walked out of Immigration toward him pushing a cart of bags, consisting of souvenirs and spices. They had managed to get through customs without being singled out.

Spencer was healthy, sun tanned, and a bit slimmer. Candice looked different too, but she had gained in the stomach with a child on the way.

After the big hugs and getting their bags into Cameron's car, they began talking nonstop.

Cameron interrupted once to ask, "Did you ever get sick from the local water or foods?"

"We were both sick twice, at different times, but fortunately not for too long," Candice said. "We both fell sick in India for several days, but at different times, even though we drank only bottled water. Oh, yes, Spencer got very sick for a day in Thailand from bad shrimp. But that lasted only a day and a half. Nothing too serious. We recovered."

"Don, Linda, and I watched the house for you," Cameron said. "There were no problems."

They pulled up in the drive.

"Home sweet home!" Spencer said. "It's so good to be back."

"At our last stop, in Malaysia, we could load up with

luggage that we did not have to lug home, and so I bought massive spices!" Candice said. "How about Saturday night for dinner here? Today is Wednesday, and that will give me enough time to get organized. I want to go to the lab tomorrow if I'm not a zombie from jet lag. I'll put some of these spices I bought to the test."

"That sounds wonderful," Cameron said.

∽∾∽∾

Come Saturday, Candice, very pregnant, put on a spectacular dinner. She had many recipes and strange seasonings to try not readily available in America. Don and Linda were invited since they had helped take care of the house. Also invited was a colleague of theirs at the medical research lab, Lawrence, who brought his wife, Karen. An East Indian OBGYN doctor friend, Kala, was also invited. Candice was rather large in the stomach, her pregnancy showing.

After dinner, Candice produced a box of prints she had made at a commercial photo lab from her digital camera. "I've not had time to organize these yet."

"You really are excellent with a camera. Some of these are worth enlarging and framing," Linda said, going through the stack of prints.

"Well, having good stuff to shoot makes the difference. The richest venue for photo material has to be India. There are so many people there doing so many things. There are many castles, the Taj Mahal, the tea plantations of Munnar, the Erotic Temples of Khajuraho, and so on—really endless." Candice left out the still photos of naked Faint Chance, and the movie as well, to preserve her privacy. However, there were a number of her properly dressed.

They began highlighting their adventures, referencing the pictures. Finally, the topic came up of what happened in Lao, and Candice said, "Then, you'll never guess what we did! We completely lost our heads in Lao! We met this absolutely gorgeous female and were so taken with her that we offered to sponsor her to come to the United States! She should be here in a few months, depending on delays with immigration. I have pictures of her and a digital movie, but some, and definitely the movie, are R-rated, so I won't show those." She laid out the still photos of Faint Chance clothed and showed them.

"She's beautiful!" Cameron was the first to compliment.

"What's her name," Linda asked.

"Unpronounceable, too tough to use," Spencer said. "So we gave her a nickname. We named her *Faint Chance*."

That cracked everybody up.

"Is that really what you call her?" Linda asked.

"It sure is," Candice said. "It refers to her own remark when we met her as to her assessment of what her chances were of migrating to America."

"Let me guess," Cameron said. She has a brother named *Slim* and two sisters, *Fat* and *No*."

That brought the house down with roaring laughter.

"You're really funny, Cameron," Kala said.

Being single herself, and admiring Cameron, she complimented him whenever possible—she considered that he was an attractive catch for her, but he had not shown any discernable, long-term interest in her yet.

"Tell us more," Don said. "Is she only a super model, or can she actually talk?"

Spencer grinned. "Well, yes, she can talk and speaks several languages. She's a beautiful mix of Laotian and German. She was orphaned at age four and actually lived with a tribal chief of animists, who are people that believe plants and objects have souls and spirits. She was then taken to the city in Lao by missionaries at age seven and later adopted by a Tamil Indian couple. We met her in a jewelry store owned by the Tamils."

"Whatever possessed you to sponsor her to America?" Linda asked.

"We had seen so much poverty in India," Candice said, "and we wanted to do something to help the underprivileged people we saw. But there was nothing we could do except for passing out coins and ball point pens, especially to the Indian children who are so beautiful and have so little. After India, we were in Lao and met this beautiful young woman, who had little, and who took time off work just to show us around. So, we decided to invite her here."

"Do you think she'll fit in?" Linda asked with a concerned look as though problems were looming on the horizon.

"There's little opportunity in Lao, so how could she not?" Candice answered. "In Lao, the future for a woman is to marry and spend her entire life caring for her family and home with very primitive means to do so, such that it leaves very little time for anything else. But now, I'll leave you for a while, and do the final preparations for dinner. Give me fifteen minutes."

Conversation at the dining table went back and forth from miscellaneous experiences that Spencer and Candice had on the trip, to various news items that came to mind about people at the research laboratories where they worked, and to some of their mutual friends.

Changing the subject, Linda asked, "How is it that you decided to go for a child in the midst of all that exotic, far away travel?"

"Well," Candice answered, "We have, of course, been thinking about it for a long time. And, we had a good deal of time to talk to one another on the trip, and we had decided that, when we got back, we would go ahead and have a child. We would not have had a child in Asia, medicine being what it is there in some places. And also, we were enjoying traveling, not child rearing. But then we were out for dinner in Lao with Faint Chance, and the most extraordinary thing happened. She gave us the most valuable thing she owned, her present from her tiny hope chest that consisted of only one thing. It was special plant leafs from a very remote area in the north of Lao that she believes has spirits residing in the leaves that give special abilities to a child being conceived."

"Don't tell me you actually did this?" Linda asked, raising an eyebrow in a suspicious quandary that her friends may have taken some hallucinatory drug in Asia and had their brains permanently fried.

"We sure did!" Candice boasted. "The whole nine yards! We had the ceremonial ritual, took the plant leaves, and had prayer strings on our wrists for three days afterward. It was really cool. We were really into it!"

"Don't tell me you ate weird plant leaves when conceiving your child?" Linda said. "Ugh! You are probably going to give birth to Medusa!"

"An alien, like in a movie," Don added. Do they have a maternity ward in Area Fifty-One?"

All laughed loudly.

"*Rosemary's Baby*," Lawrence added.

Candice smiled, ignoring the jokes, and continued, "When this person gave us this most valuable thing that she owned, with us not wanting to hurt her feelings, combined with the fact that we got caught up in this most amazing story of hers about the special plant that was meant for a tribal chief, we took the potion as though we were having a tribal chief's wedding."

"Tell 'em the truth, luv—we were drunk!" Spencer admitted.

That brought another big laugh.

"Do you suppose there is anything to it in reality?" Don switched to a bit more serious tone.

"I don't," Candice said. "We ran across many rituals. We were in Bombay and learned of an Indian sect that believes that fire is sacred, such that when they die, they do not cremate the body, but instead put it on the roof of a special building and vultures come and pick the bones clean. The remains of the bones are later dissolved in acid. We witnessed the religious significance of the Ganges River to the Indians, and how they, if they can afford it, bring the bodies of their deceased ones there, burn the remains with sandalwood and put the bones in the river. If they cannot afford all sandalwood, they buy a little and mix that with other wood. That was very eerie. We saw many such things."

"There is something to it," Spencer said. "We both had nearly the same, wild experience when we took the leaves. It was a very strong experience, whatever it was. Candice also had the experience, didn't you?" He looked to her for back up, as he was he was being challenged on the visions he had.

"I'll say," Candice said. "But I don't attribute anything to religion or the supernatural. I'm, after all, a scientist. I think the plant leaves had some chemical that gave a chemically caused hallucination. I definitely had that. It was strong."

"Wow!" Kala said. "That must have been something! There must have been something in it."

"Probably a chemically induced hallucination, and one tied by association to the superstitions you were learning of at the time," Lawrence said, acting the scientist. "Were most of the superstitions you ran into connected to religion?"

"Religion and superstition are close bedfellows," Spencer answered. "When you consider the number of monuments and major sights of interests, most are religious in nature. We saw so many Buddhas. There is a neat shrine where Buddha gave his first sermon on the Ganges River in Varanasi, India. Say, now that is an eerie place, with people burning the remains of their loved ones on the shores of the river, praying. In parts of India, in Thailand, and in Lao, there are many shrines housing a relic is called a *Shiva Lingam*, or a large phallus."

"What better thing to worship that a giant chorizo?" Kala said.

All laughed.

"There were many domed shaped structures containing relics, such as the *Shiva Lingam*," Spencer said. They are called *Stupas*. Some have a huge, gold-painted Buddha inside."

"*Stupa*? I'll show you *stupa*!" Cameron said, as he got up and poured himself another scotch.

Chapter 10

The baby was born, a very healthy boy, né Devan. There were no complications. He had no crying spells, most unusual. He had a fair complexion, blond hair, and bright blue eyes.

A month later, Candice called. "Cameron, it has been a whole month since Devan was born, and you have yet to so much as come by. We insist that you to come over this Saturday evening, and I'll make dinner. You cannot stay away forever. You have to come and see him some time. He's very well behaved. No more excuses."

"I know, I know. It's just that I don't go in for cuddling infants. But I guess I'd better get it over with. Seven-thirty, okay?"

"That'll be fine."

He hung up and shivered at the idea of holding a rodent.

೭ನ೭ನ

Come Saturday, Cameron arrived to make an obligatory, but surely to be revolting, experience. He would lie and tell them he had to do some work at home before bed so he could leave early, imagining that the entire conversation would be how cute the little cockroach was and endless topics of the disgusting of child rearing. He brought baby clothes as an obligatory gift that he let the busybody secretary at the office select, all to her great delight. As he drove up to the house, he thought that he was entirely correct, and genuine, in his dislike of anyone younger than a grown person. He realized that there should be a change in the law, which change was that to keep any unborn child, one should have to go to court and show cause why the child should be spared.

"Hi, Cameron," Candice said in greeting.

"You're trim and in good shape already," Cameron said, exaggerating, already revolted at the event. "Here, a small present." He handed her a box of baby clothes.

"Oh, thank you so much, darling Cameron." She kissed him on the cheek.

He did not like the kiss as he suspected germs were being transmitted to him from the germ infested, parasite she must surely have just kissed.

"Cameron!" Spencer came in. "How's the famous architect?"

"Just working long hours, that's about it. So, where's the creature?" Cameron said of Devan as though referring to a new specimen of incurable AIDS virus being carried by a diseased alien.

Spencer and Candice both led him to the crib.

Cameron approached the crib as though it might be a toxic specimen. He was ready for a crying, diaper wetting and fouling, obnoxious, toxic creature. He thought it should have been named Stachybotrys for toxic mold, although Stachybotrys was curable.

Cameron bent over to look at Devan. He had blond hair and blue eyes. His skin was very fair. There was something unusual about him. His eyes followed Cameron as he moved about. Devan had some coordination of his hands and could reach out and grab something in front of him, such as Cameron's finger. As Cameron watched, Devan actually turned himself over onto his side in bed all by himself.

Cameron saw and blurted out, "Have you seen him turn over by himself? He just did it!"

"I've seen him move about in the crib, but I don't think that's unusual," Candice replied.

"You both are doctors," Cameron said, "and you don't think that's unusual at this age? I do."

"Possibly," Spencer said,

"There is something uncanny about him," Cameron said. He leaned over the crib. "Hi. I'm your Uncle Cameron."

Devan looked him right in the eyes. "Hi, Uncle."

Cameron was aghast. He stepped away from the crib and turned to look at Spencer and Candice. "He said hi to me, and he's only one month old!"

Spencer and Candice came over and gathered around.

"What?" Candice asked.

"This is impossible," Spencer said. "No one-month-old infant can utilize its vocal cords to make such words, as his central nervous system is not sufficiently developed to do that."

They all bent over him, irresistibly attracted, waiting for another word.

Devan looked up at them. "Hi."

They stared at him and then at each other. Devan looked at them, as though wondering what was wrong. It was obvious that Devan was somewhat aware of what was going on around him.

"I can't believe this!" Candice said. She and Spencer looked at each other dumbfounded.

They looked down again at him.

"Do you know your name?" Cameron asked.

He looked at Cameron, "Devan."

"Oh my God!" Candice said and then went speechless.

Spellbound, the three could say little. They gathered back at the dinner table and sat.

"What could have possibly happened to Devan to accelerate him in his development?" Spencer finally said. "Could something on our trip have had something to do with it? I

mean, what are the chances of a one-month-old baby talking?"

Spencer, Candice, and Cameron, all three, simultaneously looked at each other, and all said, *"Faint Chance!"*

Chapter 11

I am, after all, a genetic research doctor with publications, and who better to analyze any difference in the DNA of Devan that the plant may have caused, than me?" Candice asked herself aloud as she sat at her lab equipment, running tests on cells she had taken from a swab inside of Devan's cheek. She had been conducting tests, using a technique called hybridization of DNA of samples taken from Devan since the discovery that Devan was unusual.

Candice and Spencer had decided that they dare not let out news about this phenomenon, as it would become a media event and there would be reporters and TV cameras stacked up outside their home. It would also be, and make them, the subject of much skepticism. Candice confided only in her lab assistant, Tadashi Uto, a Japanese man of twenty-two years of age. He was an employee of the lab, not a doctor, but a lab technician assigned to her as her research assistant and had been there two years. As far as letting him in on what was going on, she took a chance and filled him in on the studies, because it would have been impractical to impossible to do any testing at the lab where he assisted her full time while trying to keep it a secret. And, she needed someone to cover for her when she was working on this project instead of her usual work.

Candice spoke to Tadashi in the lab. "Devan definitely has differences in his DNA than ordinary people. But they are very subtle. But a tiny change can make a huge difference. The resultant differences are that he has an acceleration of the development of his central nervous system. This was brought about by one or more substitute amino acids that caused a difference in his DNA chain. Something had brought about one or more substituted amino acids."

"What can cause a change in DNA?" Tadashi asked.

"The first is who, or what, you marry," Candice answered,

Tadashi laughed out loud.

"Apart from that, the three things we know of are ultraviolet light, radiation, and poison."

"Is this one of those?"

"There was no radiation or ultraviolet light involved with Devan. The plant leaf from Lao would be somewhat like a poison, as contrasted to ultraviolet light or radiation. Pretty neat poison! But, what's a poison? Too much of something good can be poison. Then again, maybe a fourth way will be identified, and maybe this is that new category. We really need to get a specimen of the plant and study it, as now all we have is the effect, that is, Devan. Without the plant, we will never be able to do anything other than speculate on what might be in it that can cause such changes.

"These studies take time, and I've only begun. To make matters worse, whenever I run into someone that I have not seen since before I left on the trip, I have to give some condensed version of the trip to them. With all that, and now Devan, I'm pressed for time to do the research."

"Do you think that you could synthesize the chemical in the plant if you could identify it?" Tadashi asked.

"Synthesizing it would most likely be easy if I had a sample. But there is none. We look at the effect and then postulate what might cause that. Imagine if we had a specimen and could synthesize it? It could be made into a pill, like a drug, and everyone would want it. Think of the significance!

⌘

"Hi, Uncle Cameron," Devan said as he came in the door.

"Hi, Devan. How are you?" Cameron asked his two-month-old nephew.

"Fine, thank you." Devan went back to a child's puzzle he was working on.

"Come in and sit," Candice said,

Cameron went to the table as Candice was laying out a basket of bread. "This is homemade Indian bread called *roti pratha*. Actually, I did not make the dough, but I bought it ready to bake. It's much easier that way. You'll love it."

"What do you call that outfit," Cameron asked.

"It's called a *sinh*. It is the tubular skirt of the Laotians. They wear western tops there, but I chose to wear a tank top. How great do I look?"

"Fantastic! Say, this is delicious bread. What have you learned about Devan?"

Candice sat, adjusted her chair, and assumed a professional role. "It's my assumption at this time that Devan's DNA chain was altered by the plant. This is confirmed by some preliminary studies. One, and possibly more, amino acid substitutions may have resulted in a new or stronger enzyme or enzymes that accelerate development of the central nervous system. This includes the brain and spinal cord. The result is that Devan is developing his central nervous system at a very rapid rate. It must have begun in the womb—mine. I imagine that he might have heard and remembered noises from before he was born. This rapid development explains how he can walk and talk at two months."

As she spoke, Devan was proving her point by walking about the living room and was quite able to identify objects by name, know his own name, and the names of others.

"Devan has a level of talk already that seems like it should be coming from someone two or three years of age," she continued. "He does not make many noises that are not proper words in the way infants do. When he makes a sound, it is generally a proper word or a small sentence. 'I'm hungry,' for example. It's uncanny. To go along with his ability to speak, his muscular coordination is very good, and, as you can see—" she said, directing her attention to Devan walking about, "—he walks fairly well at two months. His accelerated ability to control his muscles is nothing short of astonishing.

"There was something in those dried up leaves from that special plant that Faint Chance gave us that did this to him. I'm quite certain that the fertilization of one of my eggs occurred when Spencer and I took the plant leaves in Lao. The substance taken by both Spencer and me, at the time of conception, created one or more substitute amino acids, which caused a difference in the DNA chain. The result is that the design for the central nervous system is different, such that it develops much more rapidly than in a normal person. Ability to focus the eyes, process sounds, motor skill development, ability to think and reason, bladder control, self-control, ability to learn, and intelligence itself are accelerated and possibly enhanced. This explains the ability of Devan to be able to think, walk, and talk at such a young age.

"But the significance may not just be that the child learns more quickly in life due to a more rapidly developing central nervous system. I have an idea that it may be much more significant than you might imagine. It's my notion that this may make for a whole new dimension of human intelligence. If you think of it, young ones spend years learning to use their muscles and coordination, and that, of course, includes the brain as the main component of the central nervous system. That includes speech. Humans spend—or waste, if you think about it—many years trying clumsily to learn. They are twenty or twenty-five years old before they get out of school, and then have only a short number of years, maybe twenty, of useful energy and life before things like cancer, heart attacks, diabetes, hardening of arteries, high blood pressure, strokes, Parkinson's disease, senile dementia, thinning of the bones, cataracts, loss of close up visual accommodation, hearing fading, kidney failure, arthritis, and various other maladies set in and get rid of us like beings that have served their useful purpose and should go. These show up significantly in the forties, and, of course, more so later. Brain cells actually begin to die."

"Gee, I better check my will," Cameron joked. "Come to think of it, I don't have one."

"The present design of humans is to not allow them to be able to gain much intelligence when growing, and that ability is further impeded by a lack of emotional control over the body by the central nervous system," Candice continued. "Now, this plant could be something really significant in more ways than just the fact that it can enhance the ability to learn earlier in life. It may not be just that one learns at an earlier age in life, but that one can utilize the formative years to become many times greater than an ordinary person. As an example, if this accelerated nervous system continues, a person could perhaps be in college at age seven or eight, and then go on to some level of achievement far greater than any normal human. A person will still be able to continue to learn more and more in his best formative years, and it could be as though one started out his higher learning where we left off."

"But how could a youngster have the ability to use, say, expensive laboratory or other delicate equipment at a bungling age of seven, for example?" Cameron asked.

"When the central nervous system develops, so does the coordination to use the brain. In other words, Devan should have the muscular coordination of a person of his corresponding development of brain at the same time, if my notion is correct. You have seen how he could follow you with his eyes from the crib, and now he is walking at age two months. He also uses small sentences and has an extraordinary vocabulary, considering. So, if I'm right, he will not be a 'bungling seven-year-old' as you refer to. He may be in university.

"The development of the central nervous system in this fashion will also result in earlier and better control of one's emotions. The onset of puberty, the problems of adolescence, should be much more under control and cause fewer problems. This thing may be like coming out of the Stone Age in terms of human development. You have noticed how Devan has never seemed to have fits, crying spells, or emotional outbursts like others of his age."

"What does it mean in terms of overall development?" Cameron asked.

"We can't be sure," Candice answered. "These things will not be able to be tested for some time—that is, until he gets there in age. There is no one to compare him to, unless we compare him to much older people. But his present state of development is easily compared to others. It seems obvious to me he will far surpass normal intelligence, and who knows, maybe double or more."

"Sort of like an Einstein of science or a genius in business, and at an incredibly early age," Spencer said. "A young person could achieve new heights. The person could have the intelligence of a fully matured adult at one-quarter or one-third the age of his peers. From there, he could be able to continue to use his youth and best learning years when he has the ability to acquire information and skills without his body deteriorating, and create achievements yet unknown. A new race of super humans. And, he would be in better control of his emotions, which are the cause of such a waste of human energies, especially in adolescents. Without even trying to be, anyone this way could begin applying themselves where everyone else tapered off, and still be a teenager."

"Just that, if I'm right," Candice said. "Anyone born in the future without this enhancement will be considered Stone Age. This may be the next step in human evolution. And, Cameron, you surprise me. You sound like you actually like Devan. Is this a change in my brother-in-law?"

"I'm still content to let you be the one with the baby," Cameron said. "Just because he's interesting from a scientific view does not mean that I'm going to go off the deep end and have a child. And, how can you be absolutely sure that the difference in Devan came from the plant that Faint Chance gave you? Maybe you just have a special baby?"

"From a scientific point of view, it's the only explanation," Candice answered. "Either that, or Devan just happens to be the most extraordinary child ever."

"He lives!" Cameron joked, making reference to the reincarnation of Hitler as in the movie *The Boys from Brazil*.

"Hah!" Spencer liked the joke.

"It was the plant leaves for sure," Candice said.

"What's the opinion of the famous cholesterol doctor?" Cameron asked, looking at his brother.

"I too, had an incredible experience at the time, sort of religious," Spencer said.

"You have been getting more religious lately, haven't you?" Cameron asked. "Did the trip have anything to do with it?"

"It has clarified my views," Spencer answered. "I simply cannot believe that there is not an order and purpose to the world, and to life."

"More than mathematical order?" Cameron asked, armed with math and calculus as an architect.

"Well, I think so," Spencer said. "Take an apple. It's a bright red fruit, designed to attract by its color. It's wet, suite, delicious, and healthy to eat. It does nothing for the tree on which it grows. It just hangs there until some human, or some other animal, goes and picks it. If no one does, it falls off and might be eaten by a hog, horse, or another animal, or just rot. Except for the tiny seeds inside, it makes this huge fruit which takes energy and substances from the tree which doesn't help the tree. So, the apple is clearly designed for others—in this case, humans or animals. Why does the apple tree exist? Is its existence owing to a random chance happening, or is it there because of a design or purpose? This is my view on God. It's the purpose of things. There must be a purpose."

"As you know, my good brother," Cameron said, "I cannot subscribe to the notion of some fellow sitting 'up there' in a chair guiding us through life 'in his image.' It's so much nonsense. I love the late George Carlin comedy video on that."

"Well, how then do you explain our existence?" Spencer asked.

"Does one have to?" Cameron answered. "That is the ultimate age-old question." Then he gave took up the subject to respect his brother's question. "Well, I cannot attribute any purpose to the existence of man whatsoever. Man is just another creature like an insect or anything else. The only difference is that man has a bigger, or at least more efficient, brain than other creatures on this planet. But I don't think that man has all that much brain to use, or doesn't use much of it. Most of his brain is put to use of pursuits other than the quest for knowledge. I think that Freud was totally right in that man's energy is fueled by sexual energy. Man dresses himself, or herself, to be attractive. How do you explain a person buying an eighty thousand dollar car just to get around, when that consumes a significant portion of his paycheck? Driving an expensive car is, to me, peacocking. It's an extended form of mating ritual. Women do the same. Have you noticed the news women and pundits on mainstream TV? They wear long hair extensions, have lips filled with injections painted with iridescent paint. Soon they may start using actual lights for lipstick made of brush-on nano-

LED lights. They have the brains of toad-eating ignoramuses."

Candice laughed out loud. "Can you imagine a woman on TV who has lips that actually light up?" She laughed again. "It might look good. I think Devan is the next step in human evolution," she continued. "He definitely has an advanced central nervous system and has more control over his emotions. Perhaps he's less of the Freudian person you describe, Cameron. And, I know it's from the plant."

"But the origin of Devan's difference, if it is the plant—" Spencer argued, "—it is still from God. The plant was a naturally occurring substance right here on the earth. It's not something from a computer or a lab."

Cameron rebounded. "But just because it grew from the ground does not necessarily mean that it was placed there by a supreme being."

"Well," Spencer said, "I really don't like such explanations as it's been put there by a visiting alien or a random chance happening. Have you an explanation?"

"Just leaning to a notion of a God to answer the unexplained is no answer at all, as far as I'm concerned," Cameron said. "From a fundamental point of view, the earth is almost entirely made up of things that require other things to continue. Trees take in carbon dioxide and give off oxygen. Men do the opposite. If life stems from simple cells millions, or billions, of years ago, it is my view that the division left a link open to later bring them together. If this special plant caused the change in Devan, it may have been waiting for man to find it to provide a more advanced step in his development. It is sort of like Yin and Yang. I read in a magazine that we are on the verge of making new organs from a three-D printer of human organs using stem cells."

"But aren't you necessarily conceding a purpose to the existence of the plant in your analysis?" Spencer argued.

Candice interrupted. "Hey! I'm the one that made dinner. No religion or politics at the table!"

She smiled at the two intellectual brothers that she loved.

The brothers realized that the dinner table was no place for debate on such basic matters as theology that never got resolved, only argued.

Chapter 12

Two Japanese men sat together in the 747 cabin, talking quietly in Japanese, at a level that could not be heard by anyone else over the sound of the engines propelling the 747 across the Pacific towards Los Angeles from Tokyo.

Shuji, Mario's assistant for the trip, said, "Morio, since we have the time, tell me more about the high potency marijuana we are going for."

Morio Uto looked around to the left and right, to make sure that he could not be overheard by the other passengers, and, satisfied, responded, "I'm bargaining for the Oyabun for two metric tons of marijuana with very high potency tetrahydrocannabinol, or THC, which is the rage now. We will be meeting them in California. My contact grows twenty-five percent THC that is consistently potent. There is an abundance of marijuana now in California, the price is down, and the quality up."

"Why buy from California, as Hawaii is so much closer?" Shuji asked. "I have heard Hawaii also has strong weed and a lot of it. Japanese go there just to golf since it is so much closer than California."

"Dealing with the Hawaiians is not very businesslike. They have a lazy attitude, much worse than the Americans from their mainland. It's as though they say, 'If you don't like our schedule of quantity or delivery of weed, we'll just keep it and smoke it ourselves.'"

"Are you bringing in seeds in addition?"

"Yes. I'll be bringing varieties of clones of small plants. I'll be setting up growing our own, at a secret building in the country that the Oyabun will provide. But that's in addition to the major purchase, and from a different source."

ｃｓｃｏ

Tadashi Uto felt inadequate around his brother Morio. Morio always had the most stylish clothes, alligator shoes, fashion sunglasses, fancy rings and watches, chauffeured cars, escort women, and a bundle of spending cash when he came to visit, usually once a year. Tadashi had gone to a junior college in America and stayed on rather than return to Japan. In medical research, he could easily transfer back to Japan or another country for a similar job with his English. But he had taken a liking to America and its decadence.

Tadashi thought his brother Morio was working on business investments. Tadashi knew he had an interest in a nightclub in Tokyo, but did not know he was a gangster.

Morio, from his hotel, called on his brother Tadashi. He announced his arrival and invited his younger brother to dinner. An expensive Japanese restaurant.

Tadashi arrived twenty minutes early to be polite and took a seat at the reserved table.

Mario arrived a bit late and had with him a five-foot ten-inch, blonde escort supermodel from Kiev who was so stunning that most in the restaurant stared. She only spoke a little English.

Tadashi stood when they came. Morio made the introductions. The escort's name was Marina.

"How are things going for you at work?" Mario asked his brother Tadashi.

"I'm doing well," Tadashi boasted. "My wages are small, but I have a medical plan, a 401k retirement plan, and a great future. But now I have something more for a fantastic prospect. You'll never guess what I'm working on," he said, breaking the trust of his confidence with his boss, Candice. "I'm working on a project worth a fortune. My boss is working on a special substance that, when taken during the conception of a baby, will make the baby able to develop his motor skills and intelligence at a supernatural rate, and surpass normal people in intelligence and learning faster and presumably more. It comes from a special plant from Laos. She took the plant herself along with her husband, and her own son recently born has these special qualities. He could speak words at one month and is now walking and talking at just a few months old. He is learning things that only a child of five or seven years could learn."

Mario wondered what it is that so excited his younger brother. He pretended to be interested in children and his younger brother's babble about his perceived self-importance. "What the fuck is so valuable about that?"

"If the substance can be synthesized," Tadashi answered, "it could then be concentrated, refined, and then produced. Then it can be marketed as a pill for every couple that is making a baby. Just imagine! Every couple in the world will want to have it! Governments would pay for it. Anyone who does not take it will give birth to only an ordinary child. Ordinary children will be retarded by comparison to anyone born of this substance. Everyone who learns of it will insist on taking it, unless they don't want to have super intelligent kids. Initially, it could be sold to the super rich, and eventually marketed to the ordinary person. People would pay anything to have an extraordinary child. After it's learned of, who would want a child without it? This could be the most valuable thing ever created."

"Your boss will make it," Morio said. "How could someone else go about making money off of it?"

"Once formulated, my boss can patent the process of the

formula, and it will only be obtainable from whatever source she chooses to manufacture it," Uto answered. "Major countries recognize reciprocal agreements with patents. They must honor the patent. So she, as the patent holder, will have an unimaginable monopoly. It would be like selling an expensive drug, only perhaps the most valuable ever, and legal. Think of how much people would pay for a dose! Initially the rich would pay any price. A billionaire might pay a billion! As soon as it becomes readily available, it could still be sold for ten thousand dollars a dose, or whatever price one wanted to sell it for. This thing I'm working on is really incredible!"

Tadashi was finally able to stand up tall in stature to his successful brother.

"Is that what your boss has plans to do?" Morio asked.

"Once a good deal of money has been made, she will want to make it to help the poor, like those she saw in India, by making it available to all, rather than selling it for any profit. She does not want anyone to not have it because of lack of money. She has said that she wants to control it, and she will be quite happy with just a royalty and the success that it will bring her in her research. But just think that even if it only cost a dollar a pill in poor countries how much could be made? Every time a couple has sex to have a baby, each must have it."

"Does she have it patented yet?" Morio asked, not familiar with the patent process, a legal concept, but aware that a patent could make it hers and no one else's.

"No, there's nothing to patent yet. But that's the target. When she synthesizes it, she will patent it. Then she will own it. Then all countries that recognize patents must comply. But she has no way to synthesize it yet, and so the best way will be to get more of the plant which will make it relatively easy. Then she can patent the formula and the process. This I'm sure can be done, and I'll be working on it with her," Tadashi boasted. "I'm sure she'll give me credit in the journals. I'll probably get some of the royalties too.

Maybe I could get a neat sports car. Maybe even a nice house and a motorcycle too."

"A person could make a bigger fortune with this stuff legally than illegally," Mario said. "Help the poor? Screw that! I'd sell it for whatever I could get for it. Have you already synthesized it at her lab?" He had already been told the answer, but as his interest peaked he wanted to go over it again with his proud younger brother. Whoever got this patent first would be the rich one, and that might be him.

"No, not yet. Our studies of the effects are one thing, but those studies do not leave the formula exposed, only its effects. My boss only had the plant in Lao. We have to do what seems to be an incredible amount of work to find out what the substance is, and that could take a long time—in fact, my boss has said it is not a sure thing. She has mentioned several times that she would like to return to Lao, or send someone there, to try to get a specimen of the plant. Maybe she'll send me!" He leaned back, and held his head up with pride. Hearing no praise from his brother, Tadashi continued, "Right now we're only working on separating substitute amino acids that have altered the DNA chain in her son. But synthesizing it, if we can get a specimen, should be easy compared to working on DNA chains. You'd be surprised to learn just how small, and how complicated, a DNA chain is."

Tadashi proudly went on, able to communicate to his brother for the first time on a different level than before. From that point on, Morio listened politely but did not comprehend nor did he focus his attention on the scientific aspect of how it affected the DNA, which Tadashi so proudly began lecturing on. Morio just pondered how he might get his hands on it.

By the end of the visit, Tadashi had indeed impressed his brother, but he was worried that he should not have been so boastful and revealed the confidences of his boss Candice. He said to Morio just before he left, "By the way, please do not mention this work that I'm doing to anyone, as it is done in the most extreme confidence. My boss is holding off publishing it until she either isolates the substance, or gets more of the plant and we get it synthesized. She'll then apply for the patent and then publish. It'll make us very famous in the research community. So, you must treat this in the absolute strictest of confidence. I told you about it only because you are my only brother, and I want you to know what I'm doing."

"Don't worry, you can trust your brother. I'm very impressed with what you're doing. I'll stop by the lab to see you before I go. I would love to have you show me around the lab and see what sort of instruments you will be using to synthesize the plant."

Chapter 13

Candice called Cameron again for dinner. Given the phenomenal growth in intelligence in her Devan, he figured he had better come, but he suspected there was something she wanted from him, which no doubt stemmed from the existence of the child. Only problems could come from having a child, he confirmed to himself as he drove to their house.

Inside, Candice treated him with more respect, which only confirmed his suspicions. She took his jacket, which she did not normally do, and guided him to the kitchen area that was used as the bar and offered him his choice of drink in a subservient manner as there was something to be asked of him later. "What would you like?"

Wanting to make it harder for her to ask him for whatever favor was about to come, he, in order to see if he could come up with a drink that she could not fix, said, "I'll have a Rob Roy, up, perfect, with a twist and a cherry."

To his surprise, resourceful Candice opened a drawer, took out a bartender's guide, and looked it up. "Coming up."

"I was just kidding," Cameron said. "A vodka martini will do. Why all the special treatment? There must be something you want of me with relation to Devan."

"That's easier," Candice said and went about pouring

vodka into a shaker over ice. She produced an olive stuffed with garlic and passed him his drink in a freezer-chilled martini glass, another indication of wanting to butter him up.

Cameron leaned up against the counter, sipping, enjoying his martini. He downed it fairly fast, to take the edge off what he was sure to happen, namely, something to do with the demonic notion of children, and asked for a refill.

Spencer greeted Cameron. "Hi. How have you been?"

"Fine, but very busy at the office. How's young Einstein?"

"He continues to develop his learning abilities at a very accelerated rate. He has no emotional outbursts and amazes us daily with his knowledge. We're looking for a special tutor to work here at home."

"He's truly amazing," Cameron begrudgingly acknowledged.

"Dinner is just about ready. Please take a seat," Candice said. "This is a work night, and I know you have to get home early, so I made the dinner time earlier."

At the table, Cameron could sense that something was definitely up. He realized how a wild animal could sense trouble in the wild, but he could not tell just how his combination of senses worked together to warn him.

"Cameron, you are my guinea pig for a new recipe," Candice said as she sat down in front of him a large soup bowl filed with soup and noodles, the center topped with crispy fried noodles sticking out of the broth, put on top of the other noodles. "I haven't tried this dish here at home yet. It has spices that I brought back. It's called *Khao Soi,* which is curried, coconut noodles. It's northern Thai food. It's made best with fresh egg noodles, coriander seeds, turmeric, ginger, shallot, dried red chilies, white soya sauce, black soy sauce, chicken, and coconut milk."

"Where do you get fresh egg noodles? Cameron asked, "I thought noodles were noodles, like ramen. Do they get stale?"

Candice laughed "You can buy fresh ones at oriental markets. They have to be kept chilled. The dish is a soup from the north of Thailand and has the noodles in the soup. But note that the noodles are fried noodles, and the ones at the bottom are soaking in the sauce, which I would like to think is spectacular. How do you find it?"

"You are a fantastic chef. I've never had anything like this. But this must be a lot of work for just the three of us." He was waiting for whatever it was that they wanted. Something was hiding behind the ugly head of deception.

"We've invited you this evening, and no others," Spencer said, "because we need to talk to talk to you about something."

Cameron put his drink down to make sure he did not get too drunk and agree to something involving the rodent, special or not.

"There's no practical way to ever reproduce whatever it was that changed the DNA in the formation of Devan," Candice said. "I have Devan's cells to look at, but to undertake a program to try and see if chemicals could be isolated that cause similar results is impractical. In the first place, it would be such a large undertaking that it would require a staff of people, a fortune in equipment, most likely years of work, and there is absolutely no guarantee that it could even be done at all. And, of course, experimenting in the US would be limited to mice or animals, not humans. Unless we give the project to Josef Mengele of Auschwitz, the project would never get tested on humans, essentially forever, and that assumes it could be duplicated in the first place. There will arise much opposition to it, as is obvious with all of the religious politicians opposed to stem cell research or anything involving changing humans as we now are."

"Okay, got it," Cameron said. "I'm a little slow. I've read that drug companies spend several billion now on new drugs before they can release them. So, I see what you mean."

"Frankly, it probably can't be done," Candice admitted. "Something that can make extremely precise changes in human DNA could probably never be made up from scratch, at least not in our lifetime. Something in the plant must create a different amino acid, but it is an impossibly complex thing to try to do without a model to follow. But, on the other hand, if we had a specimen of the plant, synthesizing it might be likely be done. We have instruments that can measure exactly what is in something, and what something is made of. Hopefully, they will work in this case. Duplicating something is infinitely easier than trying to backtrack from the effects of it and then trying to recreate what caused it. Then the chemical would cause the changes to the DNA when the sperm fertilizes the egg. I've now begun to realize the incredible importance of this discovery. If I could get a specimen of the plant, and replicate the formula, it could be made available to everyone and become the new dawn in human devolvement. Imagine children that spend only a few years getting a high school education. What levels of intellect a human could achieve if he could get a college degree at ten or twelve, and then utilize the remainder of his best formative, educational years to achiever after that? I believe that someone born with the benefit of this plant can possibly achieve twice the IQ as one without it!"

"Why do you think it will double the IQ, rather than just make whatever quotient of intelligence the kid is going to have come on at an earlier age?" Cameron asked. "Isn't there a name for rapid aging?"

"Yes," Candice answered. "This is not progeria. Of this, I'm certain. He is not aging, only getting very smart. Normally, the first third of a person's normal life span is for education, and there is no reason to assume that you cannot learn at a much higher rate. It's obvious when you think about it. You waste a number of early years from birth just learning to walk, potty training, learning coordination, and basics. You only begin school at five, and then start a long, slow process of education of a system that finally puts you out on the street with a degree at age twenty-two or so if you go to college or, twenty-eight if you go into medicine or some advanced field. Just think if you could do all of that in a fraction of the time. I have good reason to believe that a person can put much more into that early portion of his life if he can just learn more rapidly. It's not a matter of growing a bigger brain, but making it efficient by learning more quickly by having a more finely tuned system that can take in the data and analyze it. Some birds can fly in just a few days. If you think about it, what a waste of a third of your life just getting a basic education! Humans have the most wasteful design in that regard. You spend a good third of your life in education, another third perfecting that education, and then the body starts falling apart.

"But the chief is one hundred fifteen years old. It could be that this plant was designed to make people live longer since they will be much smarter, and to allow more time to pass on their wisdom. Maybe it even disallows cancer! I believe cancer is nature's way of keeping humans from overpopulating, sort of like cordyceps in insect colonies."

"What's cordycepts?" Cameron asked.

"It's a fascinating fungus that infects insects and arthropods. There are hundreds of different types, each for a different insect. It attacks the insect, replaces its tissues, and then sprouts long stems growing out of the head in the case of ants, and elsewhere on other insects. Once the stem grows very long, the fungus lives off the brain of the insect and then releases spores into the air, infecting others. Ants will carry off an ant that they know is infected and toss him off a limb or otherwise get rid of him. It diminishes the population of the colony. Some call eating the brain a zombie apocalypse."

"Weird," Cameron said.

"Millions of cells reproduce, happening all the time," Candice continued. "There is something in the DNA chain that directs the body after a time to stop making certain kinds of cells, or changes the way they are made, that makes us grow old and expire. Why couldn't the design just keep making us continue? Perhaps one day aging can be stopped. But to be certain as to what will happen to Devan in the future, we have to wait. As an added benefit from this potion, there's something else. From watching Devan, you can see that he's quite in control emotionally. He doesn't cry, unless he hurts himself, and has much better overall control of himself. There's an incredibly valuable added benefit in this potion. The accelerated and more finely tuned development of the central system has put him in better control of himself as well as his emotions. Today, lots of mothers work and still want kids. They have all sorts of trouble finding day care, baby sitters, and the like. The length of time of care for infants and day care would be shortened by a fraction of what it is presently. A six year old might be able to be home alone and work on his computer, rather than need a baby sitter.

"The advanced development of his central nervous system has given him more intellect and control over emotion, and he'll be able to focus his youthful energies on intellectual matters. That alone could be a multiplier of his achievements over the same period of others. You know how many youngsters, especially in adolescence, have so much trouble accepting things. This may put a stop to that, or nearly so."

"What happens when Devan begets a baby?" Cameron asked. "Will he need the potion again? Or, is he transformed forever?"

"That's a very astute question," Candice said. "I believe he's transformed, as you put it, forever. If he was to be tested for DNA in a lab to establish paternity of us over him, with the usual tests it would show that he is not our baby. His DNA is changed from ours. But we have no way to say if his children are changed as well, until it is tested. But if I'm correct, he should not need the plant to create an offspring like himself, especially if the partner was born of it too. As to whether or not his child would be the same if he had an ordinary partner, and no plant, who knows? But this is really a step, possibly the step, out of the Stone Age of Evolution, and it will be done not by a substance from outer space, but from a plant located right here on earth. It was here all the time!"

"Are you sure the plant did not come from outer space?" Cameron asked.

"If the plant came here on a meteor, for example, it could be said to be from outer space," Spencer said. "Or, it could have been here for a few million years for man to find as part of his destiny."

"Spencer, when you speak of destiny, it sounds like a religious explanation," Cameron said

"I don't buy the religious explanation," Candice said.

"The changes in Devan's DNA are so acute, and so discrete, that I cannot believe it is just random chance that it is here," Spencer continued. "How else would something exist, in the form of a plant growing out of the earth that could make such precise changes in someone's DNA, and not otherwise adversely affect him? It has changed my views about life. Whenever you have a thing growing, like an apple, there is an insect or some other critter that wants it. It's as though there is a purpose for everything growing. I have been wondering if this plant was not growing here for man to find and consume once he gained enough intelligence to realize it. It is, however, very remote, to say the least, and not plentiful. It could be that it was more plentiful at one time but got wiped out by something like the turmoil that killed the dinosaurs. It seems to me that it may be here just for that purpose."

Cameron looked at Candice, "You say the changes are from chemicals." He then looked at Spencer. "You say the matter has a divine explanation. And, from what you told me about Faint Chance, she believes that the explanation is spiritual. As another option, I suppose that one could also conjecture that extraterrestrials came and planted it for us to find one day."

Candice shrugged. "I suspect that the tribal villagers believe that the wisdom and essence of forefathers are taught to offspring of the chief by a spiritual event. As animists, and uneducated, this is what I suspect to find."

"So, the tribal people think it is spiritual," Cameron said. "Why do you suppose this plant is not growing everywhere, or that man did not run into it earlier on and obtain its benefits sooner?"

Spencer nodded. "I have been wondering if this plant has not been growing here for man to find and consume once he gained enough intelligence to utilize it."

"However, it is obviously not growing everywhere," Candice said, "and only presently found in a very remote spot, as far as is known. It could be that it was more plentiful, but got wiped out by something similar to whatever killed the dinosaurs or volcanic activity."

"Perhaps if it was brought to the planet in such a small quantity that it was not meant to be found until such time as man was able to reproduce it," Cameron suggested. "It might have come from a meteorite. An alien landing here? Maybe it was here dormant, waiting to be discovered and utilized?"

"Wow, those are wild ideas," Spencer said and gazed off into the distance deep in thought.

"If you could make up the formula for this, you could patent it and make an absolute fortune," Cameron said. "People are paying a fortune for just medications. Imagine what they would pay to have a chance at a genius offspring. Even if every person could have a chance of having some little beggar better than normal, wouldn't that be worth ten thousand? To a billionaire, a billion? Ten? Anyone wanting a child would hold off until they had a chance to buy this stuff as much as they could afford. You're sitting on the world's ultimate gold mine."

Candice nodded. "Yes, I realize that. And, I have a plan

to produce it if we can get it here and synthesize it successfully. We would patent the formula and the process and retain control over its marketing. However, I don't want to sell it for gluttonous profit. Rather, I want to control the price and sell it for a reasonable price in all places. Profits would subsidize the providing of it to those who cannot afford it, like those wonderful people we saw so many of in India, and other places that we did not get to go. Spencer and I were deeply moved by the poverty and felt so helpless that we could not give. This could be the way. Children born by this would have the intelligence not to breed like flies and would have the wherewithal to come out of poverty. This could be the most significant step in human evolution. As for Spencer and me, the two of us would be happy with just enough to be wealthy and retire to whatever limited research that we could choose to do. We are not interested in seeing how much of an empire we can build. And in our fields of research medicine, it would be the ultimate medical publication. We could literally retire and be content that we accomplished a lifetime achievement like no other."

"Even if you only charged a royalty in western countries of several dollars per dose, you would still be the richest in the world," Cameron said. "This would be crazy wealth."

"But such luxuries as being so rich as to be able to help the poor comes later," Candice continued. "I need a specimen of the plant or its leaves."

"Why not ask Faint Chance to go get some more?" Cameron asked.

"She really has no way to do that by herself," Spencer answered. "She had never been back to the village since she was taken away at age seven. She doesn't know exactly where the village is, only approximately. The journey to the village could be a dangerous one, and getting there would be an adventurous jungle expedition. Maybe the village has changed? Gone? Who knows if the plant still exists? Who knows if the chief would release the prized plant, even if there is more of it? Maybe the chief will kill whoever comes to his village to steal his special plant?"

"What is the situation on Faint Chance's visa application?" Cameron asked.

"We are still waiting for the US government to act on it, Spencer said. "We don't know how long it will take."

"Isn't there some way to expedite it?" Cameron asked.

Spencer grinned. "Maybe we should amend her visa application to: 'Please expedite this visa as the applicant is bringing back a plant that will alter the course of human evolution, and mankind cannot wait any longer.'"

Everyone laughed heartily.

"Did you go any of the villages similar to the one Faint Chance lived in?" Cameron asked.

"No," Candice answered. "We only visited one, not too far from the capital, and they had teachers and other contacts with the outside. Hers is in the very far north and has, as far as she knows, little contact with the outside. Faint Chance said her village was some distance from the nearest road, and to get there requires hiking. In one we went to, the women, even the little girls, all wore a certain dark blue homemade, one-piece dress, and a bright violet waist string around, and no other dress is allowed at all."

"And we could not communicate with them," Spencer added. "They either spoke Lao or maybe not, and only a local dialect, and the people were very timid. They ran and hid when the camera came out. As for our trip, there was no real reason to go in to the jungle too deeply. And, there were some good reasons not to. Wait until you see the warnings from the State Department."

Candice said to her brother-in-law with a big smile, "But once we have fully disclosed the dangers to you, we want to tell you what we would like you to do, and we rather think that you would like it. Spencer and I just got back from a one year long sabbatical, and neither of us can take off again to go on a journey. To compound that, I took off a few weeks to have Devan. We would definitely be in serious trouble with our positions and our responsibilities if we tried for leave again. On the other hand, you have never been to Asia, and you may be able to take off for a while and have a little adventure as well. We would like you to go to Lao, meet Faint Chance, and bring back the special plant. We think you would enjoy the trip immensely and have memorable experiences. And, if you find this plant and bring it back, we will of course, make you a full partner in whatever financial gain there is to make of it."

"That could be more than you might make as an architect in a million years or so," Spencer joked, the exaggeration designed to peak his brother's interest.

"Is that a third or a half?" Cameron asked.

"If you want a full half, you'll have to pay for your own airfare and expenses there," Spencer said with a chuckle.

"We want to make it perfectly clear that we have no assurance that everything will come to fruition, and so if you go and pay for your trip, we guarantee no more than a probable high adventure," Candice said. "Maybe the plant won't be available, maybe the tribal chief will forbid leading you to it, maybe you won't be able to find it, or whatever. We simply have no idea what to expect. It has been years since Faint Chance was there when she got the plant. Actually, once you meet Faint Chance, you may decide to run off with her and never come back. You have seen some pictures of Faint Chance, but wait until you see the digital video. Let's go over to the computer table where I can show you on the laptop."

Candice went to the coffee table and put in the memory stick of Faint Chance that was downloaded from her camera.

The scene began in the waterfall, with red flowers in the ponds below, and a gorgeous, exotic, woman dancing about in and out of the waterfall. She was naked and had a very full body with shapely legs and large breasts. The dance resembled a Thai-styled one. Uninhibited, her dance took her from side to side, and with the knees out and elevated, all very erotic. The water poured over her naked body as she went in and out of the fall.

Cameron did not speak a word during the video. After it was over, he was strangely quiet.

"Well, what'd ya think?" Spencer said.

"I'm going!" Cameron said,

"Before you say yes so quickly, you had better look at the travel advisories and warnings from the State Department about Lao," Candice warned. "And, if you go off to the remote village to look for the plant, you will be going into a real jungle, far from help and civilization. You should wear long sleeves and pants, to avoid the mosquitoes and other insects, and be careful about what you eat. As you'll be in remote areas, near the Ho Chi Min Trail, unexploded bombs dropped on Lao during the Viet Nam war remain a genuine threat. It's necessary to be very careful."

"And we still have to contact Faint Chance and see if she'll agree," Spencer said. "She puts the plant in the context of a serious spiritual ceremony, and we have not yet asked her if she will help us make it known to the world. But I think she'll do it. On the other hand, we cannot be too sure if the tribal chief is still there, or if he will give her more. Or who knows what? We cannot just pick up a phone, or have Faint Chance pick one up, and call the chief. The village has no electricity, no phones, no mail service, and no regular contact with the outside world at all. There are so, so many ifs."

"This sounds like a true adventure," Cameron said. "Okay, I'll do it. If you line it up, I'll go. But cut me in for half, and I'll pay for my trip."

"I'll call Faint Chance at her shop to ask her if she'll help. The phone service to Lao is not so great, but I'll see what I can do. Without her help, there is no plant, and no hope," Spencer said.

"No chance," Cameron corrected, smiling.

"If everything gets lined up, Spencer and I'll put together some medicines for you in case you get some bad water or bacteria in the food. We'll give you a prophylaxis for malaria as well. There are a number of things that you could get that are incurable, so it is not without risk. You must read the advisories." She went to get them from a drawer and spread them out on the coffee table. "If you find the plant, you will have to sneak it into America," Candice warned. "Had we not gone recently and learned what we did, you could have gone to all the trouble to find it only to have it confiscated by customs. Customs will confiscate any plants, looking for Medflies, mosquitos with Zika Virus, some twenty-five hundred other insects, things with viruses, and other biological threats. So, you'll have to figure out a way to conceal the plant, if you succeed in getting more. I recommend a spice packet or jar." She went to the cupboard to bring out one of the many dozens of spice packets and jars that she brought back. "Customs will allow spices if enclosed in a sealed packet or jar. You should use a jar with a label of something legal to bring in."

"It sounds like committing a high crime and misdemeanor," Cameron said.

ભૈષ

Cameron went to Candice's lab to see what she was doing on the project and to get a better feel for what he might bring back if there were to be any choices to be made. She and Tadashi Uto were there.

"Tadashi, you remember my brother-in-law, Cameron. He's an architect."

Tadashi nodded. "The Christmas party, I recall. I think that being an architect would be a great profession."

"Tadashi," Candice said, "Cameron is fully informed of the project and will be the one to go over to Lao to attempt to get us a specimen of the plant."

"We're very anxious to get a specimen," Tadashi said. "Candice has predicted we can synthesize it if we have a specimen," he boasted as though he was an integral part of the group. "I wish I could go myself, but I cannot take off from the lab. How long will you be gone?"

"I've only taken leave for a month," Cameron said. "I hope to succeed in bringing a plant back in that time."

෬෨෬

"We've successfully reached Faint Chance," Spencer told Cameron at the next Saturday night dinner.

Given Candice's interest in cooking, combined with her vast new supply of exotic spices, making dinner was the ideal way to meet and discuss family matters and grease the skids for something they wanted.

"We got through by phone, believe it or not," he continued. "Both of us talked to her. The connection was not very good, but we were able to set things in motion. She was apprehensive about getting more of the plant. When she told us when we were there that she could get more, I think she was just saying that so that we would not reject her gift of her portion of the leaves. But she agreed."

Cameron was worried. "Assuming she can go back and find the place, maybe she would be put to death if she tells the chief that she gave away the wedding present he gave her to Westerners who offered her a ticket out of Lao, and would he mind giving her another dose so her friends can give it to the world."

"Hah!" Spencer and Candice both laughed. Spencer said, "I think her apprehension comes from the possibility of offending the powerful spirits that reside in the plant."

"What'd she say?" Cameron asked.

"Well," Candice said, "She did not exactly say yes, but she did not say no. She just sort of went along with it. I told her you would be coming, and I can't imagine she would consent to all the expense and effort of you going over without telling us beforehand that she would not help or had no chance of getting more."

"We have made an itinerary for you," Spencer said, "where you meet her in the north, nearest the city with an airport. It will be still quite some distance. She has not flown before, but she has agreed to take the local airline and meet you."

"Since this is your big trip out of here, we have tried to make the trip as interesting as we can so you can see a little of another country on the way, and that's Thailand. You'll first fly to Bangkok where you will spend two days getting over jet lag and taking in the sights since you have not been there. In order to get you into the north of Lao, where we have not been, we have plotted a trip. You'll fly from Bangkok to Chiang Rai, Thailand, which is a beautiful resort area in the north of Thailand, for another two nights. You'll love that, and you can sightsee and go to the Golden Triangle. Then you will take a charted car to the Mekong River, which is the borderline between Thailand and Lao. The meeting we have planned for you is to have her come up from Vientiane, the capitol in the south, on Lao Air, which has propeller planes, to Laung Prabang, and then by boat to Ban Houei Sai. She will meet you when you come across from Thailand on a boat across the Mekong River to Lao. This is what we believe is the best and most interesting journey for you, and puts you into Lao nearest the northern part where Faint Chance once lived. You'll meet her in Ban Houei Sai, and from there, you will be as near as we can put you to the approximate area of the highland villages where her adoptive tribe is most likely to be found."

"What?" Cameron said. "Most likely to be found?"

"It was not on our Laotian map—" Spencer admitted. "—but Faint Chance says she knows where it is, or that she is reasonably sure she can find it."

"Wonderful!" Cameron frowned, concern etched on his features. "Nothing like certainty in travel. What about reservations?"

"You must be kidding." Candice laughed. "You should go soon, so you can just miss the monsoon rains, which are very heavy. You might get caught in the beginning of it."

"Of course," Cameron said. "Why would I want such certainty as a room? I can always stay on the ground with the wild snakes. Okay, assuming I'm stupid enough to go, what do I need?"

"The main thing is to check your passport, and then you need to fax the Laotian consulate for a visa," Candice said. "A visa's required."

"On the way back, you can go to the south, down the Mekong River, returning with Faint Chance," Spencer said. "We think we can get everything set up in three to four weeks. Will that work for you?"

"I'll start preparations. I must get advice on what to take. And, Candice, from you, a recommendation on what sort of camera to take. I might get some neat architectural shots for ideas."

"Only take one camera and make it light," Candice said. "When I think of all the places I hefted my cameras, if I were to go again, I would take only one and a single lens. I was on camels and elephants in India and places where toting my camera bag was a chore. And, besides, you are going off into the jungle somewhere. I recommend a single, variable focus lens, wide angle to short telephoto. You are going to be mostly jungle trekking, so don't lug heavy lenses and accessories. I tell you what, I'll buy you one."

❦❦❦

As they spoke, there was another conversation going elsewhere on the same topic, the travel plans of Cameron in Lao. It was between brothers Tadashi and Morio Uto at Tadashi's apartment. Tadashi was puzzled as to why his brother Morio, back in town, was so interested in the project that he was working on, as he had never shown any interest at all in science. But he was quite gratified that he was doing something of merit that finally gave him recognition with his brother.

Chapter 14

orio Uto pushed the button to the side of the thick, wide, solid rosewood door to the huge house. He had not been to the residence of the Oyabun before. Two cameras focused on him.

A Japanese man in his early-thirties, standing six feet tall, with an enormous chest and shoulders, weighing three hundred seventy pounds, answered the door. He wore a black, two-piece suit, a white shirt, and a black tie that was mysteriously tied somewhere in the crevice that would be a neck on a normal human. He had no discernable trace of neck.

Mario was taken back at the size and presence of the huge bodyguard. "I'm Morio Uto. I have an appointment with the Oyabun," he said in Japanese.

"You are expected," the huge man said. "I'm Kubi Nashi. Follow me. Shoes here." He pointed to a shoe rack that had leather slippers for guests.

Mario was not too surprised at the name, as the definition of Kubi Nashi is "No Neck."

There was no smile on his jaw, which was several times wider than normal. He could pass for an oversize Sumo wrestler.

Morio changed his shoes for slippers. Behind the entry was a spectacular, indoor garden, Koi fish pond, waterfall, colorful plants, and various Japanese water features, receiving its light from a glass ceiling above that had a movable panel which was partially open at the time. Considering the average Japanese family of four lived in a five-hundred-square-foot apartment, the twelve-thousand-square-foot Tokyo home was nothing short of palatial. It had its own helicopter pad on the roof, with a helicopter.

Mario was led through the indoor garden to a study. Kubi Nashi knocked and led Uto into the huge home office of the Oyabun. Kubi Nashi stood there in the doorway, waiting to be told to leave.

The Oyabun, the Japanese Godfather, was sitting in an easy chair behind an ornately carved, rosewood desk, reviewing financial records. Mario Uto walked in, stopped, and then bowed deeply in great respect to the most powerful crime lord in Japan and remained until told to rise.

"Sit," the Oyabun said and then looked at Kubi Nashi, nodding that he could leave them alone.

The Oyabun was middle-aged, medium build, with a dark complexion and a wide, heavy jowl. The side of his rough face bore a scar from a long time past. He wore a dark gray suit and white shirt, with no tie. He wore leather slippers.

"Sir, thank you for allowing me to see your beautiful home," Uto reported. "I have contracted for two metric tons of very high potency marijuana in California for you. I'm going over to check on it before paying and arranging for the smuggling. But that is not why I have come to see you as my financial reports have the details of the marijuana purchase and expense of the trip."

"I have gone over your report on the Marijuana," the Oyabun said. "I'm pleased. We have not been involved in drugs before, but this new marijuana is very popular with young people and not likely to be so much of a target by police as other drugs. I'll look to see how much eventual profit this purchase yields. I'll review your expenditures later. Now, what is this new matter that you said on the phone earlier that you wanted to talk to me about?"

"I've come across something that might have huge potential. A plant has been discovered in Lao by a genetics research doctor that my younger brother works for in America. When taken at the time of conceiving a child, it makes the child very smart by more rapid and enhanced development of his central nervous system."

"How can this be of any use to us?"

"The research doctors are sending the brother of the husband to Lao soon to try to get a specimen of the plant. When the plant is brought back to the US, the doctors will analyze it and synthesize it so that it can be made into a pill. It if works, everyone in the world will want to take it when having a child. It could be the biggest-selling, legal drug of all time. The potential is fantastic."

"How do you know that it works?"

"All that is known is that the two doctors, who are research doctors, ate the plant leaves in Lao when they were having sex to have a child and gave birth to a gifted child. The child could talk at age one month. But it is still speculation, as the doctors say they want to get a sample of the plant and then synthesize it in the lab, and then make into a pill. It is not known if they can do it. So, it is not a sure thing."

"This could be something very big," the Oyabun said, his eyebrows raised with interest. "How can we do anything with it if she is going to do it in America?"

"They will get the plant, and then analyze it in a lab to figure out what special formula it's made of. After figuring out how to synthesize it, they will apply to patent the formula and the process to make it. Most all of the countries recognize international patents, and they will then have a legal monopoly on the pill. But the plant is natural, and anyone who can get it first and get a lab to synthesize it before she does could patent the synthesized chemical formula and the process to make it, and be the one to make the fortune."

"Does your brother know where it grows?"

"Only that it comes from nearby a remote mountain tribe in northern Lao."

"How could someone find it?"

"The doctors that my brother works for met a Laotian woman in Lao who knows where to find it. She is the one that gave it to the doctor and her husband when they were in Lao. The brother of the doctor's husband is going to Lao soon to meet with her, and she will lead him to the village to get the plant specimen. I propose to follow him in, wait until he gets the plant, and then take it from him. It might be better to kill him so as not to have any witnesses."

"Where will you take it from him?"

"I think the best place would be in Lao. Then I'll get it back here, where you could have a lab set up a lab to synthesize it right away and hurry to get it figured out and patented. As the plant is a naturally occurring substance, there should be no way that anyone can challenge the person, or company, that is first to apply for a patent. The patent process would be perfectly legal and belong to who applies first."

"Do you know for sure that it can be synthesized?" the Oyabun asked.

"No, I don't. That's the gamble. But there is so much at stake that it seems like a very good risk. I do not have the resources to do it myself, and bring it to you. I want only a share in it if it works, as there will be considerable investment needed to synthesize it and produce it."

"You have done well by bringing me this," the Oyabun said. "I'll undertake to do this. What will you need?"

"I'll need one good local man who can go into the jungle, and who will have weapons and camping gear in Lao. Also, if he can speak Lao, or at least some Lao, that would help."

The Oyabum nodded. "I have a man in Bangkok named Warinton who can help. He has weapons and knows his way about in Thailand, Lao, and Cambodia, and especially the drug trade in the Golden Triangle. I will contact him and call you. This sounds like a potentially very profitable venture. I want you to keep me informed as it progresses." He turned in his chair and opened the cabinet behind his deck. There were stacks of money in it. He took out two stacks of US hundreds and handed them across the desk to Mario. "Here is expense money. You will account, as usual."

Chapter 15

Beautiful Chiang Rai in the north of Thailand made Bangkok look like a big, dirty city, Cameron determined as the hotel van drove him from the small airport to the hotel. The hotel was beautifully decorated outside with flowers everywhere. Then marbled entry was a majestic thirty feet high, and the sounds of waterfalls and fountains inside were amplified by the marble floors. A huge swimming pool outside came right up to one side of the lobby, surrounded by colorful flowers and plants. It was the most beautiful hotel he had been in, and began to realize he should travel more often, to enrich his architectural background. Cameron checked in, and his room key was presented to him in a cone made of a green leaf with an orchid in it. He told the desk clerk to phone the number of a tour agency his brother had arranged for him to inform them of his arrival. It was only ten in the morning, as he had taken an early flight from Bangkok, a short hop in a small jet. After going to the room, he went down to wait and absorb the architecture to add to his knowledge for future projects.

In short order, a short, bubbly Thai girl in her early twenties appeared with youthful, excessive energy in her gait. She had white jeans, a white shirt and vest, and a pink tie, giving the idea she was a sailor.

"Are you from the agency?"

"Yes. Are you Mr. Harrington?"

"None other."

As she approached, she stuck out her arm fully while still several steps away, an exaggerated welcome gesture, as were all her movements. She had an enormous smile, displaying large teeth.

"I'm called Judy, for my Western name. I'm an independent operator and have been hired by the agency to be your guide. I have a van outside with driver. I have several suggestions for you for today, and then tomorrow I will take you to the river where you will cross over to Lao. Is that correct?"

"Yes, that will be wonderful. What do you suggest for today?"

"Most people like to go out to some mountain villages here, which is a very beautiful drive. We can head for Myanmar, or Burma, as it may be known to you, and then to the Golden Triangle, where the three countries of Burma, Lao, and Thailand meet. Then return, which will put us back at the hotel around dark, or a little after. Will that be of interest?"

"Sounds wonderful. I have my camera, and I'm ready."

"I'll sit in the back here," Cameron said, as they approached a small, white van that was their hired vehicle, together with a driver.

Judy got in the front with the driver, and they drove off.

"You came in this morning from Bangkok, right?" she asked.

"Yes. I was there two days."

"Is this your first trip?"

"Yes, this is the first trip, and the first time I have been in Asia."

"How did you find Bangkok?"

"The floating market was very interesting. Seeing the women selling their vegetables and fruits on sampans was an experience."

"How do you find the Thai food so far?"

"Delicious. The guide in Bangkok took me to a place like a supermarket-come-restaurant where you pick your own seafood from a long row of fish on ice, and then tell the chef how to make it. You also pick your own vegetables, wine, and everything else that way. I left it up to the chef to pick the method of cooking, and he delighted me. It was spectacular."

"I'm glad you are enjoying your trip so far. What else did you do in Bangkok?"

"The guide took me to a Thai massage place. It was really neat. Do you know of them?"

"Thai massage is a specialty. You can get that here as well. I think the hotel will have that."

The little white van took them to the nearby mountains, and they wound their way up the curving roads. After an hour and a half, they came upon a rounded hill top, with a beautiful plantation off to the right side, most was not visible from the road. An industrial structure was on one side, open at the front, a residence on the left. A stone fence near the road obscured much of the view, and they might not have noticed it but for the gate open and a man walking about.

Judy quickly said to the driver, "Turn in."

He overshot the entrance and then backed up to be able to enter the open gate.

"I've driven by here, but have not noticed this place," she told Cameron. "It looks like it may be a tea plantation."

As the van turned in, she exclaimed, "Yes. Yes. I'm right. It's a plantation that I noticed on this road before. Let's see if we can get permission to look around."

The driver stopped just inside the open gate. Judy got out and walked up to the structure. She was aggressive as a tour guide, but she was so small, like a pixie, that her action of entering someone's land did not present itself as hostile.

She approached a man who was walking about near the structures. He was in his thirties, wearing off-white pants, a shirt not tucked in, and sandals. He sported a Panama hat. Short Judy approached him without fear and spoke to him.

She walked back with a huge smile. "He's the owner, and this is his tea plantation. He says we can look around. This will be cool."

Cameron got out and walked up with bubbly Judy to meet the owner. "How do you do sir? I'm Cameron Harrington. I'm from America, and my guide says you have graciously consented to let us admire your tea plantation. If you'll permit, it would be a great treat for me, on this, my first trip to Asia. Or, we can press on without disturbing you further."

"Not at all. Allow me to introduce myself. I'm the Baron Von Limbach. My tea plantation here just completed the harvest of my best teas. This special plantation grows only the finest of Oolong. I have one here that is completely unique," he boasted. "They bring an incredibly high price in Taiwan and nearly the same price in a few other places. Please look about as you wish. I love to show it off."

The estate was quite large, which was not visible from the road. The tea plants were in neat rows covering many acres of the hillside on almost all sides.

"Is this all Oolong tea?" Cameron asked.

"Yes. I actually grow several varieties, but all are extremely special. They do well here in these highlands and climate. This is my fourth year, and I'll show a profit this year."

"Are you sure we are not disturbing you?" Cameron repeated.

"Not at all. I could use a little company. I have an estate manager who is off buying supplies this afternoon. There is no harvest at the moment, as one was just completed. That is why no one is here just now except for the domestic help inside. Come, let me show you around."

They followed to the open building to the right side of the residence. Inside were four, stainless steel drums, two feet in diameter with motors to turn them by leather belts on pulleys.

"These are dryers that I had specially made. The tea is dried here. There really isn't much to it. The main thing that is special is the kind we grow, the care in growing, and the climate. Would you allow me to show off my tea by sampling it?"

"That would be a treat indeed," Cameron said. They followed him into an enclosed part of the structure. There was an air conditioner on the back wall cooling the place. The large room was undivided, and was obviously used as the office for the ranch manager. There were three desks toward the rear, and file cabinets. A young Thai girl was present, organizing some papers at a desk. Towards the front was a bar against the wall, with pitchers, tea pots and small, sampling-sized cups, although taller than demitasse.

"It's cooler here than at the lower altitudes, but as the afternoon approaches, it does get hot," the Baron said, putting his Panama hat on a hook on the wall, over an ivory-white suit jacket. "Please, have a seat," he said, motioning to a table at the front, abutting a big picture window that gave a nice view of the plantation. They sat, situated where they could look over the large plantation.

To the surprise of Cameron and especially Judy, the man spoke to the young girl in Thai.

The Thai employee girl got up and began tea preparations. She turned on an electric water-heating grill to heat up the water.

"You speak Thai," Judy said in surprise. She changed to speaking Thai. The Baron responded, confirming to Judy that he actually spoke her language. She was obviously impressed with his correct Thai from the expression on her face.

"You have quite an impressive command of languages," Cameron said. "How many can you speak?"

"Let's see. In the European languages, German, Italian, French, Spanish, Portuguese, Russian, and a wee bit of

Hungarian, Polish, and Arabic. In the Eastern languages, Thai, Mandarin, Cantonese, a little Malay which is similar to Indonesian, and Lao."

"No English?" Cameron joked.

"Oh yes, that too!"

All laughed.

"My God! We have met the world's linguist!" Cameron said showed his surprise by his look at Judy.

The Baron humbled himself with "Oh please! You are too complimentary!"

The Thai servant brought over a tray with the sampler-sized tea cups in saucers. There was a thermos of hot water and several small containers of different teas. The Baron took over and went right to work making tea himself.

"Here, I want you to try this,"

Cameron and Judy both took the small cups.

"This is spectacular," Cameron said.

"Oh yes, delicious," Judy agreed.

"It does not seem that you are here often?" Cameron asked.

"I have an apartment in Chiang Rai. I stop off there now and then. But I'm about to build a new house here, on this property, so as to have a place to come here once in a while in the north to rest and visit my teas. I also export teak wood."

"Where else do you normally live?"

"In addition to Chiang Rai, I have a place in Berlin, Taiwan, Vientiane, and on the coast of Spain. I have regular rooms where I stay, but do not own, in a few other places, such as St. Petersburg. I'm in international business. This tea is just a small thing for my ego. That tea you just sampled sells for around one thousand US a half kilo in Taiwan. But, you see, I love fine tea."

"Wow," Cameron said. "You must have a very exciting life."

"May I ask, what do you do, sir?"

"I'm an architect."

"What an interesting profession. I love architecture. Do you specialize?"

"I do small commercial properties and large homes."

"I have some plans here that I am not happy with, and I would like to show you if you don't mind." The Baron went toward the back of the room and picked up a big roll of blueprints. "I would be glad to hire you to add to these ideas that I have paid some locals to give me. The local architects, I fear, are not very creative. It seems they just want to add those funny up-turned wooded tips on the roofs to ward off evil spirits. Tell me," he said, opening the plans. "What do you think?"

Cameron was taken aback, finding a client on the other side of the planet. "Let's have a look. May I draw on these?"

"Please. I would be honored. I can get another set easily."

Cameron examined the plans. Finally, he motioned the Baron over. "I find this to be a bit boring, to be honest. I would change the entrance like this." He drew on one of the sheets with the entrance. "I would raise the interior ceiling at the entrance, right on up to the second story and delete the rooms above that area. I would add a section here, in the rear, and reach that with an interesting staircase, like this." He drew a double staircase, one on either side of the entry floor. "I would also move the garage around to the back. This will keep it out of sight, and provide a place that you can store extra cars and things that are not attractive. It will also provide a place for your helper to wash and wax your cars." Cameron paused and looked intently at the plans. "But now, if you are willing to make some more dynamic and interesting changes, why don't you make the corners round, instead of square? Like this." He drew curves over the flat and square corners of most of the walls. "Then we could have more interesting rooms, like this entry, which would wind around the curved staircase. We could then have a balcony at the upper level that the staircase leads into, and you could have the staircase and the balcony encased in interesting wrought iron. Then we could do arched doorways, instead of square ones." He switched to a different sheet of plans, adding rounded doorway arches.

"Then, in the dining room and main hall, we could do double-recessed ceilings, for an interesting effect, but also adding skylights. In the kitchen, breakfast area, and your office, let's put in solar tubes. Those are really bright. Speaking of light, I recommend LED lights, with five-thousand-degree Kelvin white light throughout. I think the entry to the dining room should have a column on either side. We could also have two columns on either side of the front door, right here, under the overhang of the roof. Repeating the round theme, we could do a round observation tower on top of the house, with a staircase to it from the top floor, with a round tile roof from which you could have a panoramic view of your entire plantation, which you would not otherwise have. Why don't we put the smaller eating area and kitchen up a step, overlooking the family room, and curve the walls into it?"

Cameron was in his own element now, and his talented hands were drawing rapid and infinitely more appealing designs than the very ordinary rooms that the locals had designed.

"This is amazing," the Baron said. "If you will stay here to finish these for me, I'll pay you very well."

Temptation rang a strange calling in Cameron's ear, but reality brought him to the purpose of his trip. "I wish I could make you finished plans, but that would take some doing, and several days at least. I'm unable to stay on for that, as I'm headed for Lao. But I tell you what. Give me another hour or two, and I will continue with the changes, making the rooms and hallways curved and more interesting, and I'm sure that your local people can fill in the details. I will leave my address in the US if you want me to do further work."

With that, the Baron and Judy walked outside to wander

about the plantation to let Cameron work, the Baron talking to Judy in Thai.

After an hour and a half, they returned to find Cameron had completed what he could without starting fresh, and showed the plans to the Baron.

"I'm most impressed," the Baron complimented. "Please allow me to give you some money for these splendid changes."

"It's reward enough that you showed us your plantation, allowed us to sample your tea, and added to my trip experiences," Cameron said. "It's fun to know that I may have contributed to a design as far away as Thailand."

"Then you must at least let me give you some of my most valuable tea." The Baron went to the shelf and took down a glass jar. He signaled for the young girl servant who came to provide fresh cups and more boiling water. "Note the leaves that have an unusual purple and orange color. This sells for two five thousand dollars per a half kilo in Taiwan." He handed the jar of expensive tea to Cameron as though it was just corn flakes.

"Wow," Cameron said, accepting it and holding it out, examining it as though it was a Fabergé Egg. "That has got to be the most expensive tea ever."

The Baron chuckled. "I believe it is."

After a silence, July, who was looking at the leaves, blurted out, "Strange color."

"It's the finest Oolong tea in the world," the Baron said. "But, of course, I am…how do you say?…prejudiced. Note the unusual aroma." He poured it into the demitasse cups.

Cameron lifted the cup to his nose and inhaled. "This is wonderfully fragrant." He took a sip. "Wow, I've never had anything like this."

"I'm so glad you enjoy it. I'm the only one that has it. Here, you must allow me to give you some. I'm afraid that there isn't much at the moment, as it was just harvested and shipped off. There won't be another crop for a while. But take this, please," the Baron said, referring to the jar.

"If you only have a little left, you should keep it," Cameron resisted politely.

The Baron gave him the jar. "Not at all. Soon there will be another harvest, and I'll have a lot. I insist."

"This is a wonderful gift," Cameron said.

"If you are ever near one of my offices, do not hesitate to call on me. Did you say you were going to Lao?"

"Yes, next stop."

"I'll be there soon, in my office in Vientiane. I export teak from Lao, in addition to tea, and also do a little business with the government. Should you be there, call me at the number on my card." The Baron passed one to Cameron. "Perhaps I might do you a favor." His card was paper-thin real wood, with lettering made part by laser and the smaller print in ink. As he spoke, a new, black, top end Mercedes pulled up in front, with a uniformed chauffeur. "Ah, here's my car. Well, you must excuse me, as I have to go leave now. I have a plane waiting. Be sure and call on me to return the favor for your expertise. I have also enjoyed your company."

The Baron exited to his grand, black Mercedes, and Cameron and Judy to their modest, white van. The chauffeur opened the back door for the Baron. Cameron and Judy watched as his black Mercedes disappeared, as though saying goodbye to someone very powerful. They then left in the opposite direction toward the Mekong River.

"What a character," Cameron said. He thought of the tea that the Baron had given him. "What spectacular tea. We have all thought that we had tasted excellent tea, but I have never had anything like that in my life."

♥♥♥

Later that day, they arrived at the Burmese border. "This is now called Myanmar," Judy said. "You used to call it Burma, right?"

"Yes, I think so. What happened to the name Burma?"

"I don't know," she said. "The reason is political, I think."

At the end of the main drag of the street before the country line of Myanmar, there were many shops close together in the last two blocks as the street ended at the border. They sold goods from Myanmar, and the proximity was a selling point to the tourists, as though that was the place to buy things from a country that one could not easily enter.

"Myanmar is still a very controlled government," Judy said, "but we can go up to the border without a visa."

As they walked about the area, window shopping, Judy pointed out what she knew of the area, having taking tourists there before. There were woven wall decorations with pearlescent buttons sewn on, mostly elephants woven into the cloth.

"One of the things that Myanmar has is rubies," Judy said. "They sell Burmese rubies here."

"Let's have a look," Cameron said, and they went up several steps from the street to what appeared to be the fanciest jewelry store. It was located only one hundred feet from the border of Myanmar, which border consisted of a black and white striped gate across the road, with a guard on either side, each with a machine gun.

As they looked toward the border from the landing just outside the jewelry store, several steps up from the street, Cameron said, "What a difference. All these commercial shops, jammed against the border. And just across the border, there is nothing!"

Inside the jewelry store, Cameron gazed at an endless display of beautiful rubies, set in gold. He asked one of the sales girls, pointing, "May I see one of these, please?"

The sales girl, overdone in makeup, wearing high heels and a tight skirt, approached. He pointed at a gold ring, which was wide at three quarters of an inch, surrounded by a winding row of rubies. The rubies were huge, three karats each, and there were eleven of them.

"Are these genuine rubies from Burma?" Cameron asked.

"Absolutely, sir." She turned around and picked up a certificate booklet of official looking papers, with various red, oriental-styled government chops on the cover and the pages inside. "We guaranty all are genuine Burmese rubies," she said, showing him the certificate book that looked very official.

"What is the gold?" Cameron asked.

"Twenty-two karat," she answered.

"How much is a ring like this?" Cameron asked. He held it under the spot lights of the store over the glass case.

She looked at the price tag. It translated into dollars at four thousand eight hundred. After looking, she turned and spoke to a man who was at a counter behind her. They said something softly to one another, and she then turned back to Cameron. "For you, a special price. In US dollars, that would be only one thousand five hundred."

Cameron turned to Judy. "That is cheap. I might get this for a present or just to hold onto. Do you think the rubies are genuine? I would not want it otherwise."

"If the store guarantees them, they must be," Judy said.

Cameron turned to the sales girl. "I thought that it was illegal in Burma to export rubies. Are you certain they are genuine Burmese rubies?"

"Absolutely, sir," she said, repeating her earlier statement. She held up the guarantee booklet again. It looked very much like an official, government book with numbers and places for chops.

"I'll look about a bit, and I may come back later to buy it," Cameron said.

The girl turned to the man behind her, and they said something he could not hear, but it was not in English, anyway. "The last price we can offer is one thousand three hundred fifty dollars."

"Thank you, and I'll consider it." Cameron led Judy out the door.

They paused and looked up and down the street, wondering about the wisdom of purchasing such jewelry with such variable prices.

"Let's go snoop about." Cameron said to Judy.

They walked up the street, away from the border, three blocks away. At that point, there was a small street crossing the main one. Cameron decided to go in that direction and walked down it. It led them to a street, more like an alley, that went back toward where they were. They came to an alley way to one side that led back to the back side of the shops on the main drag where they were. They walked down the alley and came to the back of the jewelry store they had just been in. They entered a large work area with a high ceiling. There was no air conditioning. The ventilation was from fans for the dozen workers sitting at work stations, some with small torches making heat on an already steaming hot day. Sitting at the small work stations were slender, Thai men making jewelry in various stages.

"Let's go have a look," Cameron said.

No one stopped them from walking in. Inside were about a dozen work stations, most with a worker working on his specialty.

They entered and went to a work station. The fellow there was sitting, holding red things the size of jewelry stones on what looked like cigars. They stopped and starred. No one paid them any attention, as, apparently, they thought the couple had been invited in.

The several stations where they entered had a can, a few inches in width, with a bunch of what looked like cigars in it. They were rolled-up brown papers, rolled to a point at the end.

As they watched, the worker glued one of the red objects onto the tip of the rolled-up paper, and then put it into a flame from a small burner on the work station where he sat. It got soft, and the man then shaped it into an oval with his tools. It was opaque, but as it heated it, it became clearer and clearer. After the heating, the man put it into a stone wheel that turned in water, and shaped it into a good-looking, artificial ruby.

"Look—" Cameron turned to Judy. "—these are fake!"

After the man shaped it, he passed on to the next bench, where another craftsman used much finer, wet stone grinding wheels to grind the stones into either round or oval shapes that began to shine vibrantly. At the next bench sat a man with polishing wheels that brought the stones to a dazzling shine.

Cameron, nearly in shock, exclaimed, "These rubies are fake. These are literally cooked. Did you know?"

She shook her head, looking sincere. "No."

"Seeing this, I bet the gold is not twenty-two karat as they say. I bet it is less, possibly even filled or plated."

The retreated and went to their vehicle. Cameron wondered as they drove off if Judy really did not know. How could a tour guide not know? Whether or not she knew would recur a lingering question to haunt him forever.

Their van eventually came to the high mountain cliffs overlooking the Golden Triangle, where Myanmar, Thailand, and Lao all meet at the Mekong River, eight hundred feet down from where they stopped and looked.

"Look, the Golden Triangle," Judy exclaimed, pointing down hundreds of feet below their site.

"Wow, cool." Cameron took out his new camera and took pictures.

"This was the place of major drug traffic in years past," Judy said. "And there is still activity. Life in the mountains is difficult, and dealing in contraband continues. Drugs were traded for gold, and so the name. Do you see the sandy area out in the middle of the river? That does not belong to any of the three countries. I think in English the name is 'no-man's land.'"

"This is the stuff movies are made of," Cameron said, pensively, looking down at the cliffs, dreaming of activities he had only seen in movies of drug trafficking. The sun was going down soon, and the late horizontal rays illuminated the far bank of Lao, casting shadows on Thailand and Myanmar. "I'm going over there to Lao."

On the three hour trek back to Chiang Rai, bubbly Judy offered a package of sweets, but he declined. She then turned on the portable, old fashioned, cassette tape recorder she brought along. She had recorded Western music to entertain her guests. She added to the entertainment by turning to Cameron and singing along, trying to get him to join, snapping her fingers to the beat. The first was by John Denver, "Country Roads, Take Me Home."

She sang along, facing him, adding to the gaiety, and snapped her fingers, enthusiastically butchering the lyrics as she crooned about west ginger country roads taking her home.

Chapter 16

The following day, bubbly Judy returned with the company travel company minivan and driver. Cameron was already up and waiting, ready to go. He had just come around from a walkabout of the local architecture.

Judy smiled, showing her large teeth. "Good morning! Are you ready to go to Lao?"

"I'm ready. I have all my things, including the tea from the Baron."

The trip to Chiang Khong on the Mekong River took three hours, with Judy pointing out things of interest along the way. At the Mekong River, they had to go down to the water by a steep, narrow, long, ramp to a tiny wooden dock, on which stood a building for an official the size of a telephone booth.

"Over there is Lao," Judy said, pointing to the bank on the other side. She looked sheepishly to ascertain if she had pleased her guest.

The driver got out and handed Cameron his bag. Cameron gave him a tip and then was escorted to the little hut where a fee was to be paid for a boat ride across the river. Judy went up to the man in the tiny hut to discuss the fee, got the money from Cameron, paid it, and then escorted him to the little boat.

Cameron felt that she had more than accomplished her job and appreciated her exuberance. He thanked Judy with two one-hundred dollar bills which made her eyes widen in appreciation so far that she thanked him many times, very moved.

Cameron stood at the little dock to which a strange boat was tied. It was a weathered, long, thin, canoe shaped, curved up at the front with a small, squared-off front, with a carved figurine at the bow. The widest part in the middle was less than three feet, and the wood was so weathered that it did not look safe. The length was eighteen feet, powered by one of the modern, Thai-styled, small four-cylinder engines on a swivel, with the prop shaft coming straight out the back to a propeller, such that the prop was ten feet behind the boat. The motor swiveled from side to side, up and down to raise and lower the prop in and out of the water.

The boat went very slow, barely faster than a walk. At the Lao side, there was another paved ramp even steeper than the one on the Thai side. The boat pulled up, and the boatman got out with no shoes on and roped it to a small tree trunk. Cameron got out, and the boatman got his bag for him. There was a small building to the right, up thirty more feet, the official building. On the left was what appeared to be an empty restaurant, and there was girl of eighteen or twenty sitting outside looking up the river. She appeared to be connected to the restaurant, but the restaurant had no customers or other help.

What he did not notice was that after he went ashore, the boat had returned to the Thai side to pick up two more passengers and were coming across the River to Lao. They were Oriental.

Cameron went up to the official building. It was up ten concrete steps that were very steep, so much so, he had to touch the steps above with his finger as he climbed to insure balance.

The official building above was tiny. Inside were two

Lao women in *sinhs*, one brushing the long hair of the other. Also was a small fellow, in uniform, obviously the official. None of them spoke English. Cameron produced his passport. The official then opened an old fashioned ledger that looked like an accounting ledger from many years past. He meticulously wrote down by hand information from Cameron's passport. He then pointed to a sign which had numbers on it. Cameron finally realized that there was an entry fee to come to Lao. He worried for a moment, and then took out his remaining Thai Baht. Cameron asked him how much. The fellow wrote it down and accepted the Baht. Cameron just held out his hand with the Baht in it and with trust, let the fellow take what he wanted as there was not a great deal in his pocket. After roughly figuring the fee, he calculated it to be less than a dollar. The man chopped and initialed the passport and returned it.

Cameron then saw a sign that said money exchange and the rate of exchange. He did not want to change too much, as he wondered if the change place might also be a communications device to alert some bandits. So, Cameron passed him two one-hundred dollar US bills. The official was a bit shocked at the amount but then tried to deal with it. He reached below to a locked metal box and produced new Laotian Kip bills of ten thousand kip each. The stack was huge, but fit into Cameron's satchel.

There were no taxis or anyone else waiting there at the point of entry into Lao. Cameron began walking, bag in hand, up the steep road to the town, two hundred yards up. With the hot tropical weather, he was soaking in sweat by the time he reached the top.

At the top of the steep road was the town of Ban Houei Sai. *Ban* meant village, he learned. The steep road ended there, and a level cross street greeted him. It was the main drag of the tiny little town of Ban Houei Sai. Parked at the curb was a tuk-tuk. There was very little traffic of any kind, but what little there was consisted of a few little motorbikes with little motors. No one wore a helmet. Cameron thought the helmet laws were ridiculous, and just made one's head bigger, heavier, and more likely to cause a cervical spinal cord break in the event of an accident. He momentarily wished he had his American Big Twin motorcycle there. Cameron noticed a rather nice-looking café to the right at the top of the hill, on the corner, and it had some outside tables. One of the tables had a group of five young people that were obviously college type—Cameron guessed from England or Germany. They were having beer. A *Laobeer* sign was on the building.

Cameron went over to the parked tuk-tuk. The operator got up from sitting on store steps nearby and walked over to him. Cameron showed him the name of the hotel he was to meet Faint Chance at, and the driver recognized it, *Arimid Guest House*. Cameron started to get in the back, but remembered there were no meters in the cabs. Cameron thought about the taxi cab tricks to overcharge you, and so he turned around and asked the man how much. The driver said "Two" holding up two fingers.

Cameron said "Two thousand Kip?" The driver nodded. Cameron realized the drive was around a US quarter.

The funny little vehicle's exhaust popped like a coffee percolator as they motored down the dirt road. There was absolutely no traffic, and no other vehicles, and only a very occasional pedestrian.

Although Faint Chance had been told the day he would arrive in advance, it could not be absolutely certain that he would, in fact, arrive on the day scheduled, and there was no way at all to set the time or communicate. Faint Chance was to have flown to Luang Prabang, the nearest airport to the north of Vientiane, but south of Ban Houei Sai. To get to Ban Houei Sai, it was a two day trip up the river, against the current. Faint Chance located a hotel to stay in Bang Houei Sai, where she and Cameron would meet, and gave that to Spencer by phone. Cameron was armed with that on a little piece of paper.

Ten minutes down the bumpy road brought them to a

picturesque, little compound of individual cottages, protected by a three foot high fence with many flowers and plants. A winding path led down in between cottages which were built up on teak stilts three feet above the ground. The cottages were built of teak, woven like wicker, and with a natural, reddish brown color.

The floors extended out into porches in front, which were made of teak planks, and raised off the ground an average of three feet in the air. Individual cottages on both sides of the little path went on down a gentle slope making up the compound, which had a sign in front, saying on top *Laobeer* and underneath *Arimin Guest House*, not *Arimid*. Cameron concluded it must be the right place, and that the beer supplier paid for the sign so he could use it for advertising, getting the name wrong. It was probably too expensive to do over and make correctly.

He gave the driver one of his five thousand kip notes, which was less than a dollar, and said, "Keep the change."

The driver's eyes opened wide, and he put his hands together in the prayer mode, just below his chin, bowing. *"Kop chai lai."*

Cameron entered, surrounded by flowers of the garden in front. The width of the compound was nearly a hundred feet, and he could see the winding concrete path wandering down slightly to a back gate two hundred feet away. Along the sides were the individual cottages, each with a porch with a two person, carved teak table and chairs. Teak trees protruded upwards around the cottages, and colorful flowers were in front and to the sides of each cottage. It was absolutely stunning.

A slender man, the owner, was painting the front-most cottage with a brush, dipping it into a very strong-smelling, old-fashioned natural varnish. Where he painted, the woven natural material of the cottage side took on a dark, rich natural color, contrasted with the dried out parts yet to be painted with their gray, faded tone.

He turned to Cameron. "Yes?"

Relieved he spoke in English, Cameron answered, "I'm Cameron Harrington, and I'm looking for Sangmouane Sayasithsena." His effort to pronounce the name was so bad that the proprietor did not understand, but concluded he must be the one that wanted the single woman, and said in fair English, "Number Nine."

On the porch of Number 9 were a teak table and two chairs. The table was near the edge of the porch, just behind a hand-carved teak railing. The porch to the cottage was covered by a thatched roof. Surrounding the steps to the porch were flowers on either side. A beautiful young lady was sitting at the teak table on the porch.

A tingling sensation came over him when he realized he was confronted with none other than the same woman who was naked in the exotic waterfall movie.

She got up and hurried down the steps. She wore a bright blue *sinh* and a matching Western-styled top. She put her hands into prayer with elegance and feeling and bowed formally, bestowing great respect.

"Faint Chance." It had to be her. She rose, and he could see her features more clearly, especially her emerald-green eyes. Spencer and Candice, although they had tried, had not adequately described her beauty. This, his first meeting with her, was an indelible moment he would not forget.

"You're Cameron Harrington."

"Yes, and I have heard such wonderful things about you."

"I'm honored to meet the brother of Spencer, brother-in-law of Candice, who both have honored me so," she announced like an ambassador of a foreign country making a formal introduction. "I'm here to take care of you, and to help you in any way that I may be able," she continued. "I have also heard wonderful things about you. Following your brother's instructions, I came ahead yesterday and took a room here. Your brother and sister-in-law sent me a fortune just for this trip and to help you. But it as it is so much more than I need, I'll be able to save it and still have enough to pay for my journey to your country when the papers are issued to me allowing me to come. I've taken a room here at this hotel and have prepared it for you."

She led him inside, where to his delight, she had brought in flowers from the outside to decorate the room. "I hope this will be satisfactory."

The room had something close to an American king-sized bed, although the dimensions were not the same, as it was wider and not as long, and close to the floor with no box spring below.

The floor was made of solid teak wood planks, each varying from five to six inches in width, and not quite flush together, such that there was a little slit due to their irregularities in the making. The ground below could be seen between the slits.

The bathroom was to the rear of the bedroom, done in white tile, with an angled ceiling. The back wall of the bathroom was concrete rather than wicker, with several angled slits built in the concrete for ventilation, for which there was no cover.

The shower was a wand that would spray you and the rest of the bathroom, as there was no shower curtain or enclosure. There was a western toilet, a comforting sight, and there was a short hose beside it on the wall.

"How much is this room?" he asked.

"Twenty thousand kip," she responded. A quick mental calculation put it at less than four dollars.

"So cheap," Cameron said.

"I can stay on the floor, as the bed is for you," she said. "I stayed in the bed last night, and it is very nice. But I made sure they put clean linen on for you, and I hope everything will be to your liking."

"The bed is large, so perhaps we can share it," Cameron said. He imaged a debauched thought. It was hot. "Well, let's not stay inside. It's warm in here, and the grounds are beautiful. Let's walk about the compound to admire the flowers."

They went outside and headed down the path toward the back end of the compound, a slight downhill walk lined with flowers.

"How are Spencer and Candice?"

"Wonderful, and send you their regards. They're very anxious to have you come over just as soon as you can."

"And how is Devan? I heard from them that he is indeed special. But I knew he would be."

"He's very gifted. He's only four months old, and already walks and talks. He's getting lessons from a special tutor, and has the intelligence of someone several years of age or more. He's absolutely amazing. They believe you are responsible for it. Are you aware of that?"

"Yes, I summoned the spirits and asked them."

Cameron raised an eyebrow at the notion that spirits were involved.

"I got two letters from Spencer and Candice, and they told me he was special," she continued. "And when they called me about this trip, I heard about him. But I would like you to tell me more."

"More than special, he's extraordinary," Cameron said. "When he was only a month old, he could say his name and short sentences. At two months, he was talking. He's learning at an extremely accelerated rate. He's more coordinated and mentally able than some kids are at several years of age and is now walking. He's quite in control of himself and has no fits of crying as other children do. I do not have experience with children, but I'm impressed. Frankly, he's the only child I have ever liked."

"I'm so happy everything turned out well."

"Candice is studying Devan's DNA in her lab at this time."

"What's DNA?"

He began to repeat what he knew from talking to Candice. "Deoxyribonucleic acid. It's a generic term for any of the nucleic acids which yield deoxyribose on hydrolysis and which store genetic information." Hearing himself give that ridiculous answer, he realized that he sounded pedantic talking over her head in science. He changed the answer. "She studies differences in the makeup of people at a very basic level."

"Can she detect the presence of spirits?"

"No."

"I'm to go and live with them when my papers come through, and I'm hopeful to learn from them things like science. They are both very smart."

"Yes, they are both published researchers."

"Please tell me about you," she asked as they walked among the sunlit flowers of the compound. "I understand you're a very successful architect. What sort of things do you design?"

"I design homes and small buildings."

"I'm hopeful to see your work when I come." She frowned, a crease forming between her lovely brows. "You're here to get more of the *ton mai piiset*. Spencer and Candice told me to take you to my village and ask for more."

"Yes, that's why I'm here. Are you worried?"

"Oh, yes. I am scared."

"Why?"

"Even if I can get it, I'm not sure that the spirits in the plant will follow out of Lao."

"What do you think may happen?"

"I really don't know, but I fear."

Cameron let it go. "Candice wants a sample of the plant, and believes that she can synthesize it, that is, make it, in a lab to make it available to the world."

"I don't think it will work without the spirits," she said, concerned. "The tribal people believe that the spirits either live in such things as plants, or can be contacted through them. If it is made in a laboratory, like into a pill, I don't think spirits would like to live in a pill in a bottle."

Cameron feared that if he revealed his disbelief in spirits, he would lose her trust and the mission would be reduced to failure. Finally, he decided to ease the tension. "I'm only an architect, not a scientist. I really don't know. Perhaps there's a way to add the prayers to whatever she can make in the lab."

Faint Chance did not appear to believe him and changed the subject. "I love architecture. After we go to the village, on your return, I'll show you some Laotian architecture, however insignificant it may be to you. We can see what we have in Luang Prabang on the return trip and then in in Vientiane.

Cameron worried that she might put him through an inquisition over spiritual beliefs versus scientific ones. He recalled one could not win in any such battle.

They came to the back end of the courtyard, to the hotel's small restaurant. The sides were open, without windows or doors. A skinny woman who was obviously the owner's wife was behind a small counter on a high stool, engaged in bookkeeping. Instead of letting her legs dangle down from the high stool, she had them underneath her squatting on her heels in what looked to Cameron as a circus stunt.

They sat at a table and were close enough to give her their order without her getting up. Cameron was a little afraid to take just anything, worried about getting sick, with his limited travel experience.

"Beer," he said, feeling safe with that choice.

"Coffee," Faint Chance said, and then said something in Lao.

The lady got off the stool, nodded without saying anything, and went to the kitchen.

"What was it you added to your order?" Cameron asked.

"I wanted to be sure that it was the good coffee. Lao has some of the best coffees, but the good kind is sent for export. It's grown up here in the mountains, and so it is available here."

The lady arrived with beer and coffee. "Would you like to try the coffee?" Faint Chance asked.

Cameron took a sip. "Delicious."

"Have you never had Lao coffee?" she asked.

"I confess that I've never had anything from Lao. I didn't even know that coffee was grown in Lao. For that matter, I've never heard of anything from Lao, except you." She laughed, and Cameron shifted the conversation. "Was it much of an inconvenience for you to take time off work from the shop where you work?"

"I asked my father, and he said it would be all right. He thought it would be a good idea for me to go back to my village before I leave Lao, as I may never have the opportunity again. This is probably my last chance to see him."

"How are we to go about getting this plant?" he asked, moving ahead to the mission he came for.

"The chief, my second father, if he's still alive, must agree to allow us to have the plant if we are to get it. Without his approval, we will not be able to find the place where it grows."

"Do you think he might not let us have it?" He worried his long trip might be in vain.

"I cannot say. But I'm sure the chief would not want the news of the existence of the plant to go outside, as many strangers would then come and ruin the peaceful life the villagers have."

"When do we leave?"

"I've planned for us to leave the day after tomorrow. We have to make some preparations first. We can do that tomorrow and leave the following morning. We'll need to find a tuk-tuk with the capability to go up a rough mountain road, and we'll need supplies. The tuk-tuk will not be able to go the entire way. We'll have to go in on foot after the tuk-tuk can go no farther. We'll need camping gear and have to wait until tomorrow to get that."

"Okay. What shall we do this evening?"

"Would you like a walk down toward the river to look about?"

"Sure."

After their leisurely rest, Faint Chance led him on a stroll toward the Mekong River. They came to the river, but north of the spot where Cameron had come across from Thailand. Leading to the river was a long, concrete ramp used for loading and unloading boats, and at the bottom of the ramp, in the water, were a dozen, green, wooden boats of different sizes. The larger ones had a family living aboard.

"Let's have a picture or two of you," he said to her, and lined up a shot of her with the Mekong River and river boats in the background.

Light rain escorted them back to the room, with the Monsoon soon to come.

Chapter 17

In the hardworking tradition of Laotians, the owner's skinny wife of about eighty pounds kept the small restaurant open from six in the morning to nine at night. She did not seem to speak English, or at least she was not heard to say it. It was still quite light at half-past-seven when they sat down to dinner. There were others now in the restaurant and a few moving about the courtyard. Three young women worked at the restaurant, but they had other duties as well, and the restaurant was hardly full. Cameron noticed the restaurant had an opening to the street in the back, but it did not appear to have much, or perhaps any, business from outside the compound. The few guests he saw were European students on a tight budget.

Cameron remembered once seeing an old book in his father's things called *Europe on $5 Dollars a Day*, and, although he had not read it, and it was undoubtedly very dated now, he figured that a person could actually travel in Lao on five dollars per day. Students quickly found out with their ingenuity how to get about and have adventures on a modest income, and Lao was certainly a perfect spot for that.

Behind the restaurant was a wood-fired cook stove. Apparently, the electricity was used only for the refrigeration and lights.

Cameron noticed several bottles of liquor and wine on display on a table against a wall. The owner had apparently bought them in town and kept them there for the convenience of his guests.

A Western young lady sat at the next table, reading a book. She wore ankle-high hiking shoes with canvas tops and rubber-cleated soles, the antithesis of feminine. But they certainly looked practical. She wore jeans and a rustic jacket that went to her knees. It was not a flattering outfit, to say the least. Cameron broke the silence with "Hi, I'm from the US."

"Canada. A friend and I are backpacking and only today splurged on a hotel."

"Have you been traveling long?" Cameron asked.

"Six months, so far—as long as our money holds out. We've been in China. Because we don't have much money, we're traveling only in areas where it is very cheap. Lao and China are the cheapest."

"So adventurous, camping in such places. Have you run into any trouble?"

"Not really. We have been sick a few times, but so far, so good."

Concluding his introductions, he then turned his attention to the Scotch for sale by the bottle. He became curious as to how much it cost. "How much is the Scotch?" he asked the owner's wife, pointing to the bottle so she would know what he wanted.

She answered, and Faint Chance translated, "Ten US."

"How civilized! There must be no tax!" He proudly announced his opinion to Faint Chance, who had no idea what he was talking about. He continued talking to her as though she understood, "This marvelous country is not yet saddled with the scourge of government long enough to have oppressive taxes. Europe and America have wiped out freedom with their bloating government ideas of how the government should control you by spending your money for you, and the more government, the better. Taxes themselves are Satan."

She looked on, trying to be in agreement, but had no idea what he was talking about.

He picked up two Scotch bottles from those on display for sale, and announced, "Nothing like being prepared. Would you like some Scotch before dinner?"

"Okay." Trouper Faint Chance was determined to join in any fun to be had.

There were four other tables occupied as they sat and relaxed. He did not discuss the trip, so as to not let anyone overhear. He did not want other tourists joining in the conversation to inquire about it. Faint Chance ordered for them, vegetables fried with meat.

"When your brother was here, he said you were not yet married?" she asked, probing.

"True, I'm still single." And he was glad, now that he was in the presence of such a beautiful woman. "I'll show you about when you come to America. Do you know when you can come?"

"No."

"Has anyone given you a date as to when your visa might come?"

"No."

The food arrived, and to Cameron's relief, it was not weird, like he feared, such as dung beetles. "Is there any special reason as to why you did not go back to your village before now?"

"Travel is far too expensive, and it's far away. But I've always wanted to, and so this trip will be the most magnificent thing for me ever."

Cameron thought about what she had said about a deluge of the outside world coming to the village if they found it and got the plant. "If we get the plant, we must tell Spencer and Candice not to reveal where the plant comes from. I wonder if that will work? Perhaps they could state, when it comes out, that it comes from some completely different place in Lao, or even a different country. We must not ruin the village with a deluge of outsiders who would no doubt come by thousands if news of this discovery got out."

A sense of impending evil came over Faint Chance as she thought of exposing the secret to the outside world and creating a line of people coming there.

Seeing her expression, he turned the subject to something more immediate, and asked her, "Where do we go to find the special tuk-tuk for our journey?"

"I spoke to the owner of the hotel. I asked him where to find a tuk-tuk that could take us into the north jungle. It seems that there is more than one kind. Some have a smaller motor than others, according to him, and when I told him we that wanted to go on a jungle expedition, he said we needed to find one with a bigger motor. He said he knows of a fellow who has one, and who offers his services with it for expeditions into some of the remote villages. He said he would find him for us and tell him we are interested in his services. I did not tell him where we are going, other than to tell him that you wanted to see some of the villages as a tourist."

"Can we take the tuk-tuk in to the village?" Cameron asked.

"No. The tuk-tuk can take us to the end of the road. The tuk-tuk will take us for much of the journey, but we'll have to walk in the rest of the way when the tuk-tuk can go no farther in the jungle."

"How far do we have to walk in the jungle?"

"I think I misspoke. I mean hike, not walk. Yes, hike is the better word."

"Okay, how far do we have to hike?"

"It depends on the conditions, the path, and the weather. It's in the highland jungle, or what some call mountains, and the path will be narrow and difficult at places. My guess is that we can make it in three to four days if all goes well. We could run into some very heavy rain, and that will slow us down."

"Jesus. No one told me I would be on a three-to-four-day hike."

"Spencer did not ask that in the call," she replied.

"I get it. No one asked, so you did not mention it." He smiled, making it into a joke. The worried look he had put on her face by his concern left when he smiled, and she smiled slightly in return.

"I imagined the call from America must have been expensive, so I did not want to waste money. Did you bring any suitable clothes and shoes? Those shoes you have on—" She looked at his slip-on loafers. "—will not do."

"I did bring sort of hiking-styled shoes, as my extra pair."'

"Although it'll not be very cold, the highlands at night will be cooler than here in Ban Houei Sai. I bought some things for us in Vientiane with some of the money your brother and sister-in-law sent. I bought backpacks, sleeping bags, and a tent."

"Well, Spencer and Candice did not tell me that I needed any such things. Do you think it may rain?"

"Yes, a lot. This is the wet monsoon. Let's go to downtown tomorrow to find things we will need."

Having finished their meal, they walked up to their cottage, taking the bottles of Scotch. "Let's sit out here on the table and chairs," he said, leading her to the teak table and two chairs on his cottage porch. "Would you like another drink?"

"I'll have one if you are going to."

They sat at either end of the small table and sipped the scotch. As he absorbed the tropical evening, he looked across at her, wanting to share his experience along the way. "I want to show you some exotic tea I got along the way from a baron with a tea plantation." He produced it from his bag to show her. Its purple and orange colors had not faded. He told the story about meeting the Baron. "We can try it when we get back."

"My parents are from India," she said, "and they drink

tea there all the time. They got it from the British, and, of course, it is cheap. We have it at home all the time."

"This is not a cheap tea," he said, "but I did not pay for it. We can try this tea when we get back." He then shifted the subject to her. "You must tell me your story about your life and the village life firsthand."

He prepared to relax the evening away before retiring, drink in hand. And so he did. Cameron realized, as he listened to the most interesting story, that there was a very distinct possibility of him falling for such a girl of Asian blood, something that he had not previously considered.

After the story of her past, and having come a long way that day, starting from Chiang Rai, Thailand, checking out of the hotel, then traveling by car, then boat, and into Lao, Cameron realized that he was exhausted.

He finally said, "Let's retire. I'm very tired now, but I have enjoyed meeting you and look forward to our adventure."

She bowed and said, just before climbing into the other side of the bed, "Goodnight, Cameron, I have been greatly honored to meet you."

She slept without clothing.

Chapter 18

Cameron awoke, the rays of sunlight coming through the window to enlighten them to the day. Faint Chance was sleeping beside him, very sexy. She awakened, having slept with no clothes. Cameron, now awake, looked on at her magnificent body.

"Did you sleep properly?" she asked.

"I never thought of sleep as proper, but yes, I did. And you?"

"Why, yes, thank you."

After they rose, they took an early morning stroll about the compound as the morning light introduced itself unto their day. At the back of the compound in the tiny restaurant was the owner's wife, or perhaps she was considered an owner, and she was opening the metal fold-up door that covered the restaurant opening.

They sat, but the wife did not acknowledge them.

"Coffee," Cameron said.

The owner's wife nodded, went outside, and began the process to start a fire with small logs off to the back and side of the restaurant. There was no other source of heat to boil the water for coffee. Three, thin logs forming a device to hold the kettle were over the fire and soon created boiling water in the kettle. Finally, lovely Laotian coffee was served.

"This coffee is marvelous," Cameron said to Faint Chance. "I have never had Laotian coffee. Then again, I have hardly ever heard of Lao. The only people that I know that have been here are my brother and sister-in-law, and a few pilots from the Viet Nam War that still believe they are still under orders to not reveal that they had rained bombs on Lao during the Viet Nam folly of the American government."

Waiting for the sun to fully illuminate the day, sipping the delicious coffee, he thought about the military action in Lao years earlier, and the bombing of the Vietnamese on the Ho Chi Min trail. He thought of the lack of capability of those that governed America, especially conducting a war in a way destined to lose.

He stopped thinking of such things and brought his focus to the surroundings, realizing that he should not be wasting the beauty of the trip on politics like an Irishman in a pub. The sun was now illuminating light on the picturesque flowers around the compound, turning the day into something special.

"What shall we order for breakfast?" he asked. "I'm hungry."

To help him get along, she gave some instruction. 'To say 'I'm hungry in Lao,' you say *koy heo kao*. It literally means *hunger rice*. Or, you can say *koy yahk kin kao* which literally means 'I want eat rice.' To say 'I'm thirsty,' you say *koy heo nahm*. That means *hunger water*. Or you can say *koy yahk kin nahm*. That means 'I want consume water.'"

"How strange to define 'hunger' as a want for rice," he said, trying several times to get the sayings right. She helped him as he repeated clumsily.

She looked at the menu in Lao, and recommended the rice noodle soup. "Do you like rice noodle soup? It is *mee nam*."

Trying his best to get the accent right, he said, "*Koy yahk kin mee nam*."

"That's right," she complimented. "You're doing so well."

Rays of the sun changed their angle as they sat, and the brightness of day intensified. The noodles came in steaming bowls and were placed on the table by one of the young female assistants to the owner's wife.

Cameron tried his, as Faint Chance added additional spice from a small plate of peppers provided.

"This is delicious," he said.

"To say that in Lao, say *Ahn-nee sehb lie-lie.*"

"*Ahn-nee sehb lie-lie,*" he repeated.

As they ate, the sun intensified its shining on the flowers around the compound. When the owner came by, Faint Chance spoke to him in Lao. She turned to Cameron. "The owner has told us where we can go in town for provisions for the trip, and where we can find a good tuk-tuk to go into the mountains."

After breakfast, they hailed a tuk-tuk to take them down-town. At the provisions store, the only one, they walked about looking at things they might need. The store was sixteen feet square, not exactly the sort of sporting goods store Cameron was accustomed to.

"Let's get some of these canned foods—" Faint Chance said. "—but not too much."

"How about this fresh papaya?" Cameron said, holding up one.

"If we eat it in a few days, it'll be good," Faint Chance said, and so they added that and bought fresh bananas.

"Water?" Cameron asked.

She knew. "Take as much as we can carry. If we need more, we can refill from mountain streams. We should be able to get water at the village for the return."

Cameron flinched at the idea of drinking from a stream with little black swimming critters in it.

They looked around the store to see if there was some-thing else they might need. On the shelf was a two-foot-long machete, with a crude leather sheath.

Picking it up, she said, "This may be good to have."

Cameron was taken aback at her making the suggestion of needing a weapon. He did not know what to say. He took it and moved it about as though to be cutting brush. "Okay." He added it to his purchases without saying anything.

They walked down the street to the place that the hotel owner told them to look for a special tuk-tuk suitable for an expedition. They came to a spot with a more substantial-looking tuk-tuk in front, its owner sitting nearby. His tuk-tuk had a larger motor and slightly bigger wheels.

Faint Chance talked to the fellow at some length about where she wanted to go. Finally, it looked as though they had reached an agreement, and she turned to Cameron. "I'm asking him if he will take us as far as he can go, and then come back again for us later. I think that if we allow a day in the tuk-tuk, three days to hike in, maybe three days in the village, and three back, another day in the tuk-tuk, and then add another two or three for emergencies so he doesn't leave us, that would be about right. What do you think?"

"You're the boss," he said to her. "How much does he want?"

She spoke to him further, and reported, "He will give his tuk-tuk a service today, to make sure it is in good order, and then tomorrow we'll go. He will take us in to the mountain jungles for the day, as far as he can go, and then come back for us in ten days. He'll wait for us for three more days in case we are late. The price is three hundred thousand kip. But he will charge an additional five thousand kip for each day that we do not return, and he has to stay overnight in the tuk-tuk. He only has to wait three days, and then he can return without us."

Cameron translated that into dollars. "That's roughly seventy US dollars. Tell him we agree, but let's work out how much he gets up front and how much when he collects us."

She negotiated the matter with the driver. She explained to Cameron, "We have reached an agreement. He will finish the service on his vehicle, get some extra gas in cans, and be done in two or three hours. He will take us this afternoon if we wish as he will not be able to take on any customers."

They looked at each other approvingly. They had obtained a bonus of a chauffeured vehicle to take them about that afternoon. After all, they had already collected their provisions, and all they had left to do was make arrangements at the hotel to store their bags for them while they were gone.

Faint Chance spoke again to the driver. "I have asked him where we might go this afternoon. He says there is a spot he thinks you would enjoy seeing not far away. It's a very small village, of only forty or fifty people, where there is a lady who makes Laotian liquor. Apparently, the majority of the village is supported by her, and they collect the supplies she needs for it. The money that she gets for selling the liquor supports most of the village," she continued. "We will return before dark tonight, and then make our final preparations. We'll leave the hotel at daybreak so as to utilize the daylight fully. Is that agreeable? There will be no further charge for the driver for today's service."

"Sounds perfect to me," he said.

She told the driver that they could use a ride back to the hotel to drop off their provisions and that he should come for them after he serviced his tuk-tuk at noon. They went back to the hotel to pack and make ready.

Done with packing, on the patio, sitting and waiting for the tuk-tuk driver to return for the day trip, Faint Chance said, "The ramp we went to at the River is for the slow boat. I found out that the fast boats are on the other end of town. On our return trip, I plan to take you down the river to Luang Prabang, and from there we can fly to Vientiane. You have a choice of either the slow boat or the fast boat. The slow boat takes two days to get to Luang Prabang, the fast boat only one. On the slow boat, it is necessary to spend the night half way at a place called Pak Bang. The fast boat makes the trip in one day and stops half way at a small place called Pak Bang, but only as a check point."

The tuk-tuk driver arrived at the back side of the hotel, right by the restaurant. "There he is," Faint Chance said to Cameron when she saw him pull up.

They went to the tuk-tuk and stepped up in the back. Cameron took a closer look at the back of the tuk-tuk, as he was going to be spending a full day in it. It was open on the sides, like the rest, with a metal top that curved down around the sides a little. There were three horizontal bars to hold the structure together with an occasional vertical post, all three eights of an inch in diameter. Each side in the back had a shelf seat that extended from the front to the back, and they each took a side. There were no cushions. It was a going to be a rough ride.

⌇⌇⌇

When they arrived at the tiny village, there was a woman working under a canvas tarp supported by bamboo sticks. She looked twenty-five. She had dust and smears of something dark on her pretty face. There were two, black, fifty-five gallon metal barrels busy making her brew. Each had a small dugout underneath where logs were burning. The top had a small pipe coming in, bringing in cold water from a mountain stream source. There was a pan inside the top that the cold water went in, and it drained the cold water out and toward the road.

"These are stills," Cameron said.

The cold mountain water was to condense the steam inside. Nearby were thirty ceramic pots, fifteen gallon size, covered with some sort of natural material on top tied around with strings.

A pipe stuck out of each still below the water condenser pan, from which a clear fluid dripped. The nearest one was dripping into an old, light green plastic, one-gallon British Petroleum oil container, which had the top cut off. The sight of the motor oil container to catch the liquor seemed so crude.

Faint Chance interpreted. "The name is *Lao-Lao*. The ceramic bowls have sticky rice in them, and water. Added is a special, local black mushroom."

The lady's house also served as the supply warehouse, just adjacent. The lady went inside to get one of the special, black mushrooms, returned, and passed one to Cameron.

"She says that mushroom is used in the making of *Lao-Lao* in the north, but some other things are used in the south. This mushroom only grows here in the north. It's what makes northern *Lao-Lao* different from southern *Lao-Lao*.

"Sticky rice is put in the bowls with water and some mushrooms added. The bowls are then covered, and let to stand for fifteen days. Then they are put in those." She pointed to the stills.

Cameron heard names given the things she was pointing at, but the names apparently did not translate well into English, or more likely, Faint Chance did not know the English equivalents.

Cameron assumed the sticky rice fermented and then distilled into the barrels. As they spoke, the British Petroleum plastic container filled, and the lady had to go to the still and change it. She put another in its place and brought over the full one to them. She had glasses nearby and poured out two. Cameron wondered if she sampled it often, as the glasses were handy. He looked at her face to see if there was any clue, and she did have a look like she might imbibe a bit. The lady passed glasses to them, and the heat of the freshly distilled fluid could be felt though the glass.

"This is not too bad," Cameron said, surprised, as he was expecting the taste of burnt diesel oil. Faint Chance interpreted to Laotian for the lady, but it was obvious, and the lady gave a big smile.

"How much of this do you make in a day?" Cameron asked.

"Two hundred and seventy bottles a day," Faint Chance interpreted.

They looked about at the supplies, and Cameron marveled at the differences in making an alcoholic beverage in Lao, verses in the West with the west's industrialization and health standards. They sipped the drink, and had another, as the lady tended the stills.

Faint Chance spoke to the lady and then said, "She supports most of this village, and they collect the supplies for her, in barter."

"Sort of a one-purpose village," Cameron joked.

They continued sampling of the northern *Lao-Lao*. Actually, it wasn't too bad, he thought, and asked for more. But then, the lady was the only bar in the village.

Chapter 19

The next morning, Faint Chance came out of her cottage to the restaurant where Cameron was waiting at daybreak sipping his newly-discovered Lao coffee. She was wearing faded blue jeans and ankle-high rubber sole hiking shoes. She wore a pale-blue, knit top, looking very sexy. Cameron tried to keep his eyes and mind off her body, but it was not easy. She had a natural sway in her walk that made ignoring her impossible.

"Good morning," Cameron said, greeting her. "Did you sleep properly?" he asked, returning the question to her.

"Yes, thank you, I did. And you?"

"Yes, very good. I see our driver is all ready to go," he told her. "But let's have breakfast first."

The driver was already faithfully waiting just outside the gate. They checked their gear again to make sure they had everything and then sat for breakfast. She ordered the noodle soup for two.

The owner came by, and Faint Chance told him in Lao, pointing to their bags that were stacked up against the wall, "Hold our bags for us. We should be back in ten days, or a few more."

The owner acknowledged and took them to the back side of the restaurant room where there were other bags and guests' laundry.

Collecting their supplies for the trip, they went to mount the back of the tuk-tuk for the trip. This one had a slightly larger engine, selected for that purpose, and it did not make the weak popping sound of the smaller engines; it was a bit healthier in its exhaust notes.

A few hours later, on a small, dirt and sandy trail came a fork in the road. Faint Chance told the driver to go to the left, toward the mountains. Water passing over the trail created dips, ruts, and holes, slowing them to walking speed more often than not.

There had been no other traffic or people anywhere for over an hour when finally they came upon the back end of a medium sized elephant going in the same direction with its owner on top of its neck.

"The man uses him for work," Faint Chance said. "He's very lucky to have an elephant, but the elephant eats a lot."

"Hah! 'Eats a lot,'" Cameron said. "That should be his name. Is it a he?"

Faint Chance looked. "Yes."

The elephant rider made his beast go to one side in the brush when a spot came up where he could, and the tuk-tuk driver went around the elephant. The jungle growth smacked the sides of the tuk-tuk much of the time. The sides of the back of the tuk-tuk were open except for the three little horizontal strips of round metal that did their best to keep out the slapping green foliage trying to whip in and smack them.

The road seemed to wind endlessly up a gradual trail up the mountains. It did not wind back and forth like a road climbing by switchbacks. Rather, it just curved from side to side, with an occasional sharp turn to go around some huge rock or miss a cliff.

The driver did a good job, all in all. Once in a while an obstacle would come up with little notice, and the driver would come down hard on the brakes, and the two of them in the rear would be propelled to the front part of the back of the tuk-tuk, even though hanging on with both hands.

The hard bouncing about was seasoned with occasional light rain lasting usually only several minutes.

Three hours outside the last stop at the small village, Cameron felt he was about to scream for a break when they came to a scenic spot where there was a widening of the road and a good place to stop. It was a level spot fifty feet wide, on a cliff, next to which the mountain dropped away steeply five hundred feet below. The foliage provided a natural curtain for a water closet.

On the cliff, the view surrounding the area was spectacular. The sky was a strange combination of heavy broken clouds surrounding parts of the mountain tops, but there were bright rays of sunlight coming in-between them in beautiful colors. It was an eerie sight, giving rise to the sensation of entering a strange land. As he took a picture, he said to Faint Chance, "I feel like I'm in to a strange land, looking for King Kong."

"King Kong?"

"Oh, never mind. It's from an old movie."

"Are you ready to go?"

"Yeah, let's go."

After three more hours, they came to a clearing with a small stream in its middle. There were huge rocks in the stream, and, even though it was only a foot or two feet deep, there was no way for a vehicle to cross it. And, just ahead of it was another small mountain clearly ending the trail for a vehicle.

"I guess this is the end of the trip for the tuk-tuk," Cameron said.

The tuk-tuk stopped, and Faint Chance began talking in Lao to the driver. This was clearly the end of the road. There was a pathway to the left and to the right. One would take them to their destination. The other?

Faint Chance spoke at some length to the driver as they took their gear out of the back of the tuk-tuk and made ready for the hike.

Cameron noticed that even questions did not reveal

much to the Westerner, as in Laotian a question did not end by a raising of the tone.

Faint Chance then turned to Cameron. "I've told the driver to return here in ten days. I have told him I do not know what day we will return, but that he should try to be at this spot at midday if possible so that we could get back to the main road before dark for the return trip. I've told him that if we are not here on the tenth day, that he should sleep in his vehicle for three more days, in case we are delayed. I told him that if we are not back after three full days waiting, that he should go and report us to the military to come and look for us."

"And what might happen to us?" Cameron asked.

"Well, there are a number of things that might delay our return. You could have heavy rain with the monsoon beginning, getting lost, animal attacks, and injury. Also, an encounter with H'mong."

"Wow," Cameron said excitedly.

"It's best not to think of the dangers. Let's go on," Faint Chance tried to comfort him. "I've looked at a map, spoken to some, and believe we'll not get lost. There is a pathway there, and there may be occasional hunters and other villagers working fields that we can talk to if we take a wrong turn. So, let's try it." She had a big, reassuring smile.

The driver stood by politely, as Faint Chance repeated her instructions then asked him to repeat them back to her. There was daylight left, and they set off on foot toward the village.

The driver waited for them to walk off and out of sight before he left to drive back to Ban Houei Sai.

As they walked along, she said, "I didn't tell him where we were going exactly, to protect our purpose at your instructions. I told him that you were exploring remote villages and the local ways of life, and just told him the general direction we are going in case he has to report us."

They put on their backpacks, and they set off on foot.

After an hour of hiking, a trail merged with theirs with

women carrying on their heads and, in their hands, wicker baskets of harvest just picked.

Soon dusk fell down from the sky. Evaluating spots for a place to camp for the night, they looked about into the very dense forest of tropical vegetation on all sides. Finally, they came to a place where there was a slight clearing off to the right of the trail.

"Does this look okay?" Cameron asked, assuming she might know better where to stay the night.

"I think so," she said. What looked like a fallen tree lay ahead, completely covered with green moss, at the end of a flat spot in front of it that looked perfect as a place to set up their new tent and use that for a shelter on one side.

"Let's set up the tent here," Cameron said.

They took off their gear and set up the tent just in front of the fallen tree to act as a backboard.

The tent had bows to set it up with. Faint Chance had just bought it and had not opened it yet. Cameron struggled with it for a while until he figured it out. It was a rounded shape, and just right for two people. They opened their sleeping bags and placed them inside beside each other in preparation for the night.

Cameron sat in front of the tent, looking up at the quickly darkening sky. "Do you think it will rain?" He could feel a different wind, coming from the southwest.

Just as he said it, the sky opened up like cannon fire. A Laotian monsoon rain that Cameron had never seen the likes of came down.

They scurried inside to hide from the rain. The spot they picked for their campground was a little higher than the surrounding ground, and the water did not come in. It looked like they had succeeded in setting up where they would remain mostly dry in the event of running water over the terrain.

"Are you hungry?" Faint Chance asked, rummaging through the provisions.

"Starving," he replied. "What is the *specialité du maison*?" he mused.

There was French influence in Lao, in years past, and she knew a bit. "The specialty?"

"Exactly."

She looked at him, trying to make the best of the situation. "Let's eat the meat we brought. It may not be good tomorrow in this heat."

The storm pounded on the tent as they ate. It came down so hard that it drowned out all other noise. Cameron normally loved rain, but this was so strong that it worried him. Faint Chance had seen monsoon rains every year and was not in the slightest concerned.

"We might as well go to bed and get up at first light. I hope the rain stops by morning," she told him, as she organized the food back into the bag and put things aside to make room in the small tent for them to sleep.

With the sun setting fast, and the rain clouds above, darkness enfolded them in little time. Cameron had a small flashlight, propped it up on at the corner of the tent, and pointed the light up, such that it reflected about the tent top rather uniformly in a soothing luminescence. As they rested, the heavy rain cooled down the hot day and pounded on the tent.

"It's a good thing we have these sleeping bags," Cameron said. "It's getting a bit chilly in this rain. I think I'll get in." There was no room to stand up in the tent. He unzipped the bags, took off his shoes and socks, and wondered how much else to take off in the presence of this supermodel with God only knows what customs.

"These bags zip to each other so that we can make more warmth with our bodies," she said. "Why don't we do that if you are a little chilly?"

He did not object, and she then zipped the bottom zipper of the two bags together and then the top. Once done, she then straightened them and unzipped the top half way as though to make a bed turned down and ready for the night.

"Will this do?"

"It looks very inviting."

He was trying to suppress any thoughts of sexual contact, as he was still overwhelmed by all of the newness of the surroundings. He did not know what to do. She had so little. He concluded he would not take advantage of her.

But any idea of diplomacy was not to be. Faint Chance also took off her shoes and socks, and then began taking off her jeans! As she took them off, Cameron was elevated by the sight that she wore nothing underneath. He tried to turn his head away to be polite, but the tent was small. She continued and took off her top and bra, exposing her rather large breasts. He remembered she was of mixed blood and had the best of both East and West. He did his best to pretend to continue to find something to preoccupy himself. She was soon stark naked.

She turned to face him with her breasts exposed and her legs folded. Her public hair was visible, but he tried not to look—a ridiculous notion. It was dense and formed a triangle in-between her legs, as though a pointer as to where he should look.

"I prefer to sleep without any clothes, if you don't mind."

Her nakedness was visible in the reflective light of the flashlight and absolutely beautiful. Olive skin, long and beautifully shaped legs, and full breasts with very large nipples, all engulfing.

Resisting any idea that she was inviting him to approach her, still trying to assume this was how people in Lao normally behaved, he tried to think of other things. Architecture, maybe?

She faced him as if there was anything he wished to address. When nothing else was said, she did not hesitate longer and slipped into the waiting bag. "I'll warm it up for you as you are feeling chilly."

He thought, *When in Rome*…and so he said, "Yes, I prefer to sleep that way too."

Actually, it was almost true, except that he normally wore a T-shirt at home in the cooler season. He too took off his jeans and shirt. Naked, he slipped into the double bag with her. "Actually, I'm enjoying myself immensely on this trip, thanks to you, the rain and all."

He was trying to take his mind off the senses that engulfed him in the nest that she had made. Rain continued its pounding, actually increasing, as though creating a cadence.

"I'm glad. I told your brother and sister-in-law that I would do my best to see you are properly taken care of."

Cameron's mind engaged the topic. *Properly taken care of?* He conjured up what he thought to be various meanings—suitably, fittingly, thoroughly, admirably, in accordance with social ethics and good manners, with propriety. Surely she meant something like the latter ones. On the other hand, his body was involved. He lay face up, more to his side of the double bag. He occupied more of it, of course, than she, as he was larger and had something that might be an advertisement for Cialis.

He turned off the flashlight to conserve the batteries and to put his mind into a sleeping mode to get away from the sexual atmosphere.

But Faint Chance, laying on her side, then inched her way toward him until her naked body pushed up against his. She put her arm around him and pulled herself up close. He rolled over to his side, facing her.

The rain intensified still further, the beginning of the monsoon. It soon became extraordinarily loud, pounding on the tent and anything nearby. It insulated them from all outside noises and intensified their senses. Cameron began to lose his thoughts and concerns that he should stand off from what was burning inside, as they lay and listened to the rain. Faint Chance made several movements that rubbed her alluring, warm, soft cocktail against him. She pulled herself closer in with her arm over him. In the process she positioned, and then repositioned, herself such that when they came to rest, his tumescent member was moving on its own into the warm area between her thighs, as though having a global positioning system of its own. The shape of her thighs was such that they left an opening with ample access to her welcoming sex. His member, without being touched, was beginning to enter her. In a movement he could hardly forget, she, without using any hands, made a few movements, relaxing, and positioning, such that he felt himself slide right into her without so much as moving. He considered that she had unnatural talents.

"Showtime," he said aloud.

Chapter 20

My name is Mrs. Priscilla Hargrove. How do you do," she said as she stood outside the door of the Harrington home. She was dressed in a blue suit, skirt below the knees, white shirt, and a blue and red striped, subtle tie. Her hair was pinned up, and she looked the essence of proper. She had a slender, leather briefcase in which she carried copies of her references and diplomas in a folder ready to present to her prospective employers. It was impressive.

"Do come in. I'm Candice Harrington, and my husband, Spencer, is here also." She turned and said aloud, "Come, Spencer, and meet Ms. Hargrove."

He came in from the next room. "How do you do," Spencer said. "We spoke on the phone."

"Very well, thank you.

"Please have a seat. Would you like some tea?" Candice asked.

"That would be very nice. We English drink a good deal of tea," Priscilla said.

Candice went to the kitchen for tea and returned with it shortly while Priscilla settled at the table.

"Here are my credentials and references," Priscilla said, handing the prepared folder to Spencer.

He opened it and skimmed through it. He leafed through

it quickly, as he would go through it later. "Tell us about yourself. Apparently, you decided to maintain British citizenship?" This was a loaded question to determine if she was an anti-American.

"Oh, yes, I have not applied for American citizenship. But I have a legal work permit. A copy of it is in the folder. I have a degree from Oxford in English Literature. I have worked as an Associate Professor in England in English Literature. I later married and migrated to America with my husband when his job took him here. He is an associate professor of English Literature as well. We have two children, and this year the youngest is off to college along with the first. So now I have free time, and I saw your advertisement. I rather miss teaching."

"Our son, Devan, is what one might call a gifted child, to put it mildly. We are seeking a special educator for him. Candice and I believe that communication is the fundamental first key to success, and we both feel that Devan must learn proper English, rather than just slang and adequate English. So, Candice and I both believe that someone such as you is best suited."

"How old is Devan?"

"He's much younger than you might imagine. Only four months," Spencer answered.

"*What? Four months?*" Priscilla said in shock. She leaned forward in her chair, appearing ready to rise and leave at once, as though attending a wasteful interview. "There seems to be a mistake. Your gifted child does not need someone versed in English literature. I was expecting to tutor someone in his late teens. You need a nanny."

"Please sit back for a moment," Spencer said, in order to keep her in her seat, "and hear more. And before you make any rash prejudgments, please meet Devan."

With that, Spencer went for Devan. He came back into the room leading little Devan by the hand. Devan was in pants and shirt, not nappies as Priscilla anticipated for a four-month-old. He walked by himself and put down his father's hand to continue alone.

"Devan, this is Mrs. Priscilla Hargrove. She teaches English."

"How do you do, Mrs. Hargrove?" Devan said to Priscilla, offering her his little hand. "I am Devan Harrington."

"Oh, my!" Priscilla exclaimed loudly, losing decorum. She covered her mouth in shock for fear she might say something else out of place. She regained composure after a few moments and finally answered, "Very well, thank you."

"I'm pleased to meet you," Devan said. "I hope I can learn much from you."

"Do you see now that he needs special tutoring?" Spencer pointed out.

"Indeed!"

"We think mornings would be sufficient," Spencer said. "Mondays through Fridays. We're both research doctors, and work regular hours. We have a wonderful Yugoslavian woman who is also here the entire day, Monday through Friday, who takes care of the house and prepares his meals. She will look after him in the afternoons, and you would keep him busy in the morning. We have set up a study with blackboard and suitable furniture. We'll show you now."

"Yes, this is a most unusual assignment," Priscilla said. "But I must warn you that I have no particular experience in teaching such a young person."

"We are confident that you will find Devan very much like a much older pupil and also well behaved," Spencer said. "However, we insist that you not to speak about his unique talents to others, as we do not want to draw attention to him. This is a bit like a secret job, if you know what I mean. Otherwise, there would be news media outside the door all day."

She was quiet for a time and then responded, "This could be a most interesting assignment indeed."

Chapter 21

Plop, plop, plop. The sound of huge water droplets against the tent could be heard coming from high up leaves in the canopy of the jungle after the monsoon rain was over and awoke them.

"Awk, awk."

The jungle was also awake.

"Good morning," she said to him.

Cameron held her tight, savoring the moment, realizing that he would remember that point in time, awakening in the jungle, after making love to the incredible creature beside him. Rays of sun made the tent material glow inside.

"The rain is over," he concluded.

"This is the monsoon. It will rain again at any time."

Cameron opened the tent and looked outside. A ray of sunshine struck his face, but dark, broken clouds surrounded the bright rays streaming through them. He took a deep breath of the cool, refreshing air, in the sublimely peaceful moment.

After disassembling their tent and loading their backpacks, they decided to sit in front of and lean against the fallen tree that their tent had used to prop up against. They cut a slice of juicy, bright orange papaya.

Suddenly, the fallen tree they lay against began to roll backward.

"Whoa!" Cameron exclaimed, leaping forward. The tree stopped after rolling a few feet.

He stood up and moved closer. There was a shiny plate on the tree that had been on the bottom, not covered with moss. He rubbed it with his hand to see what it was.

US Ordinance 4000 lbs.

He rubbed the object, which caused it to become loose and start rolling backward until it came up to the trunk of a teak tree two feet away. A whirring noise came from the object.

"*Jesus, it's an unexploded bomb!*" Cameron shouted.

They grabbed their packs and ran as fast as they could back toward the path to distance themselves. After running a stretch, there appeared a small cliff of fifteen feet down off to one side. They went over, sliding down the cliff, risking injury.

KA-BOOM!

The explosion shook the earth so much that it knocked them over, even down the cliff. The blast blew entire trees and rocks up in the air and some right over them. A huge, irregular rock, six feet in diameter, came down and crashed onto the ground not twenty feet away from them at the bottom of the cliff, making an enormous noise and shaking the earth a second time. Debris from the explosion rained down around them for the longest time. They stayed there, huddled up, deafened from the blast, and very scared.

When all was quiet, and then some, they finally got up, went back up the cliff, and looked around. The explosion made a crater fifty feet wide, and an even larger clearing. They could not hear a thing due to temporary hearing loss. They moved cautiously closer, into the center of the crater. It would be a while before their hearing and senses would fully return.

⌘

Resuming their hike along the sandy road, they went around a curve in the path, and just ahead, startling them, was a man pointing a long rifle off to one side. He did not see them.

Cameron grabbed hold of the handle of the machete on his belt but dared not draw it. They backed up very slowly.

"What do you think?" Cameron whispered.

"He's a hunter, and he's got something to shoot."

As they spoke, the hunter lowered his rifle, giving up on whatever he was hunting in disgust. He walked toward them.

Cameron observed that the hunter did not appear to have fear just because Cameron and Faint Chance were approaching. The man slowed his pace as he came closer, but did not appear to want to kill other humans.

Faint Chance spoke to him, and interpreted, "We scared off a turkey he was chasing. He is angry."

"I hope he's not too mad," Cameron said. "What can we do?"

Cameron could not help but look at the muzzle loader rifle of the hunter, and thought he would complement its owner. "Tell him I like his gun." *What better way*, he thought, *to possibly keep from being shot.*

Faint Chance told the hunter that her friend admired his weapon. He seemed very proud of his rusty old rifle. He lowered the hammer slowly and passed it to Cameron.

The gun fascinated Cameron. The barrel had a bore of about three-eighths of an inch. The wooden stock had brass metal bracing much like the early American muzzle loaders from the civil war period. The hunter took out a pouch and proudly displayed supplies for his weapon. He showed natural fibers and told Faint Chance it was material is to put behind the lead and explained how it worked. The proud hunter then displayed his lead balls for the shot.

Faint Chance interpreted. "He says he makes the lead balls himself."

He then took out of his pocket a stick of lead three inches long to show where the lead round bullets came from.

"He says the government required everyone had to turn in their guns, but he did not. He used to grow opium, but it's now illegal, and he is afraid. He says he needs the gun to feed his family. He says they don't have much to eat, as much of the deer are gone, but there are still wild boar, some other animals, and birds."

"Tell him that we apologize for making his family go without food today. Give him this," Cameron said as he took out a stack of Kip notes, amounting to about twenty US dollars. "Tell him it is a present that we want to give him to buy food for his family since we ruined his hunt today."

She spoke the words, and the hunter's eyes lit up at the size of the money. He took it slowly, and then stared at it. The hunter bowed humbly to them, prayed thanks for the day of heavenly sent spirts that brought him such fortune that would support his family for a very long time.

❧❧

Later on, Cameron and Faint Chance came to a stream crossing their path, twenty feet wide. It was not a fast flowing stream, and one could see fish in it. There were rocks protruded out, some big enough to walk on.

Stepping across the slippery, moldy tops of the wet rocks was precarious. Making it across the stream, they took refuge by sitting on a big rock above the stream, mesmerized by its soothing sound as a light rain began.

The rain seemed to lighten up. "We had better press on, so as not to waste the daylight," he encouraged.

They arose and began their hike. But, in no time they were greeted by another major downpour. They pressed on, clothes soaking wet in the rain.

The downpour subsided. In an hour, a small clearing on flat ground appeared off to one side that looked welcoming for them on their trip. It was time to rest, even though there was a wee bit of daylight left.

The tent set up faster for them as they had done it before. Sitting just under the rain cover over the opening of the tent, they ate some of their provisions. They finally, retired, and lowered the insect screen.

In an hour, the rain let up. The inside of the tent was illuminated by the material glowing softy from moonlight. They lay back, resting.

Faint Chance, who had been quiet, said curiously, "Is your blade nearby?"

"Yes, I have it here." Cameron trusted her instincts, and, although he did not sense anything, he rolled over, took the machete out of its sheath, and put it above their heads on the ground for easy access.

Exhausted from the long day of difficult hiking in the mountains and excitement of the bomb, the two were soon asleep.

Chapter 22

As the calming blanket of night fell over them, Faint Chance sensed something just outside the tent. She opened her eyes. Her body was tucked into Cameron's, and her arms were inside the double sleeping bag. Cameron was inside the bag beside her, but both of his arms were outside. Reassured, she drifted back to sleep.

A round object entered the tent horizontally, two feet above the ground. Its head was three-quarters of a foot in diameter. It came right over them, followed by its body which was the same, round shape and did not seem to end. It was white with brown blotches.

It was a twenty-five-foot Albino Burmese Python Constrictor.

The monster stuck its long tongue out over the sleeping couple, sensing the warm food below. Its head came in several feet then dropped down under the blissfully dreaming twosome in their double bag, encircling its meal. It began in its death squeeze, squeezing its prey so hard the prey could not breath, only to then swallow them whole.

After the beast went under their sleeping bag, it quickly wrapped itself around it. Its size and strength lifted the bag.

Faint Chance realized something was wrong, and tried to jump out, but she could not. Her arms were trapped inside as the beast tightened its first loop and began a second. "*Cameron*!" she yelled.

Cameron opened his eyes abruptly. More of the body was coming in, making its second turn around the couple in the sleeping bag. If it did make a completed second circle around them, there would be no escape. More of its length was quickly coming in, and it continued to tighten its grip. In little time, it would squeeze the last breath of life out of both of them.

Cameron was able to slither out of the bag, as he had been sleeping with his arms out, whereas Faint Chance had hers inside and was trapped by the powerful squeeze of the beast. When he got out, the snake quickly moved farther around the bag and squeezed hard to take up the slack created by Cameron's leaving.

Cameron quickly grabbed the machete above his head that Faint Chance had him buy for the trip, and which she had told him to have ready when they went to bed, as though she knew what to expect. More of the monster continued to come in and then made a third turn around the bag with only Faint Chance inside. It tightened its squeeze on Faint Chance to the point that she could no longer inhale.

Its head came up from making its third wrap around the bag with Faint Chance inside, which placed its head in front of Cameron. It was just right for Cameron to swing the machete down on it. He raised his machete with both arms, and brought to bear all of his strength down the blade just behind the neck of the beast's huge head.

WHACK! The blow cut the huge python's head off neatly. Its body relaxed, but did not retreat.

It relaxed its hold on Faint Chance, and unwound its grip on the bag. Out she came from the bag, very scared.

They went outside the tent, and witnessed its enormous length.

"If I can lift this beast, I had better drag it off. More than likely something else might be attracted to the bloody remains."

Faint Chance sat and shook without speaking, shaken by the incident.

Cameron tried to drag the snake away, but it was far too heavy to take it far. He hacked up the body into several pieces and moved them away from the tent. He gave up trying to move it farther.

They went back into the tent and sat on the sleeping bag, trying to get over the event. Eventually, they crawled into the sleeping bag, and she squeezed her naked body up tightly up to his. She held him tightly, but said nothing. It was some time before they calmed enough to go back to sleep. The memory would never leave.

Chapter 23

On the third day, the path narrowed. It became tighter with overgrown plants and trees, often barely one person wide. Walking in tandem, Cameron was first, machete in hand. They came to a decline so steep they had to use the occasional help of their hands clutching plants and branches as they descended to keep from slipping on the soaking ground.

A large black and white bird, nesting on the mountainside nearby, flew above, watching. There was a small, but fast-moving stream at the bottom. The path led them over it on rocks. Up the other side, colorful wild flowers grew.

"I think the village is not much farther," Faint Chance said. "This area looks familiar."

They were exhausted after several hours, when the path widened, and people could be seen ahead. There were clouds above, and rays of sunlight streamed through the clouds.

"Home!" she announced in the local dialect.

The village spread over gently rolling hills with houses made of teak built up on stilts several feet off the ground.

Cameron, the architect, assumed the stilts were to protect them from running surface waters from the monsoon rains, but he was not sure.

The thatched roofs were made of a natural tree material

that had dried out and were grayish-brown in color.

Four youngsters came to look at them as they came into the village. They did not get too close, following along with immense curiosity.

Off to the left, and inside the village, was a very old, small-framed woman standing over a stone apparatus. With both hands, she was turning a round stone a foot and a half in diameter around and around, by way of a stick that stuck up at the edge of the stone. The stone was on top of a larger stone base. There was a hole in the middle of the upper stone, and through the hole, she gradually trickled in a few corn kernels every minute or two.

The corn kernels came out, ground from below on one side where there was a grove in the stone, and then fell into a container.

Although she did turn to face them when they walked out, she did not greet them, nor did she pause from her work. It looked very difficult for her, and she had to put her body into it, given her slight frame. She continued at a steady pace, not letting up just because visitors came.

Faint chance spoke to her. The woman replied, but she did not break her rhythm of turning the stone.

"Corn for animals. She's crushing corn for them."

"Was that the Lao language?"

"No—local dialect."

They stood there, a few feet away from the lady who was crushing the corn, and looked all around. Faint Chance's eyes become watery.

"Do you think anyone here will remember you?" Cameron asked.

"Some may, and surely the chief will, if he's still alive." She asked the lady and reported, "Yes, he's still alive. That's wonderful."

They went on into the sprawling mountain village of a few hundred houses, the childhood home of Faint Chance.

They arrived at the chief's house. A man sat outside the house on the ground near the door of the house, covered by a drape of leather. He arose when they approached, apparently acting as guard for the chief.

"I'm Sangmouane Sayasithsena and used to live here. I wish to see the chief."

The man went inside and then came out, holding the drape open to invite them in.

Inside were six people.

She stopped at the most elder, sitting and putting her hands together in the *nop* prayer position, bowing deeply. Then she rose. "I'm Sangmouane Sayasithsena."

The chief then recognized her and smiled warmly.

"This is Cameron Harrington from America," she told him. "He is a designer of houses."

The chief appeared to be in good health. He stood and Faint Chance went to him in a warm embrace. It was her moment.

For Cameron, the chief's home was a joke of no architectural interest. It was a rectangular box, thirty feet by twenty-five feet, about the same size as the others in the village. The walls were a single layer of horizontal boards, averaging three-quarters of an inch thick, and in varying widths of four to six inches. The seams were not tight. The length of the boards averaged fifteen to eighteen feet, cut by a hand saw with irregular edges. Light seeped through edges of the boards making up the walls that were not tight. The roof was thatched tree foliage, dried, brownish/gray in color.

Two of the walls had window openings, without glass, and the overall effect was that the room was dark. It was obvious that these houses were built in the same way for perhaps dozens or hundreds of years, and the people had no other building materials, even now.

It was not immediately clear how many of the six people they saw in the single, open, dark room lived there. There was a sort of split-level effect at one side, a third of the floor space, which was elevated a foot and a half. The elevated spot was the sleeping area, and there were a number of mats to sleep on, resembling Japanese futons, rolled up and put back up against the wall so as to make floor space available for the day. There were woven blankets as well.

They took seats, short stools of wood, while the others who lived there squatted on their ankles.

Faint Chance then told the chief of the years she had been away, what had happened to her since she left, and how she was adopted by the Tamils. All in the house listened intently to what was a most interesting story. One very old lady, apparently an aunt, listened while squatting on her ankles.

Her tale took half an hour. The older woman said she remembered the young Sangmouane Sayasithsena.

When it appeared the length of the story was enough, the chief spoke. Faint Chance interpreted for Cameron, "The chief says this is a special occasion, and offers *Lao-Lao*."

The chief went to a wicker storage container against the wall and produced a bottle of clear *Lao-Lao*.

Faint Chance said, "*Lao-Lao* is not made here, and only the chief has it. He gets it from barter with a *Lao-Lao* maker at another village."

He produced wooden cups and gave Cameron, Faint Chance, the elders, and himself, all in the house, *Lao-Lao*. They sipped it, and there was much conversation, but in the local dialect, so Cameron just sat back and watched all the expressions. In Lao or in the local dialect, the chief asked her questions about the capitol city where she lived, the Tamil Indians who adopted her, and the type of work that she did. He asked her if she had become Christian since she had been taken to a mission. She said she had not.

After the reunion, Faint Chance said to Cameron, "Let's take a walk around the village."

They were politely allowed to leave, and she led Cameron on a tour. A red sky above was saying goodbye to the day. Picturesque thatched-roofed huts covered the village, and the residents seemed to hurry to finish what they had to do before the light was gone. Word was getting around the village already that one of their own had come back, and, as she and Cameron walked about, they could tell that some of the people already knew who they were.

They came to a cliff situated just above flatland below. Faint Chance pointed off to one side, "That is one of the areas for crops. To the other side are banana trees, mangos, and papayas. Let's go there." At the fruit trees, Faint Chance stopped and turned to Cameron. "This is all very wonderful. I'm so happy you and your brother and sister-in-law made this possible." She put her arms around him, and kissed him. "There is something in my karma with you."

The two kissed passionately, connecting feelings.

When they returned to the chief's hut, the aunt had organized sleeping mats for them. They found themselves sleeping with six other people in the chief's home.

"At least we won't be lonely," Cameron told her,

಄಄಄

The following day, the chief was occupied settling problems of some of the villagers. Cameron could see that he was definitely the seat of power. Several villagers came in to take up problems with him, and Cameron and Faint Chance sat back politely and listened, with Faint Chance interpreting softly to him when it would not interrupt. When the last villager had his problem addressed, the chief struck up a conversation with Faint Chance, but now the topic was just who Cameron was. Faint Chance interpreted, but Cameron noticed that the chief did not always wait for the complete interpretation—he was very astute.

Faint Chance told the chief how she first met the brother of Cameron, Spencer Harrington and his wife, Candice, research doctors from America. She explained how they were in Vientiane and invited her to come live with them in America, and that they were paying for everything. She explained that she was waiting for the government approval for her to go, and that she would then live there.

Then she apologized that she was not there just for a visit, and that she gave her new American friends her wedding present for them to have a child as a return gift for their sponsorship, they want her to ask him for more of the *ton mai piiset*. She told how she wanted them to have the special child that might have been hers had she married and undertaken the ceremony. She told how they took the *ton mai piiset* when in Vientiane, and that she performed the ceremony for them as he taught her.

The chief asked if they had a special child.

She told the chief how special Devan was.

He asked her if she was there for more of the plant.

She told him that the doctors wanted to study one of the plants in their laboratory. She told of her explaining to them that without the baci strings, and special prayers, that it would not work. She told the chief that she explained to them that they cannot make chemicals to beget special children without the prayers to get help from the spirits, but they still wished to try.

The chief told her that the discovery of the *ton mai piiset* by the West might have a greater impact on the world than she might imagine. He said that he hoped the knowledge of the plant did not bring the outside to the village, as there was much greed and evil in the world outside the village. But he knew when he gave her the *ton mai piiset* and sent her off to the outside world that he was risking an invitation to the outside.

He looked at Cameron, and she interpreted. "What do the doctors intend with the plant leaves if I let you have some?"

Cameron said, and she interpreted, "My sister-in-law intends to study what the plant leaves are made of to see if she can duplicate the substance. Her plan is to make it available to the world if she can make more of it. And, maybe there will be a way to summon the spirits over pills that they make one day."

The chief told her that if the entire world had it, it would make a change in mankind.

Cameron wondered if he had come all this way to be turned down by the chief, but, so far, he had not said no. Cameron turned to Faint Chance. "I would very much like to hear the history of the plant, if you would be kind enough to tell me."

The chief spoke to Faint Chance, who interpreted, "He tells the history of the *ton mai piiset*. His father, the *Maw Pii* before him, discovered it. It only grows in soil from ages past, which is below the top of a cliff where there are ancient soils that can be reached from the side of the cliff, well below the top layers of accumulated soils. This tells him that there is something about it that the current world is incompatible with. It's found only in that one place. That is also where he found me. I was caught there by the plant and its spirits when my first parents went over the cliff and died. He was there last year and could only see a few plants left, growing together in one spot. His father saw its strange colors and was beckoned by the spirits to sample it. He found that it put him in touch with powerful spirits. His father was the first to try the plant. The spirits told him that his wife should take the plant on their wedding day, and they would make a special child for him. He and his wife took the plant upon their wedding, and their son was born with special abilities."

"Ask him if he was an only child," Cameron requested.

"He says yes. His mother died when he was young, and his father was killed in the jungle when he was thirty-five. He was made *Maw Pii*, and has been since."

"How long ago was that?" Cameron asked, anxious to learn his age.

"He says that was eighty years ago."

Cameron asked Faint Chance to correct the question and answer, as there was obviously a mistake. She repeated his question and the chief's answer. Cameron hesitated, wondering whether or not to ask a third time. Perhaps there was something that was not translating correctly. Perhaps he should ask it another way. Cameron looked at Faint Chance. "Ask him his age."

"He says one hundred fifteen."

Cameron was taken aback. "Ask the chief if he has achieved the age of one hundred fifteen because of the plant?"

"He says yes. He was intended by the spirits to be the *Great Maw Pii,* the leader of those who speak to the spirits, a Shaman, and also the wisest. Only a person of many years has the experience to be very wise. The spirits of the plant also give longevity so that the person born of it can accumulate great amounts of experience and have the extended years to gain and pass on his wisdom to others."

"My God," Cameron said. "This plant is the next step for mankind. Ask him if anyone else has taken the plant leaves besides him."

"He's the oldest one born unto it. His widow was not born unto it, but she also took it at their wedding. She was killed in an accident. Their son was born unto it, and he lives here."

"Ask him why no one else has taken it."

"He says there is not enough for all the villagers, and thus it was saved for his son to become *Maw Pii* to follow him. There is very little of it left."

"Do any other village chiefs in other places have the plant?" Cameron asked.

"He says not."

Cameron changed the subject. "I was told missionaries have come through here. Do visitors come to the village often?"

"He says it has been some time since the village has had a visitor. Sometimes a military scout comes by. A few years ago, Christian missionaries from Australia came, trying to spread their religion to the village, but he would not let them. The Lao Government does not allow them to come in and try to convert villagers. They were posing as educators to the government, pretending to be educating, but, in reality, only trying to spread religion. The military came here afterward and asked him about them. That is when he found out that they were arrested for trying to spread Christianity. He does not want Christianity here."

Cameron was quiet for a time, wondering about such a place. To break the silence, the chief asked a question of him.

"He wants to know of any new wars."

Cameron had to stop and think as there had been so many. Faint Chance interpreted as best she could, although some of the places she had not heard of. "There has been fighting in many parts of the world, some over territory and oil, but now many with people of different religious faiths killing each other. Most of these include Muslims as they are backward and waging their idea of killing for their God. They like suicide attacks. Many are one type of Muslim killing another type. They are jealous of the luxuries of the Western world, and prefer to rid the world of such ways so no one else can have them. There are continuous suicide bombings in many parts of the world. India and Pakistan are in conflict on the border of Kashmir over a continued border dispute. There are endless wars in Afghanistan and Iraq. Some wars are Muslims fighting other Muslims. There is war in Syria. There are Muslim groups that continually bomb Israel. Muslim terrorists commit acts of lethal terrorism against innocent people done in what they think is for the glory of their God. There is something like a civil war in Venezuela where the people are fighting the dictator. North Korea is about to boil."

"So many have been slaughtered, and many in the name of religion," the chief said through Faint Chance. "No doubt that all carry the notion as they create wars, that they have their notion of their God with them. He says now you can see why he doesn't want religion here. He believes all leaders of countries believe that they have God on their side, no matter what religion. Or, even if they don't, they say they do."

The chief asked about developments with nearby Vietnam, Thailand, and Cambodia opening their countries to the world, and Cameron told what he could, but he was not so well informed. To Cameron's surprise, he found the chief to be relatively well informed about the world, considering that he had access to news only on the rare visit to his village from outsiders. The chief then changed the subject, and asked if there had been any developments in curing cancer.

"Yes, but all very small. The answer is basically none."

"He says medicine from the outside is the one thing he would like to bring here, if it could be done without bringing in religion and outside cultures," Faint Chance told Cameron.

"Can the villagers read and write?" Cameron asked.

"Only he and his son. But that may change. The government is hiring educators to come to remote villages, and one day a government educator will probably come here with government orders to educate the young ones. These villages of *Lao Sung*, or the highlands, are more difficult to get to as you may have witnessed coming here."

"That's an understatement," Cameron said. "What sort of spiritual beliefs do your people have?"

"He says the villagers are animists and believe that living souls reside in or are reached by certain natural objects, in a spiritual world. The people believe that they may make contact with their ancestors."

"Do you think it would be appropriate for me to ask the chief if he, himself, is religious? Please tell him that I am not but that I was raised as a Christian."

"I do not think it is bad to ask." And so she did and also told him about Cameron. "No, but he knows that certain spirits are real. He says that when Christians pray to God, no one is listening. He says that if you were to take the *ton mai piiset*, and you ask the spirits to come to you, you will definitely experience something extraordinary."

"Tell him that I know that to be true, based on the fact that my brother and sister-in-law took the plant and had such an out-of-this world experience. Ask if he considers belief in spirits to be the same as religion."

"He says no. Many people have a need to believe in a religion. Some leaders use it to control people. However, religions, as he knows them, are largely invented by man as an excuse to take a day off work."

Cameron was taken aback. "Religion invented to have a day off? That is profound, and it makes sense. Ah, and so delightfully simple. A day off work required for religion. Christians take Sundays off. Jews, Saturday. In many Muslim countries, they take off Fridays. Hindus take off various days for religious activities. I took philosophy courses in the university so I could sound more intellectual at cocktail parties with elaborate and lengthy theories of philosophers such as René Descartes and St. Thomas Aquinas as to the existence of God. What nonsense. Religious people claim it would offend Jehovah, Jesus, Mohammed, or God by many other names to work on their Sabbath. How ironic to come to a village in the middle of nowhere, where there is no electricity, no internet, no TV, no newspapers, no mail service, and learn such a lovely definition of religion. It's like having an audience with the High Llama in the story of Shangri-La."

Not much of that was interpreted, as it was beyond the ability of Faint Chance to interpret all of that, as much of it was not part of the Laotian language and certainly not in the local dialect.

"Ask him if the villagers have a day of the week that is taken off from regular work?" Cameron asked, this time more slowly.

"He says no. No religion, no days off. If a villager wants to rest a day, he just does so. Of course, it reflects on his abilities to perform."

The chief smiled a little, and for the first time, as though he understood perhaps much of what Cameron had been saying.

"Ask him if he intentionally does not bring the outside world to his village."

"He says, not that long ago, your government was dropping bombs like rain very near here in the war. There was madness and killing. He can take you on a fairly short journey from here where you can see for yourself several large, unexploded bombs dropped from airplanes. He's still waiting for the government to clear all dangerous bombs that did not go off when dropped. A number of his people were killed by bombs during the war, and even recently there have been deaths to his hunters who came upon an unexploded bomb unknowingly."

"We slept next to one without knowing it on the way in, just a few days ago," Cameron said. "I'll always remember that. We were nearly blown to pieces."

"He says undoubtedly your civilization will one day be here, but he does not believe that keeping it out so far has been a mistake."

Cameron nodded. "I'm sure he is right. How presumptuous of me to assume that civilized ways are better. How about inventions and the luxuries of the west? Is he aware of much of these?"

"He says he is not aware of many of these things, but along with these come bad as well as good. His people were able to stay out of the carnage of the War by being in this remote village. One day the village will be in contact with the rest of the world, but that should come later. He leaves such changes for his son when he becomes Chief, as he wishes. Or, to his son, if he does not wish it. Such major changes may be best left to the younger ones. He knew that my giving the wedding gift to me might bring outsiders here. And so now you have come. Others will follow. He hopes it will not bring trouble, but he fears it will."

Cameron decided it was time to leave the heavy conversation. "Please thank the chief for his wisdom, and ask if I may walk about the village."

"The chief would like to show you about," she said and, with a smile, added, "I'm invited, too."

The chief led them on a walk about the village. He and Faint Chance spoke in the local dialect, and so Cameron just fell in behind and enjoyed the vistas.

Although picturesque in their hillside settings, the thatched roofs on all the houses, made Cameron, always the architect, asked her to interpret, "Aren't those natural roofs impractical? They must have to be replaced often."

She interpreted, "Sometimes, parts of the roofs have to be replaced, but the roof material is readily available just paces away. It's light in weight, and requires no large beams to hold it up, and no cement or other materials to make it work. It is easy to find and gather, easy to take up on the roofs, and requires no maintenance, other than occasional partial replacement. And, just because it dies off and needs to be replaced, now and then, does not mean it is not worthy as a building material. Everything you take out of the earth eventually goes back there."

Cameron was taken aback by the answer. He repeated, "Everything you take from the earth eventually goes back there? How wonderfully put. I deal in building materials all the time, and the useful life of materials is, in some cases, something that has to be certified by an engineer. His statement is not just profound, but inspiring."

ℰ⁓ℰ⁓

Outside the village, on a high spot, sat Mario Uto and Warinton, camping. Looking through binoculars, they kept watching.

"What do you think, Kumi-cho?" Warinton asked.

"There is no sign that they have the plant leaves yet," Morio answered. "When it appears that they have them, we'll make our move."

❧❧

In the chief's house that evening, he finally announced his decision.

Faint Chance interpreted, "He has made his decision. He'll take us to the place of the *ton mai piiset* so we can get some of its leaves. He will allow them to be taken across the ocean. But in order for the spirits to follow you, it will be necessary for you to pull the plant leaves out of the ground yourself. He will later conduct a special prayer to ask the spirits to follow the plant leaves across the ocean. He does not know for certain that the Spirits will follow, but he will ask them. He has a few conditions."

"What are they?" Cameron entered the subject cautiously rather than simply saying "of course," or otherwise promising before he heard the terms.

"If the doctors are successful at making more of the *ton mai piiset*, and it works, you are to bring enough to the village first so that everyone here can have it. Then their offspring will be special. He wants his village people to succeed and not fall backward while the world passes them. Right now, there is too little for everyone to take it. The second condition is not to tell anyone the spot where the plant comes from so as to keep the world out, as many will surely flock here if the information gets out. "Do you agree to these conditions?"

The chief looked at Cameron as Faint Chance interpreted.

"Yes, I promise." Cameron assured him.

"He says that I must promise that some of what I will give you will be used for my wedding, and not given away again. I promised him. He says we will start out in the morning for the *ton mai piiset*. His son is still on a hunt, so we'll go without him."

The chief went for an antique-looking muzzle loader against a wall.

"He wants you to use this. There are dangers along the way."

"Yes, if he will show me how to load it."

"He says he will. He prefers his bow and arrow."

Chapter 24

"Please wake up," Faint Chance said as she shook Cameron lightly.

The chief had arranged food for them to eat along the way, in their backpacks. The chief carried his own in a bag attached to his belt. He put his bow and quiver of arrows over his shoulder and a machete on his belt. He handed Cameron the muzzle loader, and Cameron familiarized himself with its primitive flint lock mechanism.

They started out with the chief in the lead. The village was only making a few noises, slowly yawning, as they left it behind. The sun was hinting that it may come up soon in the Eastern sky. The jungle that they were led into by the chief was obviously uninhabited.

"Awk, awk!" A strange bird screeched loudly, scaring Cameron. He looked for it, but the bird could not be seen in the dense jungle. Cameron considered it to be an alert of intruders. The security of the village was no longer there, and it gave Cameron cause to fear what they might encounter. He had, after all, already encountered a huge snake and an unexploded bomb. Thinking of the snake, Cameron decided he should be quieter and adjusted his steps to make less noise.

The pace the chief kept was exhausting, his physical shape extraordinary at one hundred fifteen. There was little breeze in the dense trail below the canopy of trees above and large plant leaves. The trail widened into a small clearing. The chief stopped suddenly.

Eating the carcass of an unlucky animal was an enormous tiger. The animal was six feet long without adding the tail. It had not noticed them yet, its sense of smell apparently satiated in the flesh and blood of the unfortunate creature that had not outrun it and the fact that the humans might be downwind.

The chief got his bow and arrow ready and backed up a few paces with extreme slowness, so as not to make noise by crumpling the fallen leaves on the ground.

It didn't work. The tiger stopped eating and turned its huge head toward them. Everyone, including the cat, went motionless. Cameron realized he was not breathing.

Blood from its prey dripped out of the beast's mouth. A piece of the prey's skin hung from one of the cat's giant teeth.

The chief continued to back up, ever so slowly, Cameron and Faint Chance also backing up just behind him. He brought his bow up slowly and then took an arrow from his quiver. He put the arrow slowly into place and began to draw the bowstring.

Cameron held up his muzzle loader slowly and pointed it toward the cat, but he kept silent as best he could so as not to cause any reaction from the cat. He dared not pull back the noisy hammer unless there was no choice but to fire.

The chief increased the tempo of the backward motion, moving away to make the cat think that they were not going to try to take away its catch.

As luck would have it, the tiger decided it had enough in its new kill to eat, and these humans were not going to try to take it away. It turned its huge head back to the kill and tore off another bite of raw flesh.

The chief turned and led them quickly back. He told Faint Chance that they would go around.

They soon came to a cliff going nearly straight up twenty-five feet, with vines on it from trees above. The chief went up the cliff, pulling himself up a vine like Tarzan, showing no obvious signs of age.

Faint Chance grabbed a vine, but could not go up without help. The chief took hold of her vine and pulled her up. Cameron went for it and did his best to go up, but needed help too, and the chief did the same for him.

They sat above the cliff. The tiger was nowhere in sight. Was he likely to attack? He had a meal already. They huddled together and looked all about before continuing their trek.

❧❧

After several hours, they stopped for a break at a small clearing with huge trees and a jungle canopy providing welcome shade. Large roots came out from the trunk above the ground for some distance before they went underground, providing makeshift seats for them against the trunk. Cameron took a bottle of water out, handed it to Faint Chance, and then took some himself. The chief had his own.

While resting, Cameron looked just in front of him and noticed an interesting line of identical insects approaching, each an-inch-and-a-half long, with long, skinny legs, marching toward him in a neat column. Cameron watched intently, very hot from the hike and the temperature. There were only seven of them. Each stood just over an inch tall, and had a bright-blue colored bump on the head. They were getting closer and closer to Cameron. He put his finger down in front of the column to see if they would stop or go around like some do with ants. They did neither, and the one in front was a matter of inches from his finger, when suddenly something startled him.

WHAM!

The sound of a rock smashing in front of Cameron startled him so much that he jumped. Faint Chance had picked up a rock and smashed the first insects in the column.

The chief came and joined Faint Chance, and the two of them then scurried about smashing the remaining insects with rocks. After killing three more, two were missed, but instead of running off, they continued to pursue Cameron at a faster pace. The insects were hunters! Cameron backed up while Faint Chance and the chief pounded at them with rocks in hand, smashing at the remaining two that had been initially missed. The chief smashed the last one, only inches away from Cameron, who was now backed up against the tree and could retreat no farther. Cameron's heart pounded, puzzled at such actions over mere insects.

"What's all this about?" Cameron looked to Faint Chance for an explanation. "It's a bunch of bugs. Are they dangerous?"

"Those insects are extremely poisonous," she said. "If one bites you, you will either die or become totally paralyzed for life. One or the other, for sure."

"One of those tiny little insects? It can do all that? One bite?"

"Yes. I had a friend who lived in Vientiane, who went on a jungle expedition and became permanently paralyzed from the bite of one of these."

The chief began to speak, and Faint Chance interpreted. "He says he has witnessed the results of their bite. Just one has killed more than one member of his village."

"Good Lord," Cameron said.

The air cooled as the sun lowered. They continued on until the chief selected a place to sleep for the night. He came upon a spot he liked.

"He says that it will be dark soon, and we will sleep here. The place we are going to is some distance away, and we will go at dawn. He will watch for danger."

Cameron and Faint Chance set up their little tent, but the chief was apparently going to sleep on the ground, taking no extra baggage to make him more agile in the jungle.

"I wonder what other dangers lurk about," Cameron said to her.

They fell asleep, holding each other.

❧❦❧

Cameron's eyes opened, and it took him several moments to remember where he was as he had slept so soundly. Faint Chance lay next to him. He opened the tent and stuck his head out to see if the chief was ready.

He leaned back over Faint Chance. "Are you up?"

Her eyes opened, and she looked at him. She hugged him and then sat up and yawned.

Outside, the chief was alive and well and seemed anxious to tell Faint Chance something. She came outside and asked him, "What?"

"Look where he's pointing," Cameron said.

A black object, five feet long, was lying on the ground near the edge of the clearing where they slept. The chief went to it and picked it up by the tail, which added to its length, and held it up. It was a black jaguar with an arrow in its chest.

"Oh, my God! What happened?" Cameron exclaimed.

Faint Chance interpreted. "He sensed the cat coming, and positioned himself to the moonlight that lit his eyes so he could see him close."

"Was he going to attack?" Cameron asked.

"He was attacking."

"Why didn't we hear anything?"

"He was silent."

"It is a good thing we didn't come here alone," Cameron said. "What is the word for that fearsome animal in the local dialect?"

Faint Chance asked the chief. "Cat."

❧❦❧

Later, they came to a cliff atop an eight hundred foot gorge. This was the spot. The chief stopped at the cliff and looked over. The drop-off angle was a few degrees farther down than just vertical. The cliff went down eight hundred feet to a river at the bottom. A dizzying sight, it was no place for someone with vertigo. As the cliff went down more than ninety degrees, it was difficult to see what was growing on the side of the cliff down from the top.

"Jesus!" Cameron said. "This must be the end of the earth."

Faint Chance interpreted for the chief. "This is the place of the *ton mai piiset.*"

"Where?" Cameron asked.

The chief led them along the scary cliff's edge. He stopped, and pointed down.

Cameron could not see below the cliff's edge. "I don't see it."

The chief pointed down once again. Cameron lay down on his stomach and put his head over the edge of the cliff so he had less fear of falling over. He could make out the purple and orange plant down about twenty-five feet.

"Down the edge of the cliff?" Cameron asked in dismay. "Are you fucking crazy? This is a suicide mission!"

Faint Chance spoke, more involved than just an interpreter. "You have to remove it in order to ask the sprits to follow it."

"What is it about this place that grows the *ton mai piiset*?" Cameron asked.

Faint Chance interpreted. "As you can see, the soils are many feet above the plant, piled on over many years from rain water flowing down toward the gorge. There is something in the soils below where it grows, which is from ages past. Only those ancient soils grow the *ton mai piiset.* The soils above have accumulated over many years, but are not the same as those on top of it."

Cameron tried to look again by just getting near the cliff and could see the river a zillion miles below. He became dizzy. Snapping out of his dizziness, he backed up away from the cliff.

"He says, to follow him," Faint Chance told him.

The chief led them to a cutout in the cliff, probably from water erosion, fifty feet farther on. Below the cutout was only the suspicion of a path, only a foot wide in some places, sloping downhill, traversing across the vertical cliff down toward the plant.

"Oh God," Cameron said. "We have to get it from down there? This looks like the place where mountain goats with severe depression come to commit suicide. I'm glad that he's here to do it. There is no way I could do that."

The chief and Faint Chance spoke for some time in an involved conversation. Finally, Faint Chance turned to Cameron. "There's a problem. First, the chief says that you must be the one to remove the leaves from the special plant and from the soil so as to put yourself in touch with the spirits, or, otherwise, they will never communicate with you to cross the ocean."

"Me? Won't they just understand and come along? Can't they make an exception?"

"No. And, there is one more problem," Faint Chance continued. "There are a few very large, dangerous birds that nest on these cliffs. They may attack any game they can find for themselves and for their young, which includes people. The chief says that if you go down for the plant leaves, he will sit on the cliff's edge with his bow and arrow and shoot any bird that attacks you."

"You mean that I have to go down there?" Cameron asked frantically.

"He says you must go."

"Jesus, I'm an architect, not a rock climber!"

Cameron went to the cutout and took deep breaths, as though that might help cure the fright. He could not take the muzzle loader, as he would surely fall if he did not have both hands free to touch the tiny things on the cliff that resembled handles. Anyway, that ancient beast of a gun would blow him off the path. The chief returned to the point just above the plant and sat on the cliff edge, bow and arrow in hand.

"Oh, well," Cameron said, self-emboldening his resolve. "There is only one way to do this, and that is to just do it and not think about it. He began side-stepping very slowly along the narrow trail, moving down the cliff toward the plant. He had his arms outstretched along the side of the cliff as he inched along, grabbing on to what little plant life, rocks, or crevices, available on the vertical wall. Only his fingers would fit in to hold him on the path. The chief sat on the cliff's edge, just over where the plant was situated, watching for the birds.

When Cameron had nearly approached the area of the plant, inching his way, Faint Chance saw a huge, ten foot wingspan of a black bird with red wingtips flying out over the gorge. "Watch Out!" she yelled.

Cameron, nearly petrified, looked around as far as he dared without losing his grip on the crevices he was holding onto. He could not see any bird as he could not turn around enough to get it into view.

Above, at the cliff's edge, the chief readied his bow and arrow, but the bird then made a turn as it flew in toward the vertical wall of the cliff and used the updraft of the air along the cliff to propel it very fast as it surveyed the situation and flew past. It was obviously aware of Cameron. It then flew out over the gorge and turned around, coming in to attack Cameron. It was moving in from one side, not straight in. The chief could not get it with his bow and arrow as it was below the line of sight of the cliff's edge.

It struck Cameron with its talons on his shoulder from behind. The impact nearly knocked him off the ledge. The talons made deep scratches in his shoulder, drawing blood. A sharp pain rammed his shoulder.

The monster bird bounced off Cameron on its first strike and then went out, away from the cliff, flying very fast. In just moments, it was a quarter of a mile out, nearly to the other side of the gorge. But it was not yet content with having a prey too big to take back to the nest, and it turned and came straight on for a frontal attack. Cameron could then see it coming, straight, and very fast. As it came in close, it rotated its neck up to put its large feet and huge talons in front of it to tear into its human prey. This time the chief could see it from where he was sitting on the cliff.

There was nothing Cameron could do. He could not back off the cliff quickly enough to escape. But the bird was unaware of the chief's archery skills. The chief did not have to calculate lead in his shot since it was coming straight in. All he had to do was hold steady and shoot very true. He pulled back his bow string as far as it would stretch, requiring much strength, waiting for the shot—there would be no time for another.

The monster bird rotated up all the way as it came in close to it prey, its talons open and ready. In rotating, it exposed its chest fully. When it was frightfully close to Cameron, the chief released his arrow. In a perfect shot, the arrow went *thiiiiiiiiiip* and hit the huge bird squarely in the chest, going through the bird half way down the length of the arrow shaft. The huge bird lost control and smacked into the cliff only a foot off to the side of Cameron, its wing hitting him, and then it tumbled down toward the bottom of the gorge, eight hundred feet.

Cameron's heart was beating a thousand times a minute. He looked about, wondering if Godzilla had a relative. Seeing none, he continued to traverse the side of the gorge toward the plant.

The chief shouted out, Faint Chance interpreting, "It's just below you. Reach down to it, but don't take the entire plant, as there are no more—just take some of the leaves."

"Hah, just reach down to it," Cameron said softly to himself. "Here I am on a little ledge, eight hundred feet high, with nothing to grab onto, being attacked by a monster bird that hunts humans, and he says 'Just reach down!'"

He worked up the courage to look down. He could see

the colorful plants of purple and orange growing out just below the ledge he was standing on. There were a few plants in a cluster. He dropped to one knee and reached down as carefully as possible to get hold of the leaves of one of the plants.

He pulled some of the leaves off, folded them, and put them in his pocket. He took another few, being careful not to strip the plant completely so as not to kill it and eradicate it into extinction.

Having removed what seemed like enough, he stood up slowly and began creeping back, inching his way, just on the edge of falling.

When he finally arrived back at the starting point, the chief was there. He took Cameron's arm and helped pull him over the cliff top. Cameron crawled away from the cliff, and lay down on the ground to rest. His shirt was torn from the bird's talons, his shoulder bleeding. He rose and took out the bright purple and orange plant leaves from his pocket, showing them to his companions with a huge grin.

"What beautiful colors these leaves have," Faint Chance said. "You are very brave."

"We should get out of here before that bird's mate starts looking for him, or maybe her," Cameron said,

The chief looked up at the sky and said something. Faint Chance said, "He says it's going to rain. He says that's good because it will keep our scent down." Then she added, "I think he is talking about your and my scent, as we are perspiring much more than he."

"Now I have to worry about sweat?" Cameron asked sarcastically.

They started out, and within an hour, it began to pour rain. Water ran across the trail at many points, and rapidly in some, as the water found its way down the mountain.

Cameron's scratched shoulder hurt when the leaves of the overgrown foliage smacked it on the trail at the more narrow points.

At sunset, Cameron and Faint Chance set up their tent

again from Cameron's backpack, and made ready to retire. After the cat incident, Cameron wanted to stay up with the chief but realized that he was far too tired not to sleep and went into the tent with the comforting knowledge that the chief was on guard.

∞

Late the next morning, they arrived at the village, its protection welcome to Cameron and Faint Chance. After settling in at the chief's house, the chief told others about the cat and the bird attack, as it was a custom of the villagers to tell of what interesting events happened on any hunt or journey. Some of the stories were legends in themselves. And, sometimes hunters did not return.

After dinner, when the village people had mostly retired, the chief had Cameron and Faint Chance gather around him inside his house where he had laid out the plant leaves on a piece of cloth.

After obtaining quiet in the room, the chief spoke. Faint Chance interpreted, "He will now communicate with the spirits of the plant and ask them to follow us to America."

Cameron straightened up and got ready to be respectfully silent. Faint Chance was already in form.

The chief began a chanting prayer. At some points, the others in the room joined with a noise, adding emphasis to something. Cameron did his best to follow along with the chant and the sounds the others made.

"He says he has asked the spirits residing in the *ton mai piiset* not to stay only in Lao, and to follow the plant across the ocean and work their powers there."

He crushed the purple and orange leaves in his hands, and put part of them into a little cloth bag. He handed the bag to Faint Chance.

She translated. "He says this is for me for my wedding." He was obviously displeased that she had given away the first batch he had given her years earlier. He put the remaining portion into another bag. "He says that the remaining portion can be taken to and used by the doctors. If they are successful in making more, we must bring more back here for all in my village first." She then told Cameron, "He wishes to speak to me alone. If you don't mind, could you please take a short walk outside?"

Cameron got up and went outside to let them be alone. He took a lovely stroll about the village in a very light rain. When he returned, Faint Chance had the bedding ready, and what could be better than her in a bed?

Chapter 25

The next morning, a young villager appeared at the chief's house. He brought news.

The chief looked at Faint Chance and asked her if there any more people in her party still coming.

"No."

The chief sensed an emergency, and he told the messenger to go and get help. A sense of danger permeated the air. The chief went for his machete that was leaning against a wall.

Two dangerous men had been observing the area of the village with binoculars, unseen to anyone, and now were approaching.

Before help arrived, the two stormed into the house. Their clothing was soiled and filthy from lying outside the village on the ground observing. It was Morio Uto and Warintorn.

Uto took his pistol out of his jacket, as did Warinton, which they had not brandished when they walked through the village, preventing whoever might see them to think that they were dangerous intruders. Uto and Warinton both took out their nine-millimeter pistols once inside.

The chief approached Uto with the machete in his hand as Uto came in. He went right into the middle of the house, with Warinton remaining just inside the door.

Warinton saw the chief raising his machete, and yelled out a warning, "*Kumi-Cho! Abunai!*"

Uto raised his pistol and shot the chief squarely in the chest just before the chief could get him with his machete.

The bag of plant that was for the doctors was sitting like a prize on top of a small, square piece of wood where the chief had placed it. Uto grabbed the bag and began to back out toward the door, all the while holding his pistol in front of him in case anyone else attacked.

Warinton was ahead of Uto, also backing out. Warinton was now just one step outside the door.

Suddenly Warinton's head split open from the top down to the neck, with blood spattering everywhere. The gunshot heard was the call to action, and one of the village hunters had arrived with his axe. He had brought his axe down with all his might onto Warinton's head. The force of the blow opened his head like a ripe melon, all the way down and the axe was sticking out of his neck.

Uto turned and shot the hunter times in the torso, killing him instantly. Several of the other hunters arrived and swarmed Uto. He struggled and fought with them, and, having to use both of his hands in the fight, dropped the bag with the plant leaves. He broke free and began running for the jungle, with several hunters in hot pursuit and more following. Uto stopped and shot the closest one, killing him. The others stopped the chase for the moment when faced with the pistol. Uto resumed his running escape like a scared rabbit into the jungle. Several hunters came to join in the chase, slowed by their fallen friend who was shot. Several chased Uto into the jungle, but he had a head start.

Faint Chance, knelt over the slain body of her first adoptive father—he who saved her from dying from exposure when she was four—and wept. It was and would remain the saddest day of her life. She realized that she had brought this evil upon her village, to her father, and now to the chief's son. And, it was occasioned by her desire for advancement in life, to get the plant for her sponsors to America. She considered it her fault. At age one hundred and fifteen, the chief was now dead, and it had been brought about by the concentrated evil that followed her into the village from the outside world, just what the *Great Maw Pii* feared, or perhaps knew, would happen.

She considered taking her own life, not allowing the plant to leave, and not trying to keep the new chief from putting Cameron to death, which he surely would.

Chapter 26

The slain chief's son arrived from his hunt to learn what occurred. He took charge and placed Faint Chance and Cameron under arrest, but allowed them to stay inside the house, not able to leave.

Villagers swarmed about everywhere, guarding the village parameters, looking very fierce. Things were in turmoil. Hunters were coming in, and moving about the village, looking for anything suspicious.

Night fell on the village, village hunters about, standing guard for a return of the remaining bandit Uto, or anyone else that might come.

Cameron looked out the door opening. There were two guards on duty, to make sure the bandit would not return and also to make sure Faint Chance and Cameron did not leave.

Over the next few days, Cameron and Faint Chance saw ceremonies begin that they would never see the likes of again. Not only all the villagers, but those that knew of or had known the *Great Ma Pii* came in from other villages. Hundreds came. He was thought to be a great shaman, with powers to reach the Spirits. Chanting, dancing, and ceremonies were everywhere. Women made food to feed all those involved. Occasional rain did not slow them down.

The chanting and dancing were made louder by noise-making instruments, mostly metal rattling bells and drums.

For several days, a huge amount of outsiders from villages several miles away, came to join in the prayer to the Spirits for the fallen *Great Ma Pii* and his fallen villagers as well. At one point, Cameron and Faint Chance were sitting on the ground in the crowd, chanting prayers in unison. Sometimes each would touch the person in front of him or the person next to him with the tips of the fingers on one hand only, the hand extended, usually touching the side or the back of the person while chanting some part of the prayer. They, including Faint Chance, were talking to spirits, and to the spirits of the slain men. Cameron participated as best he could by humming the extended syllables.

Chapter 27

The son of the chief, already designated by his father, took over as the new chief. He had not married, and lived in the same house.

While the shaman ceremonies were still underway, in the house, he summoned both Faint Chance and Cameron inside. He spoke to Faint Chance in the local dialect. "Knowledge of the *ton mai piiset* has already brought death to my father and two village men. We caught one of them, but not the other. If we capture the other one, it might bring our village back to safety, provided news of the matter does not go out."

She interpreted for Cameron, who was struck with fear. He asked of Faint Chance, "He is going to kill us, right?"

"I think so, but he will decide," she answered.

Cameron then realized that the new chief had the power of life or death over them and that there was no other form of tribunal for their fate. They might not be allowed to live, so as to keep the location of the plant a secret forever. He and Faint Chance, if put to death, would never be heard from again, and no one would know, not even Spencer and Candice, what happened to them or even where to look for their ashes.

The new chief gave some commands to his men, and an armed group commanded Cameron and Faint Chance to get up and follow them to a small hut that was empty and only ten feet square inside. It had no windows, and four of the men stood guard by the doorway. The door was made of vertical sticks. There was also a cloth drape over the door. It was dark inside, except for little rays of bright sunlight that shown through the cracks in the wooden sides and a few knot holes. Cameron realized that now they were no longer guests, but prisoners. Whatever the hut was normally for, it was now a jail.

"I guess all we can do is to wait." he said in despair. "We have brought evil to the village and caused the deaths with an avarice of the outside world. He may put us to death."

Faint Chance remained quiet, calmed with an inner peace, unlike Cameron, as though to take in stride whatever was to come. How could he, an architect from the bustling city, become involved in such an ordeal?

He lay down on the dirt floor and wondered if this day would be his last. He thought of back home, his air-conditioned office, his brother Spencer, his sister-in-law Candice, and his luxuries. He became very frightened, realizing he may be at the end of his life.

ഇൗ

Two hours after first light, the door was opened, and two guards came in. One spoke to Faint Chance.

"We are to go back to the new chief's house, which is the same house as his departed father," she told Cameron.

"Did they say anything else?"

"No."

At the new chief's house, they were led in and pointed to where they were to sit, in front of and below the new chief. He was sitting on the raised portion of the built up floor, where his father used to sit. Presiding over their lives was exactly what he was doing.

Several locals came in to testify, but Cameron had no clue what they were saying.

For his defense, Cameron had no police to call on, no court-appointed public defender, no twelve jurors of peers, no public trial, no media attention, no precedents, only the final, singular, last word of the chief. No doubt, the sentence of death would be carried out that same day, as there were no appeals.

Several elders were behind them, and many of the village people outside. The old lady identified as an aunt was squatted on her heals over against the wall, observing. Standing in the back were four fierce guards with machetes and knives, the village equivalent of court bailiffs. They looked like they could handle any situation that might arise.

The new chief spoke collectively to the group of respected elders and the accused. Faint Chance sat next to Cameron, interpreting. It was similar to a court announcing its verdict in an English court of Old Bailey.

"The new chief says the pursuit of the *ton mai piiset* brought evil from the outside to our village which his father had been wise enough to avoid until now. He has not known such evil since the skies nearby rained with bombs in the War. His father, the *Great Maw Pii*, is with us now in spirit. He granted Sangmouane Sayasithsena, his adopted daughter, the right to summon spirits at her wedding to make her a special child. He gave her the way to contact the Spirits in the *ton mai piiset*. But she traded the powers of the *ton mai piiset* to those who would take her to the West, where the world travels at a pace unknown to us. That world has wars, evil, and crime that we do not. She then led them from the outside here to get the *ton mai piiset* to make it available to the rest of the world for her own benefit."

Faint Chance shivered in fear as she determined that they were about to be given a sentence of death. She continued to translate for Cameron. "Knowledge of the powers of the *ton mai piiset* is now out in the West. He says if he kills all who have the knowledge of how to find it, he may be able to keep others from coming. There is little *ton mai piiset* left. Sangmouane and her Western friend wish to take some of it to the outside world to see if more of it to put the entire world in touch with the spirits. But Father is now dead, killed by evil outsiders in their greed. It is now his decision what to do."

He paused, and looked at Faint Chance and said to her, Faint Chance interpreting, "He wants to know what either of us has to say."

Faint Chance discussed what he said with Cameron to make sure that they got it right.

Cameron realized that he had a few moments to make a plea, and perhaps only hours to live if the plea did not work. He could feel his heart pounding away, realizing that what he would say would determine if his head would be chopped off or he would go back home.

Faint Chance said to Cameron, "I think you should speak to the new chief."

"I better say something," Cameron said.

Faint Chance said in the local dialect that Cameron Harrington, designer of houses, requested the right to speak.

The new chief acknowledged Cameron's last right to speak.

Cameron gathered his wits for his one and only chance to say something that might determine his fate. Faint Chance did her best to translate. In English, he said, "You are now the *Maw Pii,* the wise one who talks to the spirits now that your father is gone. As now the leader, you must decide if you are to hide the biggest secret of the world, or let it die here as the plant is small and will not grow much longer. There may be enough for you and your wife to take, but probably no more. If you believe that the next generation of men should have the powers of the *ton mai piiset,* then you will release it to us. If you do, you will surely become the greatest *Mai Pii* ever, the one who brought the powerful spirits to the rest of mankind."

Although Cameron thought he had done a pretty good

job of making his final plea, the new chief did not seem impressed. It did not look good.

The new chief spoke, and Faint Chance said, "He says that if news of the spiritual powers gets out, the village will be swarmed like a beehive with unimaginable numbers of people from everywhere. Life for the village will never be the same."

It appeared to Cameron that the new chief had decided to put them to death and retain the secrets in the village. Cameron had lost his plea.

Just as the edict of death was about to be passed, ending their lives, Faint Chance spoke in the local dialect. "I demand my right to hear from the spirits of the *ton mai pii-set!*"

The new chief sat back, disrupted in his death sentence, and raised his eyebrows quite surprised. Then he spoke.

"He says that is my right," Faint Chance said.

Both Cameron and Faint Chance were astonished at the success of the last moment plea. But it was a right that could not be refused under tradition.

The new chief got up and went to the bag of the *ton mai piiset.*

He brought the bag of the plant leaves to a small wooden table. He opened the bag and put its contents on a wooden plate. He then took a healthy pinch of the leaves in his fingers and put them in his mouth. He produced a black mushroom and ate that next. Then Faint Chance took some leaves and a mushroom as well.

They both sat quietly. After waiting a while until the plant took effect, he chanted a prayer to summon the spirits of the *ton mai piiset.*

Faint Chance's eyes were not focusing, and she appeared to be in another world. She put her hands in the prayer position, and chanted something.

Cameron remembered the stories from Spencer and Candice as to what happened to each of them when they took the plant. There was something very powerful in it.

Absolute quiet deafened the room. The new chief began to gaze out into the room, not focusing on anything, but quite absorbed in something. Then he put his hands in the prayer position and began to speak very softly. After what seemed like an eternity, he bowed his head in a position of respect and remained motionless. Finally, he stopped, raised his head, and spoke, something indistinguishable to Cameron. He then opened his eyes and looked at Faint Chance and Cameron.

She translated for Cameron. "The new chief has been told to allow you to leave with the *ton mai piiset* as you wish."

Cameron thought he might pass out.

The new chief then spoke to Faint Chance at some length.

Finally, Faint Chance turned to Cameron. "Father says we may leave and take the *ton mai piiset*."

The new chief spoke to her again. Faint Chance translated. "He says that the bandit may be in pursuit, and he will send some of his best men with us, who will take us to the end of the path. We are not to tell those on the outside where our village is or where the *ton mai piiset* grows on the cliffside."

Faint Chance assured the new chief that she would not disclose the location of the village or where the *ton mai piiset* grows on the cliff. "He says that the bandit knows of the village, but not where the *ton mai piiset* grows. The location where it grows must remain a secret. He says that the bandit cannot make it work."

What is he referring to? Cameron wondered. *Oh yes*, he thought, *the prayers that Faint Chance knows. That must be it. Without the special prayers, it will not work.*

Cameron and Faint Chance got up and went outside into the sunlight. The rain had let up. They walked to the cliff side overlooking the valley of the crops and sat down. Cameron realized his heart rate had been so high for so long

that he was sweating and exhausted, and now it was slowing.

"That was nice going on your part," he said to her.
"There is a criminal justice system here—at your trial, you
get to call on spirits for your witnesses!"

Faint Chance did not respond. Cameron lay his head
down in her lap and wondered how close he came to being
executed. This trip was not supposed to be so dangerous.

Chapter 28

The new chief arranged an armed escort the following morning for them. Four were with muzzle loaders, the other four with bows and arrows. All had machetes slung from their waists.

Surrounded in the front and back by the escort of guards, Cameron and Faint Chance left the village. Because the hunters knew the way and were setting a faster pace, they made much better time than on the way in.

"It's quite impressive to be in the center of an armed escort that will kill on sight, with no Miranda warnings," Cameron said to Faint Chance when they were walking.

"What are Miranda warnings?" she asked.

Cameron pondered and then came up with what he thought would work as an answer. "Warning shots."

When they came to a resting place for the night, Cameron, exhausted, lay down to ease his aching muscles. The guards explained that they would not be making a fire which could be seen, in case the bandit was following. Fruits and dried jerky brought with them was the menu. The guards slept around their charges in a circle to protect them, both from the bandit as well as from the jungle, with four awake and on alert at all times.

On the second day, they traveled even more distance than they had the first day. It rained, but they continued on,

and the hunters were not bothered by it. They saw occasional wild birds, but did not shoot any of the game they
saw en route, as they wanted to be prepared for human
targets. The guards would be able to look for something to
take home on the way back to their village.

At mid-morning the third day, they reached the end of
the path. And there was the tuk-tuk driver, loyally waiting
for them. Such a welcome sight!

Faint Chance and Cameron said goodbye to the hunters
and wished them well. Once again in the tuk-tuk, they were
off on a bouncy trip back to the safety of the hotel in Ban
Houei Sai.

Faint Chance said to Cameron, "On the way back, I'm
going to have the driver take us back to the lady that makes
the northern *Lao-Lao*. I want to get some."

Chapter 29

Cameron awoke at daybreak, delighted to find that he was back inside the now-familiar little hotel cottage in Ban Houei Sai. The first thing he did was to smile. They had made it. The events of the past several days raced through his mind, and especially the moment in front of the new chief when the decision was made as to his future—whether or not he would have a future.

Then his thoughts shifted to the Japanese bandits. Who were they? How did they get on to the knowledge of the plant? Somehow they had learned of their trek into the jungle to get the plant, but how? Were there more than two? The hunters chased the bandit that was not killed into the jungle. Maybe they finally caught him?

There was no way to find out, with there being no communication whatsoever to the village. The discovery of the plant had reached others. How many? Since the attempt to take it was by bandits willing to kill to get it, most likely the knowledge of it was only known to a few—otherwise, some officials would have come to the village, rather than bandits. Most likely it was some sort of leak from back home, but who?

As he became more awake, he realized that without confirmation of the death of the remaining bandit, he and Faint Chance should not linger around. He turned and looked over at Faint Chance, who was sleeping next to him.

"Faint Chance, we had better wake up and get going," he said.

Her eyes opened, and she rolled over facing him, to embrace for a short while before taking on the day.

"We should go early, to stay well ahead of the bandit if he's still following us," he said.

After a dose of the proprietor's wife's lovely noodles and coffee, they were ready to start the next leg of their journey.

Faint Chance spoke to the proprietor and then told Cameron, "I asked him for the fastest way to Vientiane. We have to go down the Mekong River to Luang Prabang, where there is an airport, and we can get a plane to fly to Vientiane. There are two ways to get to Luang Prabang, the slow boats, which are those larger ones we saw before to the north of the village, and the small, fast boats, which are at a dock to the south. The slow boats take one day to get to Pak Bang, which is half way, where we would spend the night, and then they take another day to go on to Luang Prabang. The fast boats make it to Luang Prabang in one day."

"Let's take a fast boat," Cameron decided. "Find out how to get to the fast boats, and let's get going.

After five minutes in a tuk-tuk heading south of the little village, the driver pulled off to the right of a small concrete-block building, painted green. There were window openings, but without glass, and a doorframe with no door. It hardly looked weatherproof, which, no doubt, accounted for the fact that the only things in the building were two tables, each with a chair, somewhat back from the open windows so as to stay dry when it rained. The rooms were otherwise utterly bare. On one side the fast boat tickets were for sale, and on the other, an official-looking person who took passports and wrote down the information in an old-fashioned ledger as to who came and went. Cameron figured the official must take the ledger home with him at night. There was no electricity in the building, the light provided by the openings. Several young men, who were obviously the pilots of the fast boats, stood about outside. It was unclear if the fast boats were government owned or belonged to some agency.

Cameron and Faint Chance did not enter straightaway to get tickets. They instead walked over to the cliff at the edge of the Mekong River, twenty feet high. Going down to the boats were a series of steps, but not made of concrete or even wood—the steps were simply cut into the hillside with a shovel. They were irregular, somewhat soft from rain, and treacherous at points. Cameron looked at the fast boats. What a difference from the slow boats!

The slow boats had a large cabin, whereas the fast boats were like inexpensive racing boats. Eighteen feet in length, three feet in width, only a foot deep, with a flat bottom. They had many colors, decorated with painted geometric shapes. On the back, sticking up from the boat, on each was a four-cylinder Japanese engine, out of a car, with "sixteen-valve" on top of one of the valve covers. Each engine had a four-into-one exhaust collector that ended in a completely un-muffled megaphone that pointed back and slightly up, pure racing style and very loud. They seemed completely out of place in Lao.

The engine swiveled from left to right as well as up and down. Sticking out of the back of the engine was a ten foot long shaft with a completely exposed propeller on it. The method of steering was a handle on the front of the engine, with a twist throttle. The pilot would take this handle, which looked something like the collective on a helicopter, and move it from side to side, or up and down. There was no seat for the pilot, who would sit to one side of the engine on the rear deck of the boat with his feet in the engine well. The pilot would keep from falling out by holding on to the steering rod.

The fast boats could hold as many as eight people—two abreast—but with no leg room at all. The seats had removable wooden seat backs that slid down into wooden guides on the insides of the thin hull to hold them in place. With the wooden seat backs in place in front of another seat, there was only a little space between the seats. Cameron balked at that, as sure to be torture sitting in a yoga position for an entire day with seven other people. He said to Faint Chance, "Let's go back up to the building and see if we can rent an entire boat for just ourselves."

It turned out that was no problem at all, and cheap. After negotiating for an exclusive boat to go the entire distance to Luang Prabang, he gave his passport and she her identity card to the official to write down their information in his ledger so they could legally take the trip.

Cameron looked out the door and noticed the group of boat pilots that had arrived, who were talking to one another. He said to Faint Chance, "I think it would be a good idea to ask which of the pilots is the best and fastest. The bandit may be following us. Ask the group of pilots over there which of them is the fastest and best."

She walked over to the group of pilots, "Which one of you is the fastest and best boat pilot?"

They moved together and pointed to one young man of their group. He blushed with the compliment. The others laughed somewhat, but it was clear that this was not a joke. This young man that they pointed out was clearly their best.

Cameron told her, "Tell that man inside that we want this man."

The pilot agreed, and they then agreed on a price, very cheap. They stepped down the dirt hillside to the place where the final perilous dirt steps were all different sizes and shapes, and walked to one of the fast boats.

In keeping with his reputation for being fast, the pilot hustled on down ahead of them with their bags to where the fast boats were tied to the shore and started his preparations to the boat before they got to it. He took out the extra boards for the seat backs, leaving only one in place for his two exclusive passengers. They had to get into the boat carefully, as it was light, and stepping on the edge might capsize it, especially with Cameron. The pilot had taken off his shoes, rolled up his pants, and stood in the water a foot deep to give them his hand and assistance to get into the racy yellow boat. He put two vinyl-covered cushions side by side where they were to sit, which the pilot had determined so as to get the best planning and performance out of the fast boat. He placed them just back of the center, put their bags in the bow, and then tied them across with some thin rope. He offered them each a life jacket, orange in color, rather small for an American.

"Can you swim well?" Cameron asked Faint Chance.

"Yes, I can."

"Take one if you want, but I'll pass," he decided.

"I prefer not to wear one," she said.

Cameron waved the life jackets away, disliking such things. He did not want to spend the day with an orange Mae West around his neck. The pilot next offered them helmets. The helmets were full cover, with no face shields, and had no strap underneath, perhaps missing from use. Cameron declined those also.

The pilot made his final preparations and secured two cans of extra gas, and then, standing in the water, he turned the boat toward the center of the river. He gave it a big push, took a few steps, and jumped over the back and into his steering position. He then went through the procedures of starting the boat. He turned on the gas, primed the engine, and put on the choke. The engine fired to life, extremely noisy with no muffler, and he began to warm it up by putting around in a circle not far from the shore. This was the mark of a good pilot, Cameron thought as he watched, to check and see if there was going to be some mechanical problem with that particular boat—if there was, they would not be a mile down the river and have to paddle back for another against the strong current, or paddle over to the shore and walk back, either of which would cost them a good deal of time. The Mekong River was fairly narrow at that spot, one thousand feet wide. On the other side was Thailand. But there was a visible current in the river, most easily seen where there was a branch or rock sticking out, as the water made a wake around the obstacle.

The pilot made a second circle in completing his check ride and concluded everything was functioning properly. All seemed to be in proper order, and so he yelled something back to another pilot standing by on shore, waiting and watching to make sure all was well as the pilots did with one another. If the motor failed, they might need a rescue if the current was too strong, as the current might take them downstream before they could get over to the shore to moor. After the engine warmed up, the pilot revved it up a few times, with the long shaft of the propeller up and out of the water, the propeller spinning and throwing water all about. He then positioned the boat downstream, and waved over to the fellow pilots as a salute to say he was off and on his way!

The river was not cleared of rocks, like navigable rivers in the United States. There were dangerous rocks of all sizes—from small to large, the large as big as ten to fifteen feet high—jutting up out of the water in spots in the shallow river. There were also sand bars, some above, and some below the surface.

As the monsoon was not yet fully underway there, the river was low and narrow compared to what it would be several weeks into the monsoon. Currents formed as the water flowed around the rocks, and it was obvious from the way he navigated about them that this pilot knew the river very well. Their fast boat had a flat bottom, obviously designed to be able to navigate the shallow river.

On occasion, the pilot went rather frightening close to the big rocks. Cameron wondered at first if that was daring or careless, but as the trip continued, he realized that the pilot knew exactly where to take the boat, and Cameron became comfortable with the pilot's ability.

As fast as they were going, they could easily demolish

the boat and get killed if they smashed into one of the rocks.

The shoreline of the Mekong River consisted of rock formations and cliffs, dense jungle in-between, and also, and oddly, clean, white sand on the shoreline as if on an ocean.

Most of the sandy shores had roped off squares of crops growing in neat rows, tied to bamboo stakes. An occasional water buffalo roamed about. The rope was natural fiber wound around the bamboo stakes to form a fence, to keep out the water buffalo and perhaps other critters.

To speak over the engine exhaust, Cameron had to raise his voice. "What are these crops?" he asked, pointing.

Faint Chance got up close to the pilot so she could be heard, and repeated his answer to Cameron. "Sweet potatoes and peanuts."

And so, they continued down the Mekong River, turning in and out of the rocks at times, traveling at sixty miles per hour. There were occasional mists of water from broken clouds of light rain, and there were also distinct sunny portions between them—an unusual sky.

Hours later, the driver slowed down. Faint Chance interpreted. "He says this is Pak Bang. We're half way. Here, we stop to rest and get food."

There was a floating boat dock to the left, thirty feet long, moored only a few feet from the shore. It had no walls. There were fifteen or more boats docked there, not like the fast boat. They were slow boats for inexpensive transportation, and for hauling things. A hundred feet up, on a ridge, overlooking the river and the dock below was a cottage hotel where the slow boat people in transit stayed overnight. The steps were only cuts in the dirt with no concrete or wood.

Inside the hut was a wooden outhouse built on top of the dock at the corner toward the river. Inside, there was a simple hole in the floor four feet above the river.

Inside the open-sided dock were several tables of varying sizes. The food preparation was done in the center of the floating dock toward the rear by a short, heavy woman and a young, female assistant, probably her daughter. Several of the tables had customers, some of which were local river people, and there was another table with four European students.

Faint Chance told him, "Better not take the water here. You might get sick."

"Please order me a beer. And how about getting us something to eat? You pick."

Faint Chance ordered beer for the two of them, and also rice noodle soup from the cook.

Cameron drank his beer quickly, and ordered another. The clouds were disappearing, and the sun coming through. As they drank the soup, they could see their boat pilot checking the boat, adjusting the ropes on the baggage and transferring gas to the main tank from his extra can. Faint Chance had her hair forced back by the wind, and looked very sporting.

After forty-five minutes on the dock, the woman who ran the place told them their boat was ready, passing a message from their pilot. They boarded the boat for the remainder of the trip to Luang Prabang, another three hours away.

They noticed across the lake, near the other side, another of the fast boats. Its motor was off, and it was just sitting in the water as though waiting. It had a single passenger in it, in addition to the pilot.

Chapter 30

They pulled out of the dock for the next part of their adventure in the little fast boat. The sky continued to be mixed with heavy patches of dark clouds with rays of sun coming in between them off and on, rain occasionally falling in short bursts.

Twice they saw slow boats coming up the river, against the tide, en route in the other direction, heading from Luang Prabang to Pak Bang. No one overtook their fast boat going down the river.

After an hour, the pilot turned his head to the rear, off and on. Cameron did not think anything of it at first. He did not have the vantage point that his pilot did as he was down lower in the bottom of the boat, whereas the pilot was sitting up on the deck near the engine. The bumping up and down, the very fast speed, and the turns in-between the occasional rocks made it impossible to stand, or even get up on his knees without risking falling out. But eventually, he realized that something was bothering the pilot.

Finally, after half an hour, when they were in a turn so Cameron could see around the engine behind him. He saw what the pilot had been turning to see. There was another fast boat up the river, behind them one hundred yards.

At that part of the river, there were large rock formations jutting out. The pilot slowed and maneuvered around them.

Cameron could then see that the boat behind them had one passenger and a pilot, and it looked like it might be the same boat that was sitting across the river from the boat dock earlier.

After they cleared the rocks, their pilot went back up to speed. There were more turns, and slower sections of the river to navigate through. The boat behind was catching up, and, finally, Cameron could then see that the passenger was a Japanese in his late twenties. It was the bandit!

Cameron shouted excitedly over the engine noise to Faint Chance. "That's the bandit. Tell the pilot he will kill us and to go as fast as he can!"

She spoke loudly to the pilot over the roar of the engine, and he sped up to his maximum speed, wide open. The boat behind did the same. Both boats raced on down the river, bouncing up and down, on a wild ride.

The bandit took out a semi-automatic pistol and began shooting at them. One of the bullets hit the boat just a few feet ahead of Cameron and Faint Chance, making a hole above the water line.

The bandit and his pilot got into a scuffle as his pilot did not want to continue with the bandit shooting, worried about the law. They fought on the boat, and, finally, the bandit successfully knocked the pilot overboard into the river. His boat slowed, as no one was at the throttle. Then Uto took over the throttle. The chase was on again!

Cameron and Faint Chance's pilot expertly maneuvered through the rocks and the sand formations sticking above, or nearly above, the water as they raced down the river. The bandit had an advantage of having a lighter boat with only one person and was doing a good job of slowly catching up.

They heard two loud whistling noises beside their heads, and they turned around to see that the bandit was shooting his pistol with one hand while holding the control stick with the other. He was eighty yards back, at that point, and there was a straight stretch that allowed him time to aim.

Cameron said to Faint Chance, "Tell the pilot to weave

back and forth without losing speed, and to try to lose him in the rocks ahead with tight turns."

She yelled at him over the roar of the engine. He understood, and expertly turned a little from side to side, weaving, as the bullets continued. One bounced off the engine making a load metallic sound.

Cameron leaned over to Faint Chance, and said loudly, "Tell the pilot that the man chasing us does not know how to pilot one of these boats well and that he should try to outmaneuver him in the rocks."

Faint Chance could not be heard well by the pilot from where she was, so she turned to the rear to face the pilot, got up on her knees inside the hull of the boat so as to brace herself from being thrown overboard, and yelled the instructions to the pilot. On the second try, he got it and acknowledged with a nod. The pilot leaned farther forward into the wind and closer to his control stick, as though to pick up even more speed through better aerodynamics. Cameron and Faint Chance held on tightly to the sides of the boat and to each other, as the pilot stopped slowing as he turned around the rocks in the middle of the river.

Just ahead, there were two huge rocks that protruded out of the river fifteen feet high, dividing the river into thirds. The natural tendency was to go in between them. However, with the river low, there were dangerous rocks just inches below the surface, in between the large protruding rocks. If you knew this, like their pilot did, you could miss them. But if one went too fast and went into one of the rocks, it would not just slow your boat but stop it at once. At sixty miles per hour, it would flip or destroy the boat. Their pilot knew this all too well, as he had been going up and down the river often. He formulated a plan.

The pilot looked back at the bandit. He was holding the gun and shooting with his right hand and steering with his left by holding the steering stick that stuck out straight in front of the engine. He was sitting on the right rear of the boat to the side of the engine where the pilots always sit.

Going through the rocks slowly was the only way to safely pass. It could not be done safely very fast, let alone at sixty miles per hour. However, their experienced pilot, without slowing, went in between the tall rocks wide open. The bandit lined up to follow, trying to aim his pistol in his bouncing boat, and unaware of the danger just below the surface.

Traveling at sixty miles an hour, their pilot entered in between the tall rocks sticking out of the water, just in the middle. He then executed his planned move. He suddenly cut the throttle and leaned back and out to the right, such that he was nearly horizontal, at the same time pulling the control stick over his mid-section, much farther than it would otherwise be able to go with his body there to prevent it. He pulled it right over his chest with both hands on it, forcing the boat to turn left so hard it nearly flipped over, and ever so narrowly missed the rocks just ahead, inches below the surface. Had he not cut the throttle, or been clumsy in the maneuver, the boat would have hit the rocks below the surface and cracked up or flipped over, destroying it. As it was, Cameron and Faint Chance were nearly thrown out in the amazing maneuver.

In the instant before the event had the bandit seen or understood what the pilot had done, he would have cut his throttle at once. But he did not, and he went through the tall rocks at full speed in pursuit, unaware he was led into a trap. He steered with his left hand, his gun in his right, held up, still hoping to get a good shot as the water sprayed all over him and the boat bounced wildly.

After entering between the tall rocks sticking out of the water, he turned to the left, assuming he would be following those ahead.

But his turn was not nearly enough to avoid the rocks inches below the surface.

The bottom of the bandit's boat, smashed into those rocks. It flipped up and summersaulted two times, much of it breaking into pieces.

The man was propelled thirty feet high and a hundred feet downstream, landing in the water.

Cameron, Faint Chance, and their pilot saw the flying Uto, saw the debris from the crash, and felt sure that he was hurt, if not dead. However, they had no weapons, and dared not stick around to confirm.

Cameron told Faint Chance, "Tell the pilot to go on fast and not to stop. Let's make good time the rest of the way to Luang Prabang."

They took off once again, full throttle, and went on, the excitement over. They finally reached the little dock of Luang Prabang. There were no other boats at the primitive dock.

Faint Chance told the pilot, "If you report the incident, we'll all be detained until it is sorted out. It's better to say nothing."

He spoke with her and quickly determined that freedom was better than jail.

Cameron turned to the pilot. "Good work!" He put money in his hand. When the pilot looked down, there were three one-hundred dollar notes. His eyes opened wide. His regular pay was a tiny fraction of that. It was the most he had ever made.

The docking area was some distance below the banks, and it was necessary to climb another steep dirt path with more of the dirt steps. At the top, off to the right and back away from the cliff was another check point. It consisted of a wooden roof, six feet high, with four posts holding it up and no walls.

Sitting behind a desk underneath it was a man in a uniform, with another ledger like the one the official had upriver at Ban Houei Sai.

They gave him Cameron's passport and her identity papers, and the man took down the information in the ledger. The government logged who embarked and disembarked. There were no communication devices.

Not far away from the official was a single tuk-tuk and

its driver, waiting, hoping to get a fare from someone off a boat, like theirs, that might arrive that afternoon.

Cameron said to Faint Chance, "Tell that tuk-tuk driver we'll hire him, and he is to take us to the airport. We don't know for sure that the man is dead. There'll be an inquiry if the bandit shows up alive and gives a story. We should go at once to see if there is a flight that we can still take today to miss any such inquiry."

Luang Prabang airport was a half hour away. The road for the first part of the journey towards the airport away from the river was a narrow, sandy, bumpy dirt road ten feet wide, totally undeveloped.

All of a sudden the tuk-tuk driver stopped, the deceleration jerking Cameron and Faint Chance forward in the back of the two bench seats.

Jumping out in front of the tuk-tuk were three men, holding weapons. One came up and held a gun on the driver, and the other two moved in. The man holding the gun at the driver yelled at him to get out, and then he looked at Cameron and Faint Chance in the back. They had machine guns, appearing to be well worn AK-47s.

The driver did not hesitate, totally afraid, jumping out quickly. Two of the bandits moved in closer with guns pointed and motioned them out of the vehicle. All exited the vehicle.

Cameron and Faint Chance got out, hands raised. They were motioned at gun point to stand off to one side with the driver, with one of the bandits standing guard while the other rifled through their backpacks that were taken from the back of the tuk-tuk.

Standing back with their arms in the air, Cameron asked of Faint Chance, "Who are they?"

"H'mong."

Cameron and Faint Chance talking came to the attention of the H'mong, and one came over to them, machine gun raised, and shouted something that Cameron did not understand.

Hearing nothing from Faint Chance, he asked her, "What's he saying?"

Since Cameron had not obeyed his command to shut up, the one who said it came around to the back of Cameron, raised his machine gun butt and hit Cameron over the head from behind.

Cameron fell unconscious.

Chapter 31

The throbbing of his head was his first sensation. He saw the world upside down.

As his senses slowly returned, he remembered. Had he become dyslexic? He wanted to rub his eyes, and tried. That did not work, and he realized he could not move his arms.

He was hanging from a tree by a rope tied to his bound ankles, his arms tied behind him. The ground was several feet below his head. He saw his backpack and that of Faint Chance, and all their contents, lying in a pile, rifled through. He could not tell if the bag with the plant leaves was still there. One man with a machine gun sat on a rock close by, standing guard.

As he turned his aching head, he saw Faint Chance strung up similarly, close by, hanging from another limb from the same tree.

She saw him move. "Are you all right, darling?"

Cameron said aloud in his dizziness, "She called me darling!" Then he answered, "Yes, I think so. Now I know why hotel rooms are only four bucks in this fucked-up country. Where are we?"

"They brought us to a campsite not far from where they met us."

"Do you know what they intend to do with us?"

"Not yet. A group of them have gone off somewhere and will be returning soon."

Cameron looked around and could see no sign of the tuk-tuk driver. "What happened to the driver and his tuk-tuk?"

"I don't know. They either let him go or killed him."

"Who are these people?"

"H'mong."

"What is 'H'mong'?"

"You don't know?" Then she realized that he actually did not know. "They worked for your CIA in the Vietnam war." She heard something, looked around, and then back. "Be quiet!"

There was rustling in the jungle nearby, and someone called out a signal to the H'mong man guarding them, who responded. Soon a group of four additional men appeared in the clearing, weapons in hand. Their weapons were also aged machine guns, Vietnam Era.

One of them barked out something at Cameron. He came over and hit Cameron in the stomach with the butt of his machine gun. Cameron let out a groan of pain.

Faint Chance told them in Lao, "He does not speak Lao. I live in Vientiane. He's from America and is a designer of houses. Please do not hurt him."

The same man said, "I can see that he's from America. Where have you been, and where are you going?"

"We have been to the village in the far north where I'm from," Faint Chance answered, "and we are going to Vientiane."

"What business did you have in the northern village? Are you looking for us to report our whereabouts?"

Faint Chance knew that the government troops would come after these H'mong and kill them if they got word of where they were. The H'mong would now almost certainly take their possessions, kill them, and burn them in fire with no trace.

Time was now. "We are not seeking H'mong. We have

just come from visiting my father in the far north at his village. He was killed by an evil man when we were there and entered the spirit world. Now my father is more powerful than ever before. He was the *Great Maw Pii.*"

The man moved backward, as though struck by something. "You are the daughter of the *Great Maw Pii*? I don't believe it!" The chief's powers were so legendary among the H'mong that his reputation had spread all around as the greatest shaman. The most devoted shamans on Earth were H'mong. The *Great Maw Pii* was a legend, almost folklore, as they had never had the experience of the honor of his presence. Many H'mong thought he was only legend.

"The *Great Maw Pii* adopted me as his daughter and raised me," Faint Chance said. "Now I live in Vientiane. He is now in the spirit world since several days. Before he entered the spirit world, he attached his spirit and his ancestors to the *ton mai piiset* that he gave me. He's traveling with us in the *ton mai piiset*, and if you harm us in any way, or take his gift to me, he will curse you with his magnificent powers forever, and you, and all of your ancestors, will be all be removed from the spirit world forever, or, if not yet entering the spirit world, will never be allowed to go there."

This contact with the spirit of *Great Maw Pii* was the most profound thing that could ever happen to him. He shook with fear. He and the other H'mong began talking among themselves.

They would, under no circumstances, offend the greatest spirit of all, the legendary *Great Maw Pii*, the ultimate shaman. They untied her and Cameron from the tree and lowered them to the ground.

Cameron's world spun in dizziness as he went from being inverted to right side up after so long. Eventually, he sat up and found himself sitting next to Faint Chance with his hands still bound with leather straps.

The same man came over to them. He spoke to Faint Chance. "Exactly where is your village in the north?" He was testing her to see if she was lying, and also trying to find out where the residence of the *Great Maw Pii* existed, the legend that few had ever experienced.

Faint Chance described where the village was.

"What you have described may be the way to the village of the greatest shaman, the *Great Maw Pii*." Becoming more convinced, the man untied her hands. "Show me the *ton mai piiset*."

She went to her things that had been dumped out of their back packs and found the bag with the plant leaves. She held it up and opened it only a little, saying, "This is it. You must not touch it now that you have done this to us, and you must help us leave. If you do not, you and your ancestors will be cursed forever by the great spirit of the *Great Maw Pii*. If you help us, I will speak to the *Great Maw Pii* and tell him to forgive you and your ancestors."

He spoke to the others, and they all agreed. They then brought them water and untied Cameron.

The same man said apologetically, "We did not know you were the daughter of the *Great Maw Pii*. Please do not curse us or our ancestors. We return your things."

"Will you escort us back to the road to Luang Prabang?"

"Yes."

"I'll speak favorably to my father in the spirit world about you."

Cameron's things, including his money and camera, that had been taken by one of the men, were then returned to the pile of their things apologetically. Her chain and locket were returned, and the H'mong chanted when it was handed back to her.

They began their hike back to the main road to Luang Prabang, only this time traveling with an armed escort of four of some of the meanest guards on Earth.

As they walked along to Luang Prabang, escorted, Cameron could finally speak in safety to Faint Chance. "So, what's a 'H'mong'?"

"I'm surprised that you do not know. We all know all about them here in Lao. H'mong is a northern Lao race of people of eighteen clans. They worked for your CIA during the war, fighting the Viet Cong, and doing dangerous things for like rescuing downed American pilots. They are the bravest and most efficient warriors ever. Many years ago, they were a wandering group in central Asia, and eventually ended up in Lao fleeing persecution in China. When not fighting, they settle and burn forest patches to grow rice, corn, and, of course, their cash crop, opium. But especially now, having become such fierce fighters, it is hard to take that away from them, and a small number of them are a challenge to the government. Lao has actually hired Vietnamese troops to come into Lao to help find the remaining militia groups."

"This is all completely new to me. How many of them are there, and how many were involved in the Vietnam War, if you know?" Cameron asked, wondering how he could never have heard of these people.

"Three hundred thousand now live in Lao. Twenty thousand died in the Vietnam War. Many died afterward in Lao. After Vietnam, many H'mong were gassed with toxic gas in some places by the communists and had to flee to avoid death. One hundred twenty-five thousand, which was nearly half of them at the time, went across the Mekong River into Lao or Thailand, hoping to go to America, and waited in refugee camps for years before being allowed to go there. Some did not leave, and remain here or in Thailand. The Lao government discriminates against the H'mong, and they have very hard lives. Under the communist government that took over in 1975, of those that remained, over forty-six thousand were arrested and put in re-education camps where three-quarters of them have died. Others have died of hunger and disease."

"Since Lao became a republic, what's it like for them?

"Even after our government became a republic, the H'mong did not believe that they were receiving the same benefits as other Laotians, and they have organized militia groups that receive money from their own kind in America, which they use to buy weapons in Thailand. Those in America send money to those here for support as well. These militia groups now cause terror to the Lao government."

"This is the first I've ever heard of them," Cameron repeated. "What do they think of Americans?"

"By and large, they are still loyal to America as many now live there and are supported by the US government. But that is not the same with all. Some years ago, there was an attempted assassination of the then US Ambassador to Lao, Wendy Chamberlin."

"I suppose that working here as an ambassador does have its risks," Cameron said.

"Yes, but the attempt on her life was in America when she was giving a lecture."

"My God." Cameron realized how little he knew of world affairs. No one he knew ever spoke of anything like that. The Middle East was the main topic of foreign affairs news, and so little was heard of places like this. No wonder he hated the mainstream US news and refused to listen to it. They had their own agenda and tried to make ridiculous things into a mini-series, completely omitting major parts of the world. "Now, you must tell me what it is that you said that got us out of there. Whatever it was, it was very clever."

"The H'mong are said to be the strongest of shamans."

"What's a shaman?"

"Shamanism is the ancient Laotian practice of contacting spirits of the dead. It is also practiced outside of Lao. A shaman is one who can do that. The H'mong go to a shaman to talk to ancestors, to obtain healing."

"Does the Lao shaman have his own special ceremony?" Cameron asked.

"Oh, yes, certainly. They chant and jump about, using a ring of metal disks in front of an altar for several hours to summon the dead. They were at the funeral of the Great Maw Pii."

"I recall all those people with the noisemakers. So what did you tell those H'mong that was so moving? They cut us down at once then acted apologetic, let us live, gave us back everything, and are now providing us with an armed escort to the road."

"I told them who my father was, the *Great Maw Pii*. H'mong know of him as one of the greatest shamans, even though most have never met him. They are from the north, but not as far as his village, and they know of his legendary powers to talk to the spirits, and also of his wisdom. I told them that he died during our visit and that his spirit lives and is being carried in the *ton mai piiset* with us on our journey."

"I remember the part where you showed him the plant."

"I told them that they had wronged us, and if they touched the plant and did not let us go, the *Great Maw Pii* would curse them and their ancestors forever."

"Wow," Cameron exclaimed. "That's fantastic. And they believed it?"

She looked at him very seriously. "Why not? It's true."

Cameron became quiet, mesmerized by the concept that the plant or whatever was in it, was certainly very powerful, and so had been the late *Great Maw Pii*—or was he still with them?

Chapter 32

Cameron slept so soundly he could not remember where he was when he woke up. He then remembered yesterday, with the high speed chase down the Mekong River, with the Japanese bandit shooting at them, and then being captured by the H'mong. But they had finally made it to a hotel in Luang Prabang. What a day to remember!

He looked over at Faint Chance, who was sitting on the edge of the bed.

"I've checked with the airline," she said, "and there's a plane to Vientiane at five o'clock. That means we have the day to show you about here at the old capital where you can find some interesting architecture. How does that sound?" In her hand were brochures from the hotel lobby. "Here is what I have for you. We will see the former Royal Palace, the Wat Mai architecture from the eighteenth century, the Wat Xieng Thong and the Buddhist architecture from the sixteenth century. Would you like to do that?"

"Maybe I can get some ideas," he said, realizing it was, in fact, an opportunity, and he got out of bed. He went to Candice's camera and began to dust it off in preparation.

⌘

Later at the tiny airport, they stood at the counter of the

only airline, Lao Aviation. He looked at the girl behind the counter, wondering if she spoke English and decided to give it a try-after all, it was an airline. "How much is the fare to Vientiane?"

The girl did not answer, but she did understand what was being asked, turned slightly to one side, and raised her arm, pointing it to a white board hung on the wall behind her where the fare was handwritten with a broad green marker pen. It read:

Vientiane US $100 Cash Only

"One hundred dollars," Cameron said aloud as he read the crude form of rate announcement.

The girl did not respond. Cameron pulled out his wallet and handed over a credit card. He was warmed by the fact that they were now back in his world with credit cards.

"Two tickets to Vientiane, one way," he said, holding out the credit card.

She did not reach out for the card, leaving him holding it out in the air, and once again turned slightly to her side and pointed up at the same sign with the rates.

"Yes, I see that," he said. "Here. We'll take two seats. Charge it to this card." He pushed it toward her.

She continued to point to the sign, not accepting his credit card.

Faint Chance broke the standoff. "Cameron, I think she only accepts cash, not credit cards."

"What about Laotian kip?" he asked, hoping to get rid of some of the kip in his pocket, somewhat resentful that he could not use his standard form of currency when traveling in America, which was plastic.

Faint Chance spoke to the girl in Lao, and said to Cameron, "No, only US dollars. No kip."

"This is amazing," Cameron exclaimed to Faint Chance. "An airline that will not accept credit cards or even its own country's currency! What about other tourists who might not have the cash? Who would know that Lao Aviation will not accept its own country's currency, and no credit cards? It's a good thing we're not carrying yen or some other money. We would have to hire an elephant to take us there."

Faint Chance frowned. "I'm sorry, but I do not travel, and do not know of such things."

"What would we have done if the H'mong had not returned our money? What if we had lost it? It's a good thing that I have some money left. We might never leave!"

⋐⋑⋐⋑

After arriving at the Vientiane airport, Cameron said to Faint Chance, "If the bandit is still alive, or has accomplices, they will try to find us here as they would know we are coming back here. You pick a hotel and don't tell the driver which one, in case he might be asked where we are staying. Have him take us a block or so from the hotel, without mentioning its name."

At the hotel, Cameron phoned Spencer and Candice. No one was in, but he left a message. "I have the plant, and am now back in Vientiane at a hotel. Faint Chance and I shall be coming soon."

In the hotel room, Cameron opened the bag and produced the very special plant that had already caused murders. It was now somewhat dried out but still had its purple and orange colors.

"Look at this," Cameron said. "These leaves have the same color as the Baron's exotic Oolong tea!" He took out the Baron's tea leaves that he got in northern Thailand, which had survived the trip, to compare. "Check this out."

Faint Chance came over and looked at the comparison of the Baron's exotic Oolong tea leaves to the *ton mai piiset* leaves. "How interesting. They are almost the same."

"I'm worried that if the bandit is still alive, especially if he has other accomplices, and they find out where we are staying, they'll come for the plant, Cameron said. "I'll carry plant leaves in my pocket rather than leave them here." He put the exotic Oolong tea gift from the Baron into a plastic bag. "I'll put the tea into our luggage. If someone breaks in, he will think it is the special plant."

That done, they were exhausted. He showered and sat in the room, quietly thinking of the day's events. Cameron poured himself a scotch whiskey obtained from a local store, put it beside the bed, and lay down. Faint Chance came out of the shower in a hotel terry robe.

"Drink?"

She nodded. He poured. Then followed a deluge of rain, the monsoon season bringing rainfall, more often.

"There is some massage cream here in the bath. Would you like a massage for your sore muscles?" she asked.

"That would be wonderful."

She came to the bed with the cream. "Turn over on your stomach and relax, and I will give you a massage."

She took off her terry robe, naked underneath. Cameron took a gulp of the whiskey, relaxing his muscles, and Faint Chance began her massage technique.

As she massaged him, he asked, "I've been wondering. When we were before the new chief, how did you know that he would be told by the spirit world to let us live?"

"I didn't."

"Then why did you ask him to communicate with the spirits?"

"The new chief was going to put us to death. I relied on my father to save us. He did."

"All this spirit business is new to me, dear."

"But you can see that it is real, can't you?"

"I really don't know what to believe at this point," he said, so as not to offend her, but still clinging to his skeptical analysis of any spiritual world.

He rolled over on his back as she continued the massage. She could tell he was resting, but that he had other energy left. The rain was becoming very strong and providing insulation of outside noises and a background for intimacy much like they had in the tent on the trail to the village.

"I can give you a special massage now."

He wondered what on earth that might be. Faint Chance put her legs on either side of his feet and squatted over him without sitting on anything, in the sitting manner of the Laotians. She then lowered herself slowly over his feet and began squeezing one of his feet, using only her incredibly talented nether lips. She went up, squeezing from the foot up the leg, a bit at a time, and then back down the same leg. Then she moved over to the other leg, repeating. She then moved up to his front and, still using only her nether lips, continued in what was the most extraordinary massage he had even heard of, let alone experienced.

In a short time, he changed his views on the reality of the spirit world. He concluded that Faint Chance could definitely summon spirits of ecstasy not found on planet Earth.

<h1 style="text-align:center">Chapter 33</h1>

The heavy monsoon rain continued. One hotel widow in their room was open part way for ventilation, and the noise of the heavy rain pounded away all night. Cameron awakened in the morning at first light. Faint Chance came out of the shower, wearing the hotel robe, and drying her hair with a towel.

"Good morning, luv," he said to her.

"Good morning. Did you sleep properly?"

"Yes, I did," he answered that unusual question of hers.

"I ordered coffee."

"Sounds wonderful." Cameron rolled back into bed to absorb the ambiance of the moment, if not the experience.

The delicious Laotian coffee came, and was served by the hotel person.

"I should go to the shop," Faint Chance said, sharpening the day into business. "My father will be worried about me, and he will need me there so he can do needed errands."

"Is it going to be very difficult for you to move to America?" Cameron asked after a pause.

"Yes. But, if I stay here, the best I can do would be to find a husband here, marry, and have a family. In Lao the wife takes care of the husband and the home, and that takes all of her time. And, if I don't marry, it's not fair to my parents to have them supporting me forever. If I might make it to America, I have heard that I could find work that would pay so much that I might be able one day to send a little home to my parents when they are too old to work. So, it will be like my leaving to marry, except that I will be far away. I'll write often, and after a few years, I hope to have saved up enough from working hard to be able to come back and visit them again. I love them very much."

Cameron could not help himself. "Would you consider living with me instead of Spencer and Candice?"

Faint Chance stopped what she was doing. Cameron was putting her in a predicament.

She followed what she had been taught to do. "I am to live with Spencer and Candice. If I was to live with you, they would have to consent."

Cameron knew they wouldn't mind, but there was no way to relate that to her.

"I want to look into expediting your visa. Would you consider living with me in America, assuming Spencer and Candice consent?"

"I will follow my new parents, Spencer and Candice, as to their wishes."

Cameron side stepped the answer. "I'll go over to the embassy and see if you can come under some expedited tourist visa. I would like you to come back with me, ahead of your immigration, if that is possible. Would you like to come over earlier?"

"Yes. I did not think it would take so long for me to get approval to come. I thought I would have it some time ago."

"Good. I'll go to the American Embassy tomorrow and see if a tourist visa can be arranged for you. Today, I think I'll rest."

Her face glowed. He then wondered after he said it if it could be done. He realized the importance to her of what he was talking about, and he hoped he had not suggested something he could not deliver.

Across town at a hotel, Morio Uto, the *Kumi-cho*, quite badly beaten up from the crash with fresh cuts on his face and arms, a broken arm in a sling, was talking long distance to Japan. He told the Oyabun enough of the story and the status and asked if the Oyabun had instructions.

"I'll arrange to put pressure on the brother and the sister-in-law in America to tell their brother in Lao to give you the plant," the Oyabun answered. "I have people there who can do that. Call me back in two days."

Uto hung up, and felt good that he was working on this project for the Oyabun, who had impressive and far-reaching influence.

തതെ

Bang, bang, bang, came the knock on the front door of the Harrington household. That was unusual for ten a.m.

Priscilla Hargrove was giving lessons to Devan. Rina, the housekeeper, heard the noise without concern that it might have been out of the ordinary and answered the door.

Three outrageously aggressive men in ski masks stormed in.

"Don't move," one of them yelled. Each had a pistol pointing.

"Where's the baby?" another said.

He found Devan before anyone answered. He was sitting in his chair where he had been receiving his lesson.

Their actions were swift and decisive. One stuck a gun in Rina's neck, and another put one in Priscilla's face. They went for the baby, quickly wrapped him up in a blanket, and carried him outside toward their waiting car. They walked backward out the door, and one left a folded letter on the table near the door. In just a few minutes, they had success-fully kidnapped Devan.

The note had typing on it. It was addressed to Spencer and Candice Harrington:

Do not call police or the FBI. If your brother does as we

say, you will get your son back. If not, the baby will be killed.

Priscilla Hargrove called Spencer at once. "Mr. Harrington! Three men just came in here and kidnapped Devan. They left a note." She read it to him, and then asked, "What shall I do?"

"Just sit tight," Spencer told her. "I'll get Candice and we will be there immediately."

Candice had ridden with Spencer that day, and he got her in the lab. As they hurried toward home, he told her, "Candice, it's the plant. It has already started. Word has leaked out, and the criminal element has already learned of it. That plant is evil."

"I wonder just where Cameron is," Candice said. "Would he have the plant by now? We really have to wait for him to contact us to know what is going on over there. He must have the plant since they refer to him doing what they demand. Oh God, I'm so worried about Devan!"

Chapter 34

Faint Chance was working at the jewelry store, allowing her father a chance to run errands. A messenger came in. "Is this where I can leave a message for a Mr. Harrington?"

"Yes, I will give it to him," Faint Chance said. She accepted it for him. "What's it about?"

"I do not know. I was instructed to leave the envelope at this shop, nothing more."

Soon Cameron arrived. She held out the envelope for him. "Here, this was delivered here for you."

He opened it and read:

Cameron Harrington: Call your brother and sister-in-law at once. Be at the Euro Café at 2:30 p.m. tomorrow with the plant. Contact no one else.

He showed it to Faint Chance. "It must be the same man, or an accomplice. I had better call at once."

The only phone in the shop was in the center of the store, inside at a desk that was surrounded by a square of jewelry cases, and was not private. He hurried back to the hotel for the call.

One could not dial out directly from the hotel room overseas, as the phone system was primitive by western standards, and so Cameron placed the call through the hotel operator, and after five minutes, the phone rang and his call was put through.

"Cameron!" Spencer exclaimed, breathing hard. "I got your message that you got the plant. So, the knowledge of it must be out at least to someone. Devan has been kidnapped! Have you been contacted by anyone? Your relationship to me is mentioned in a note that was left."

"I've been given a note to call you, and to bring the plant to someone at a café tomorrow called the Euro Café. What happened there?"

"Some masked terrorists came into our home when Candice and I were working, when the tutor and the maid were there, and took Devan at gunpoint," Spencer answered. "We have been told not to contact the authorities, and we have not done so yet. We believe that these people will not stop at murder to get the plant leaves. Whoever wants the plant and has kidnapped Devan, knows about us, and has international connections. Can we really risk Devan's life? Candice and I would never be able to live with ourselves if we allowed our Devan to be killed just to get the plant specimen. As important as the plant is, I would not be surprised that they might kill Devan just to make a point. Devan is of no value to them, only the plant. Then they might come after either Candice or me or both of us."

"There may be another problem with contacting the police," Cameron said. "We'll have to reveal the ransom of the plant and the news of it will get out. As it just a natural plant, not yet a patented process, it could become known to the world that such a thing exists, and there will be the whole world to hear about it. Then the village where it came from will be invaded by the outside world, which we promised not to do, and we have already caused violence to come there—murder, in fact."

"Candice is worried sick," Spencer added. "I think you should relinquish the plant."

"I've been sent a message to go to a meeting tomorrow,"

Cameron said. "I think the only thing to do right now is for me to go and then I'll call you." He then gave the number of his hotel, and concluded the call. He sat back, wondering what he should do, and contemplated the stakes, his future, and Faint Chance.

✁✁✁

Cameron went back to the jewelry store for Faint Chance and led her to the nearby café to be able to talk.

"Devan has been kidnapped. This is definitely the same as those who killed your father the chief. These people have the ability to send gunmen to Lao and simultaneously have someone kidnapped in America. They would kill again in a heartbeat to get the plant. I don't want to be responsible for the death of Devan. I think if we don't give them the plant, they will kill Devan to make their point, and then kidnap Candice or Spencer and repeat the ransom demand as the next step until they get the plant."

"Is the plant all that valuable?" Faint Chance asked.

"Whoever synthesizes it first can patent the formula and process. Whoever gets the patent first can make billions," he said.

"But if they stole it from you, how could they have it legally?"

"Stole what? If someone gets the naturally growing plant leaves and has it analyzed first at a lab and then synthesizes it and makes it into a digestible potion or pill that can be taken when creating a child, that person will own the formula if he patents it. It would be impossible to go to court to claim it is ours since it comes from a natural plant. And we must not forget, with the kind of muscle behind these people, we will likely run into some accident and never finish a court challenge. I'd bet on that happening for sure. So, I think we had better show up with those strange purple and orange plant leaves tomorrow at the Euro Café, or we can expect them to kill Devan, and then come after Spencer or Candice. They have already come after us."

Silence prevailed for a time as they looked at each other, trying to grasp the scope of the events. Finally, it was Faint Chance who came up with the solution. "Do you know what? The Baron's special Oolong tea leaves are the same color, purple and orange."

Cameron's eyes opened wide. He was silent for a time. "Do you think we could substitute it for the plant?"

"Who would know the difference?" Faint Chance said.

"You are a genius," Cameron said. "It would take some time, days or longer, for them to get the leaves to a lab, analyze them, and finally determine that the leaves are only tea. But then again, who is to say that the power does not come from tea? Devan would probably be returned once they get the tea leaves. Do you think we dare?"

❡❡❡

Cameron called Spencer from the hotel room. He decided not to tell the truth for security reasons. "I'm going to turn over the plant leaves tomorrow afternoon, Lao time, as I have been told to. If they contact you, go ahead and tell them what I said."

He dared not mention that he was going with the Oolong tea substitution.

"We haven't called the police," Spencer said. "We doubt if there is anything they could do in a short time. They would probably want to monitor the phone line to trace the calls coming in. I'm sure these bastards are aware of that and would take precautions from where they call. Here's Candice. Please reassure her. She's a basket case since Devan was kidnapped."

❡❡❡

That night Cameron had a nightmare about Devan being

kidnapped and killed, his dream merging with the Lind-
bergh baby story after a movie he had seen. His eyes
opened, and he discovered it was just a nightmare.

As he lay in bed, he realized he might be responsible for
Devan's death if he did not give up the plant. How could he
ever look Spencer and Candice in the face again if he
caused Devan's death? On the other hand, coming to Lao
and finding the biggest discovery for mankind and simply
letting it go, with the chief murdered, would make it impossible for him to live with himself if he did nothing. This was
the biggest decision he would ever make, his defining
moment.

He looked over at Faint Chance sleeping next to him in
the hotel bed. He lay back down and tried to weigh the
risks.

Chapter 35

It was early morning. Cameron sat in the hotel room chair, sipping coffee sent up from room service.

Faint Chance stirred. She moved about and then saw him. "What have you decided?"

"I'm going to go for it. I can't let the death of the chief be for naught. The gangster gets Oolong tea. That's my decision."

"I want to come along," she said. "I want to be part of it."

"These people are dangerous," he warned.

"I know the Euro Café. I want to be there with you. This is my karma."

⁂

At midday, Cameron put the Baron's exotic purple and orange tea leaves in a silk jewelry bag Faint Chance brought from the jewelry store.

"You hold this. He gave it to her, and she put it into her purse."

When it was time, they called for a tuk-tuk to go to the Euro Café. It was a neat, wooden cottage café. It was newly decorated in beautiful teak, inside and out, and had a large western-styled bar inside. The dozen tables were covered in table cloths of blue and white checks. The motif of the newly decorated establishment was designed in a European flare. At an off hour, no other customers were there. The gangster picked a perfect meeting place.

As they sat at one of the empty tables, the waiter approached with menus.

"Just two coffees," Cameron told him.

At two thirty-five p.m., Morio Uto walked in the door. They recognized him as the same man that they had seen in the house of the chief. His face was very scratched up, and he had a cast on his arm.

Cameron had immediate ideas of jumping him as the earlier scene at the village went through his mind. The Euro Café had western utensils, as it catered to westerners. There were knives, forks, and spoons on the table at each setting, and Cameron thought of taking one of the knives and plummeting it into him. Faint Chance also had an intense reaction of hatred and desire for revenge. They both could sense the coldness of the gangster.

"What's your name?" Cameron asked.

Uto looked Cameron straight in the eyes and said coolly, "You do not need to know my name. What you do need to know is that I hold the power of life or death over your brother and sister-in-law's baby. If you do not give me the plant, he will be found in a field, very dead. Then harm will come to your brother or sister-in-law next. You can be sure of it."

The threats were convincing as there seemed to be no reason to assume that these people, whoever they were, who had already killed in Lao, and had kidnapped on the other side of the Earth, would stop short of another act of violence to get what they wanted.

After a few moments of silence, Uto asked, "Did you bring the plant?"

"If I give you the plant, how soon will the baby Devan be returned?"

"Within a few hours after I call. I will call as soon as you give me the plant. We have no reason to hurt the baby if you give me the plant."

Cameron had no reason to suspect otherwise. If they killed the child, there would be a very great motive for the FBI, police, and international authorities to track all involved. But if the matter was over and done with in just a few days, the baby returned safely, the matter would be treated completely differently even if reported. So they had no motive to harm Devan if they got the plant. But Spencer and Candice sure as hell would have to take some protective measures once the gangsters found out they had Oolong tea!

Faint Chance noticed the very edge of a multi-colored paper sticking out of Uto's shirt pocket. Only a little bit stuck out. Faint Chance recognized the colors, but kept quiet. The colors were pastels. It was the edge of an airline ticket.

Cameron took the silk bag of the Baron's exotic purple and orange leaves out of his pocket and put it on the table. The gangster opened it. He smelled it as though he might recognize it but he obviously could not. The tea had a fragrance, but who would know? He could have no idea what the odor was between one and the other.

The distinct purple and orange color was present, although dulled somewhat from being dried out as he had anticipated it would be. "If this is some sort of trick," he threatened, "or if you notify any authorities, you can be sure of swift and certain retaliation."

In order to divert the gangster's attention from studying the plant, Cameron introduced his own form of drama. "It's no trick. We have not contacted any authorities anywhere. However, if Devan is not returned in a few hours, the FBI will be notified, and worse for you, I will fixate on you for the rest of my life and utilize all of my resources to locate you and put you in the ground."

Uto was used to living in a world of threats, so he did not feel particularly threatened, but the FBI would be a problem, and he did read in Cameron's statement a very firm resolve. It took his attention off the plant. He closed up the bag with the plant. "I'll make the call." He got up and left the café.

The waiter came with the coffees. "I hope I have not made a big mistake," Cameron told Faint Chance, worried. "Let's hope that he doesn't find out what we have done before they release Devan. I wish I could find out who he is," he said, frustrated. "As it is now, we have no idea who he is, what country he lives in, or anything about him. There is little we can do, other than try to get the plant leaves out of Lao and get back and take precautions against retaliation."

"Did you notice the paper in his pocket?" Faint Chance asked.

"I saw a paper with some pastel colors on it."

"Right. Those are the colors of a newer airline out of Singapore. It is called SilkAir. The only flight from here on SilkAir is to Singapore. To get a ticket on it, you must go to the office, which is only two blocks from my father's shop. It's new and has only one girl full time with an assistant girl helping. The girl in charge is my very good friend whom I went to school with. Let's go there."

"Can we get her to help us?" Cameron asked, wondering if her friend would jeopardize her position for Faint Chance.

Faint Chance smiled. She had the tuk-tuk driver take them near the ticket office, but not right in front, in case the gangster might have gone there himself. There was no sign of him. The same pastel colors of the ticket in the man's pocket decorated the place, the airline's colors. The tiny size of the airline was obvious from the office which was only twelve feet wide and had a staff of two.

They went inside where the SilkAir staff, two Laotian girls in their twenties, sat behind a small counter. They had a single computer behind the desk. A young Asian couple was there and walked out when their business was completed. No one else was present. There were large books of schedules around them. Scheduling for international flights in Lao had to be physically done at the ticket office, old-fashioned style. However, connecting flights were necessary to go far away, such as to America.

One of the girls recognized Faint Chance and jumped up with a big smile on her face. They began talking in Lao, good friends that they were. Finally, Faint Chance switched to English and said, "This is Cameron Harrington. He's from America."

The SilkAir girl also spoke English and looked approvingly at him. "I'm pleased to meet you."

"Likewise," Cameron said. "Is this a new airline?" he asked.

"Relatively new. It's Singapore based, and at this time, the only flights out of Lao are on Mondays and Thursdays, and those are to Singapore."

It was Tuesday, Cameron thought. Just maybe the Japanese man had already booked a flight out, knowing he would get the plant, or had just planned ahead in case he got it so as not to delay in the country where he had already killed three people. Booking in Lao was not something you did from your hotel room, and so maybe, just maybe, the man would be in the reservations information.

Faint Chance took over and switched the conversation to Lao. She told her friend that they wanted to find a Japanese man whose name they did not know, and would she please look and see which of the passengers were Japanese on this week's Thursday flight out of Vientiane to Singapore.

Without so much as a hesitation, her friend turned to her computer screen to check. The plane was obviously not a big one like a 747, as the number of people going to or from Lao was small. Cameron thought it would not be too hard to locate a Japanese person.

"The next flight is Thursday, at nine-thirty a.m.," the girl said. "It's SilkAir, Flight Number Two. It is a direct flight to Singapore. There are no other flights until next week." As she looked at the screen, she said, "There are only two groups of parties with Japanese names. One group is four people, and the other just one person."

"Do you remember them buying tickets?" Faint Chance asked.

"Yes. The four people are two couples, the Kannos and the Omori's. They are traveling together. They did not buy tickets, as they already had them. They came in this morning together to confirm their flight."

"Can you describe them?" Cameron asked.

She started speaking in Lao, and Cameron was not sure if she realized it or not. Faint Chance interpreted. "They are elderly, probably retired. Who is the other person?" Faint Chance asked her in English.

"That is Morio Uto. He's a young man. He came in this morning also and bought a ticket."

"Uto," Cameron said aloud.

Both girls looked at him. Cameron thought he had better not say too much in front of the SilkAir girl. He recognized the name, that of Candice's assistant, Tadashi Uto, who had been to two parties at Spencer and Candice's home. The connection came together. It must be a brother or close family relative of Tadashi Uto who worked at his sister-in-law's lab. Tadashi knew of the plant, as the only one that Candice had confided in. He'd talked! Was he involved? He had to be.

"That is the person you want?" the SilkAir girl asked.

"Yes," Cameron said. "When's he leaving?"

"He's taking the Thursday flight to Singapore. He is traveling on a Japanese passport."

"Do you know where he is staying?" Cameron asked.

"Yes. We require a number to be reached as part of the reservation. He is staying at the Manoluk Hotel, in room twelve. Here's the phone number." She wrote down for Cameron.

"Do you have his passport number as well?" asked Faint Chance.

"Yes, we get that on international flights." The friend

added that to the paper, which she then passed to them.

Faint Chance thanked her girlfriend, who did not think it was any big favor at all.

Quaint place, this Lao was, Cameron decided. They left and went back to the little café next to the shop only two blocks away, where they sat to talk.

"So, we know he's going to Singapore for sure, on Thursday, unless he changes his plans," Cameron said. "The only flights out are on Thai Air and SilkAir. It takes some doing to make or change a booking, and he will probably keep the one he has made. So, we have only until then to report him to the police for the murder of the chief, or he will be out of the country. I'm afraid that if we report him to the police, and he is arrested, three things will happen that we do not want. The first will be that he might let his contacts know, and if he finds out we are his accusers, he may leave word to have Devan killed. The second is that they will detain us as well until they make their inquiries. By the time they go to the village, obtain witness information, and conduct an inquiry, many days will have passed, and we may be held here as witnesses. And the third is that, once they find out about the value of the plant, they will seize it.

"There is corruption at high levels," Faint Chance added. "If the value of it was found out, they would take it and not let you out of the country with it."

"So, reporting to the police is out," Cameron said. "He thought for a while. "I think I have a plan that may work. I visited the Golden Triangle coming in from Thailand and heard of the drug trafficking. Is there still drug trafficking in Lao?"

"Yes," Faint Chance said. "It was not illegal to grow or deal opium in Lao until 1996. It has been a major crop, and there are many people that make their living off of it today."

"Do you have any contacts who know where to get some opium or heroin?"

"Yes, I do. There is trading here in Vientiane."

"We might need a pound or so."

"That amount should be very easy. I know some people who will know where to get it. Do you really want to go buy that?"

"I have a plan that I believe will solve everything, but it will take some quantity of a strong drug such as heroin. Do you know how much heroin costs here? I have never bought anything like that, but back home it is very expensive, according to the papers and arrests that I read about occasionally."

"I do not know exactly, but I doubt that it is very expensive as long as you buy it in Lao. I think it gets expensive once it's smuggled out and arrives in its destination country."

"If I come along, will those people sell it to us, or do you have to go alone?"

"I think they will, as I will be introducing you as a buyer from America," she said.

"What is the penalty for possession of heroin here in Lao?"

"I imagine jail for a few months."

"First, let's go back to SilkAir," Cameron said. "I want to get a phone number in Singapore."

Back inside the SilkAir office, Cameron asked the girlfriend, "Do you have a phone number for the Singapore International Airport where the SilkAir plane lands?"

The girl looked in a book. "Here it is. It's called the Changi International Airport. There are several numbers. What department do you want?"

"Customs," Cameron replied.

The girl wrote down the number for Cameron. He and Faint Chance went to buy the heroin. In a residential area, Faint Chance recognized a house and told the driver to pull over. "Please stay here," she said.

In a few minutes, she came out and gave the tuk-tuk the next destination.

She told Cameron as they drove off, "That was a fellow

who knows where to buy such things. We're going there now."

The next destination was another residence. Inside were a man and his wife.

Faint Chance and Cameron went in. Faint Chance introduced herself and spoke to them for some time, during which Cameron could hear some numbers being discussed. Finally, the man went to the back and came out with a plastic bag of white powder that looked to weigh perhaps a kilo. Faint Chance told Cameron, "For this, he wants two hundred dollars. He says it is pure heroin, not cut, and of the best quality."

Cameron looked at it and had no way to determine if it was real or diluted. He asked Faint Chance if she knew if it was real.

"I have heard of this man before," she told him. "He has a reputation for selling heroin, and I'm sure he is selling the real thing."

Cameron took her aside so the dealer could not hear. "From what I know of it, the price is too low for it to be real, or concentrated. I would expect something like this to be many times that price, even in the country of origin. But don't tell him I think it is cheap—just tell him I'm concerned it is not pure."

Faint Chance looked surprised at that, as though she had thought that two hundred dollars was not cheap. She spoke to the man again. After a time, she said to Cameron, "He says he has heard of people cheating by reducing heroin by adding things to it. He says there is no need to do that in Lao as there are many poppy fields, more than there are people to harvest them. And he would like your repeat business."

Cameron chuckled. "Nothing like relying on reputation for repeat business."

He gave the man two one-hundred-dollar bills, and he split the heroin into two bags, instead of one, after obtaining another empty bag from the dealer, as the larger one would not fit into one of his single pockets well without sticking out. Cameron put a bag into one of each of his front jeans pockets, and they returned to the hotel under a late afternoon sky of pink and red.

Inside, Cameron said, "It may be a little early to call Spencer and Candice. Maybe we should wait a few hours, given the time change. This will also give the gangsters time to return Devan. I want to somehow get into Morio Uto's bag or bags at his hotel before he leaves the country to put the heroin in. I don't yet know how to do that. Do you have any friends at the Manoluk Hotel, like the girl at the SilkAir office?"

"No, I don't. I have only been by that hotel, never inside it."

"We must give Uto time to call and for his accomplices to return Devan before we do anything to get him caught," Cameron said. "So, tonight is out. I think the best time would be to wait until tomorrow. Perhaps he will leave the room to eat or do something, and we can find a way in. Tomorrow is Wednesday, and he leaves Thursday."

☙❧

After dinner in the hotel, Cameron asked her, "It's still too early to call the United States. It would be best to wait a few hours before calling. Do you have any recommendations on how to pass the time?"

"Why don't we have a drink? I know you'd like that."

"Sounds like a winner."

She poured drinks from their bottles in the hotel room, while he went for ice. Halfway through the drinks, she went to a bag she had brought along with her. Inside were clothes and things, which she took to the bathroom.

She showered and returned in her change of clothes, a silk dress. It had long, flowing, silk to the floor, patterned with flowers. It was blue with flowers of lighter blue and cream. She then took from her bag a small, metal incense cup with a lid with holes in it. She removed the lid and lit a match, then held it on the incense until it was going well. She covered it and put it on the floor in the middle of the room.

Smoke began to come out of the holes in the cup, which then turned invisible after the incense heated up. It made a delicate, wonderful fragrance. Cameron would soon learn that the fragrance's method of transportation to his senses by her was not quite what he anticipated.

"Would you like me to dance for you?"

His eyebrows raised. "Sure."

There was an old fashioned radio in the room on the side of the bed, built into the teak night stand. She turned it on, and there was a station playing a combination of modern music and Lao, or who knows what? It might have been from neighboring Thailand.

Faint Chance went to the middle of the room and began a traditional dance. Her hands moved about in circles with the fingers wide apart as she rolled her hands around at the wrists. Her head moved from side to side in the traditional style, as though she had a double jointed neck. She danced about the incense, occasionally turning full circles. As she did, her loose silk dress was so thin he could see through it somewhat, and he could see that she was wearing nothing underneath.

As she went around and danced, she occasionally crossed over the burning incense, and paused over it, while moving her hands, arms, and head about in the traditional moves. As she paused over the incense, he realized that the purpose of the incense was not only to enhance the dance, but to provide additional stimulation. It was for her to take on the fragrance of the incense herself for his delight.

He wondered if what was going on could actually happen to him. As he watched from the bed, her movements became even more suggestive, and she began to move her steps in more closely to the bed where her spellbound audience awaited in anticipation. She pushed him down on the bed, got on top of the bed, and stood over him, her dress going over his head occasionally. She lowered herself slowly. The fragrance had arrived. And ah, what a fragrance!

Chapter 36

Cameron made the call to Spencer and Candice. Candice answered, "Hello?"

"It's me. Done." He wondered if he should reveal at that time what he had done with the tea. Possible retaliation if Uto found out was a scary idea. It would take some time for the gangster to find out he had Oolong tea. But how long?

"Have you got Devan back yet?" he asked, not telling them what he was doing.

"Yes, just minutes ago. A Japanese woman came up to the door. When she rang, we went to the door and saw her entering a car and leaving. Devan was left at the front door. We are so relieved. I've been worried sick! He's fine. We didn't call the police. Do you think we should call them now?"

"Not yet. I'm working on something here and will call you soon." He then spoke to Spencer, who repeated how relieved he was that Devan was safe and sound.

"Was the event traumatic for Devan?" Cameron asked.

"Actually, no. In fact, something they may not have known, but Devan is so smart that he can recognize who did it if the police can show him suspects."

"I must warn you of something," Cameron said. "A man named Uto is involved. He must be related to your Tadashi

Uto. Do not confide any further in Tadashi Uto." The call ended. He turned to Faint Chance, "So now it's done. The kidnapping is over. Devan is safe. But now it's payback time, for the chief's life, and for what Uto and his accomplices have done."

☙☙

The next morning, Cameron put the heroin that was in two plastic bags into a shopping bag. They hailed a tuk-tuk to a spot down the street from the Manoluk Hotel. The hotel was a two-story building of white stucco. It sat back from the street forty feet, separated by a flower garden with short palms. It had balconies trimmed in teak. There was a small, circular drive in front.

There was a row of some little shops across the street. One shop was a little stall, with a rack of sundry items in it. Behind was a lady with an infant in her arms. The store had a modest inventory of things like toothpaste, tissue, combs, chewing gum, candy, soaps, and things like that. The lady behind the counter was moving about, bouncing the infant up and down to keep the infant from crying. Next to that was another shop, farther away from the hotel, that appeared to be a new business. Some fellow was bringing in cardboard boxes off the back of a motorbike. Another man was inside organizing things. There were boxes in the shop not yet opened.

Cameron and Faint Chance discussed hiding in the new shop, behind the boxes to wait and see if Uto would leave, as from there they could clearly see the front of his hotel.

Faint Chance asked the man unloading the boxes if the two of them might wait inside there for a while. He agreed and left for another load. They went around behind boxes in the front that formed stacks four and five feet high, which provided cover as they watched the hotel entrance.

They waited for an hour, with the young man returning

twice more with additional boxes tied on the back of his motorbike. Cameron noticed the boxes contained small appliances, as one was opened and had an electric fan in it. It was a small appliance shop, and the owner or someone working for him was bringing in the appliances to set up to sell.

"There he is," exclaimed Faint Chance, the first to see him.

Uto walked out in front of the hotel, looking around, smoking. He did not seem to be in any hurry to go any-where. Cameron and Faint Chance ducked in tightly behind the appliance boxes, spreading two of them ever so slightly so as to just barely be able to see through the crack, Camer-on on top and she below. All the while the man unloading boxes was curiously looking on. After Uto had smoked half his cigarette, he raised his arm to a passing tuk-tuk. Uto spoke to the driver, which took a while, no doubt for the difficulty in explaining where to go with the language barrier. He then climbed in the back of the tuk-tuk, and they drove off.

"So far, so good," Cameron said.

Once Uto was out of sight, they came out from behind the boxes with the man inside now quite puzzled as to just what they were hiding from.

As they approached the hotel, Cameron said, "We know his room, number twelve. Let's just walk in deliberately like we are staying there. The morning desk operator will assume we came in last night, or are perhaps meeting someone. Just look like we know where we are going."

The entry was handsome teak. Just inside to the left was a wide spiral staircase leading to the second floor. It was only a two story hotel. Opposite the staircase on the first floor was the reception desk. Cameron took Faint Chance's hand, made an abrupt turn to the stairs, and led her up as though they were going to their room. Up the spiral stairs, there was a huge sitting area, with teak floors. It was appar-ently for parties or gatherings. There were windows on the arched stucco openings on the two outside walls, but no glass. Rain was kept out by an overhanging roof. Against one inside wall was a huge bar, but no one was there. Behind the bar were cabinets with locked glass sliding doors in front of various liquors the hotel was displaying, but only one bottle of each.

They went into the sitting area near the outside windows and sat on a couch from where they could see outside the front of the hotel through the open window.

As time passed, Cameron began to get anxious that Uto might return. They could not be seen by him, or he would know something was wrong—he would realize they knew who he was, and his plans would no doubt change.

Finally, a cleaning lady came along pushing a cart full of towels, soaps, and things for the room. A mop was carried in front of it, and there were brushes in a bucket. She went right on in number twelve, leaving the cart partly in the doorway so as to keep it open from shutting and locking.

"Get her out of the area somehow for a minute or longer if you can," Cameron said.

Faint Chance went to the room, stood at the door, and said to the cleaning lady that she was waiting for some hotel guests, and needed to use a bathroom. The maid told her about a bathroom on the first floor, but Faint Chance acted like she could not understand where it was and asked if the maid would show her. The maid said yes and led her down the spiral steps toward the first floor lobby area.

Cameron had to move quickly. He jumped to his feet and quickly entered the room. Inside on a luggage stand was a soft bag, already packed. There were a few articles of clothing not in the bag on a chair.

In the bottom was a pair of jeans that were soiled and rolled up. Apparently, Uto had not given these to the laundry, not knowing when and how quickly he might have to move. Since Uto was leaving tomorrow, he would not be giving these for laundry, or he would have done so by now. It looked like a good place to stash the heroin. Cameron took out the packages of heroin and put one each of the two small plastic bags in the front pockets of the dirty jeans. He rolled the jeans back up and replaced them as they were.

He hurried quickly out of the room, and as he did, he could hear someone coming. The cleaning lady had returned. He walked right by her, trying to look natural. He went over to the wall adjacent to where he had been sitting, which had a window facing the front of the hotel overlooking the courtyard and street.

Uto was getting out of a tuk-tuk. He must have decided to turn around for some reason.

Cameron quickly ran to the steps, taking them two and three at a time, only slowing as he came in sight of the front desk so as not to attract attention. He asked the female clerk at the desk, "Where is the bathroom?"

She pointed to a hallway just past the elevator. There was a turn in the hallway, just before the bathrooms.

He went into the bathroom, even though it was marked for women, and found Faint Chance. "Uto is coming," he told her softly.

They hid just behind the door, listening.

Uto came to the front desk, and they could hear him ask, "Any messages for number twelve or for Uto?"

"No, sir," the clerk said.

Uto went to the steps and climbed on up. Cameron and Faint Chance walked at a fast pace outside, turned left, and began walking down the street trying to look normal, although their gait was really too fast to be normal to a cautious observer.

There was nothing more to do about the retaliation for the moment, according to Cameron's plan. "Lunch?" he asked.

Chapter 37

The next morning at ten a.m., Cameron and Faint Chance returned to their hotel room after breakfast to use the hotel phone. Faint Chance called her girl friend at SilkAir to make sure the plane to Singapore was on schedule.

"Everything is on schedule," Faint Chance reported.

Cameron dialed the hotel desk and took the piece of paper he got from the SilkAir office the day before. "I want you to call this number in the country of Singapore," he said and gave it to him.

After ten minutes, the phone rang. The clerk said to Cameron, "I have Singapore on the line for you, sir."

"Is this the Singapore Government Customs Office at the Changi International Airport?"

On the other end, the person who spoke English, a comfort to Cameron. "Yes. It is. How may I help you, sir?"

"I do not wish to be identified, and so I prefer not to give you my name," Cameron said. "This is an anonymous tip, but a very good one."

"Yes, sir, we welcome anonymous tips," the customs official said. "What is it you have to report?"

"En route at this time to your country is a Japanese man named Morio Uto, traveling to Singapore on SilkAir from Vientiane, Lao. He's on SilkAir Flight Number Two. It left

Vientiane at nine-thirty this morning, Lao time, which was thirty minutes ago. He will be arriving in two hours in Singapore, at the Changi Terminal. He is in his late twenties. His passport is Japanese." Cameron read off the number he got from the girlfriend at SilkAir. "He is smuggling into Singapore over a pound of pure heroin. It's in his jean pockets, rolled up inside his bag. He's a dangerous gangster and drug trafficker."

The customs officer on the other end wrote down all the details. "We thank you for this tip. Can you give us a description of the man?"

"He is Japanese, five feet, six inches tall, with dark, medium length hair. He's traveling alone. He has a broken arm in a sling."

"Very good, sir," the customs official said. "I'll make the alert."

Cameron hung up the receiver and turned to Faint Chance with a sense of accomplishment.

"Why did you wait to turn him in to the authorities in Singapore, instead of here?" Faint Chance asked.

"Don't you know about the Singapore Government and drugs?"

"No, but I heard about some stewardesses that were executed for bringing in drugs to Singapore. But won't he tell them that the heroin was not his, and that someone put it in his bag without his knowledge?"

"Sure," Cameron answered. "But then all the smugglers say that. No one admits to it. He's obviously a gangster, and he will never be able to convince the Singapore Government that he did not know about it. The Singapore Government is known for not making exceptions in drug smuggling cases. He will be hung within six months. It's a sure thing."

Chapter 38

The SilkAir jet flew en route over Thailand and then over Malaysia on its way to Singapore. Just over Kuala Lumpur, Malaysia, the stewardess announced, "Ladies and gentlemen, we have just passed Kuala Lumpur, Malaysia. We will be landing in thirty minutes. The captain has asked me to tell you to return to your seats and prepare for landing." After a short pause, she added, "Please be advised that the laws of Singapore prohibit drugs. The penalty is death."

Uto listened to the stewardess and said to himself, "Only the stupidest guy in the world would try to smuggle drugs into Singapore."

He strutted off the plane into the modern Singapore airport terminal with a swagger. He had gotten what he came for, he thought, and was feeling good. The Oyabun would reward him handsomely with a percentage of the proceeds from the synthesized plant formula, and he would never have to work again. He thought of buying a red Ferrari. He imagined he would look very cool in Tokyo in such a car.

The automated people conveyor belt moved the passengers down the long hallways of the Singapore Changi Airport to the customs area. His baggage consisted of two carryons which he carried, with nothing checked in. The precious cargo was in one of them. At a mirror on the wall next to the conveyor belt, he checked himself out to see if he looked as cool as usual. With a quick fix of the hair, he satisfied himself that he did and put on his sunglasses.

At the first check, the passport checkpoint, there were several of the numerous stations staffed with personnel. Several anxious Singaporeans got ahead of him, and he stood in line patiently to have his Japanese passport chopped.

When it was his turn, an attractive Indian female official in a uniform shirt with epaulets took his passport. She ran it through the computer scanner and waited. On her screen appeared a warning visual signal, designed not to be seen by or alert the person entering the country. She saw it and nonchalantly pushed a hidden button with her knee that no one could see. "Please go to the customs area with your bags for inspection, sir," the pretty Indian official said.

Instead of the usual white card, she put in a light pink card into his Japanese passport, and its length made it stick out of the passport, such that it could be seen ahead of him as he held it.

Six police were already waiting ahead, standing in the general path of the incoming passengers.

Nearby in a room were ten more airport police waiting, drinking sugared coffees and teas. Due to the almost total absence of crime in Singapore, whenever a pre-known criminal event was to occur, an abundance of police were always available and came out for the crime as though they had no other, which was basically true. A buzzer rang in the room.

One of six standing officers held out his arm with his neatly white-gloved hand pointing over to the section for inspections, as opposed to the section that permitted people to go through on their honor that they had nothing to declare.

All of the rest of ten officers came out and went to the customs inspection area. They covered the exits so as to block any attempt to escape. Several slowly moved closely in toward Uto, but not so much as to let him know he was their target for an arrest, just yet.

"Place your bags up here, sir," the attending customs inspector told Uto. Uto hoisted his bags up on the examining bench. "Please open your bags, sir," the polite customs inspector said.

"Sure," Uto said.

"Have you anything to declare, sir?"

"No."

The customs officer took out several articles of clothing, some soiled, and began leafing through them. He came upon the plastic bag of the Baron's exotic purple and orange tea leaves, and held it up. "What is this, sir?"

Uto, experienced at crime, without any change in expression nonchalantly said, "That's an herbal remedy for a certain pain. You mix it in hot water and drink it."

The Chinese, the predominate race in Singapore, took all sorts of such remedies, Uto recalled, and it would not seem unusual to the customs official that someone would travel with such a potion. Uto thought there would be no way the customs officer would have any problem with some plant leaves, which might very well be thought by the Chinese to be a herbal remedy. The customs officer set it aside, to determine later what it actually was.

The customs officer looked further. He came to mud soiled jeans, rolled up. He looked in the front pockets, where he had been told to look. Out of each front pocket came a bag of white powder. He held them up high for the other armed officers in the room to see.

Uto's eyes opened wide as he stared in amazement. He said, in high panic, "Those are not mine!"

All of the officers moved in and surrounded Uto. Uto looked about to see if escape was possible, but realized it was useless.

Chapter 39

Cameron had the plant, and Devan was returned to his worried parents. With the Singapore Police holding Uto, no doubt thinking he had the plant with him in Singapore, there were now a few days available for a short holiday before returning to America with his precious cargo.

And with Faint Chance. Which was more precious?

Cameron walked to the American Embassy. Inside, he approached the counter. "I must have a temporary visa for a Lao citizen to come to America. Whatever it takes. The person has already applied for a permanent visa some months ago, so it should be no problem."

The lady behind the counter, Asian but English speaking, said, "Did you say the person has already applied for immigration?"

"Yes. Not long ago. So, it should be no problem to get her over early. I'm here to take her back."

"Oh, sir, I'm afraid you have been operating under a misconception. Once a person has applied for immigration and is waiting for papers, Immigration will not grant a tourist visa. They find that people who enter America in that manner tend to stay if the immigration visa is not granted."

"What? Just because she has applied to come in permanently, now she can't come early as a tourist where she might have otherwise?"

"I'm afraid that is the case, sir. I'm sorry."

"What else can be done? I must have this person in America right away. How long should it take? Months? Years? I can't wait for that. I want the person to come over right away."

"You and many millions of others, all over the world, sir. I'm sorry. But as much as I would like to help you, it is not the embassy that makes these judgments, but the Department of Immigration and Naturalization in America. I believe that you may have had an unrealistic idea of this Lao citizen coming to the US. There are quotas, and frankly, I would not depend on her coming for quite some time. It could take a long time, and there is no guarantee at all. I want to be candid with you. And there have been several changes in immigration policy recently, so it is much more difficult to get a visa. It could take a very long time, even years."

Cameron remained silent and motionless like a statue for what seemed to be the longest time, and then he said, "Thank you. I appreciate your help."

Down and out, he walked very slowly back toward the hotel. What had happened? He concluded that Spencer and Candice were misinformed about her chances of coming over soon. Years? Never? He concluded that was not acceptable. The idea of just going back home to architecture and forgetting Faint Chance was not an acceptable option.

෬෯෬෯

Later, after her work, Faint Chance came to the hotel room. She came in with a smile but sensed something was wrong. Cameron had a very sober expression that telegraphed bad news.

"I'm afraid I have some very bad news. I'll not be able

to take you back with me. And worse, they told me at the embassy that your visa is not certain. There has been a change in immigration policy to curb immigration to America. It'll take a long time at best. However, I'll go to work on it when I get home, and see what I can do from there. There must be something I can do."

Her eyes watered, and then turned to tears. "It was all really too good to be true. I won't get to come to America, after all. It is my karma to live and die here. The wonders of the West are not to come to me."

"I'll not lie to you or mislead you. When I get back, I hope to find a way, but I don't know what to do from here."

Faint Chance sat down quietly, her hopes of magical future in a mystical foreign land all gone, and she wept. And wept.

Chapter 40

Two days later, Uto was allowed to make a limited number of supervised calls in order to assist in his defense from the Changi prison where he was being detained, pending his court date in Singapore. He called the Oyabun on a special number the given him by the Oyabun for such calls.

Uto knew he was being monitored in Singapore, but he felt that he could communicate his message without compromising himself. He explained where he was and then said frantically, "Someone planted heroin in my luggage. I'm in big trouble and in the Changi Prison. Can you get me out?"

"Not out of Singapore," the Oyabun answered. "I'll send money to a barrister for you. That's all I can do. What happened to the thing you were supposed to bring?" He did not mention anything by name or description, so as not to alert anyone listening.

"All I know is what I have been told me by the police in interrogation sessions. I'm told that I bought in with me over a pound of pure heroine and also some Oolong tea!"

"Oolong tea? What are you talking about? Tea?"

"That is what the police have told me. Pure heroin and Oolong tea."

"Do you think that the American and the girl still have the item?" the Oyabun said.

"Well, I can't do anything to find out here in the Changi prison!"

"Leave an instruction to give your things to this person." He gave the name of a courier. He wondered if he could get the tea turned over to him as part of the personal belongings of a condemned man, in case the tea might be the plant. Uto was as good as toasted history.

"Is there anything you can do for me?" Uto pleaded.

"Singapore does not allow bail in such cases—" the Oyabun answered, "—where there is a death penalty. And, the Singapore government is not open to influence."

"But I'm innocent," Uto pleaded.

"Maybe you can convince them of that. But everyone caught in Singapore at the airport says that, and all of them have been hung in six months. I'll send money for your barrister. And, if there is anyone you want money to go to, let me know."

That was the tradition with the gangsters and the Oyabun, to provide some assistance to any family. But Uto had no wife or children, only a brother in the US.

Chapter 41

Cameron awoke at daybreak. He called room service on the hotel phone, but no one answered, as it was still too early for the restaurant in the small hotel to be staffed. He wondered what it was that made it impossible to get someone into America. He would have to go home without her. Time would pass, maybe years. He would lose her. He moped about the room, trying not to wake her up.

He looked at her in bed, innocently sleeping. She owned nothing, apart from her hope chest. At least now she had her hope chest restored. Some dowry! The richest men in the world would want her for making a special offspring. Perhaps if he became rich, he might gain the influence to get the government to allow her to come? But how long would that take? Years?

He sat at the table and began organizing his passport, tickets, and papers, tossing things he did not need into the wicker trash basket. As he organized the nearly useless Lao Kip money, he came upon the wooden card of the Baron Von Limbach. Cameron looked at it intently, remembering the dandy from Chiang Rai. The impressive card had writings on both sides in many languages.

Then he remembered. The Baron said he would be at his Vientiane office at this time for his teak and tea exporting. Maybe he might know someone who could give them some help. It was worth a try, and, it was not as if he had other options.

Overly anxious, at eight a.m., he phoned the Baron's office, and someone answered A receptionist said only that he was not in. Cameron asked when, but she would not give his schedule. After a time of pleading for an audience, he was able to convince her that he was someone that the Baron might talk to. She agreed to phone him.

In an hour, she phoned back and said that the Baron would see him at nine-thirty a.m.

He went over to the bed where Faint Chance was sleeping. "Faint Chance. Wake up. There's someone I want you to meet."

જ⌒જ⌒

Cameron and Faint Chance wore their best clothes, however modest, and headed out to Baron Von Limbach's Lao office. There was light rain, and they walked there under an umbrella loaned by the hotel.

The Baron's office was in a single-story commercial trade building, trimmed inside in teak, very handsome with old fashioned high ceilings. The reception was not overly large, and had only a single, secretary/receptionist.

She looked at them to see what they wanted, sizing them up. Cameron surmised that she could handle simple communications in several languages, working for the master linguist Baron. So, he spoke English, rather than have Faint Chance use Lao. "I'm Cameron Harrington, and this is Faint Chance—I mean Sangmouane Sayasithsena. We would like to see the Baron von Limbach."

"Will the Baron know what this is about?" she asked in absolutely perfect English with a slight British accent.

"No, but he knows me. Tell him I'm the architect he met in Chiang Rai. Cameron Harrington."

She picked up a phone and announced them. In just moments, the Baron came through the door dressed in a very smart dark-gray, three-piece, silk-and-wool suit with discrete, dark-red pinstripes.

"What a pleasure. I'm so glad you came to see me. Please, come in. Mr. Harrington, you must tell me, just who is this beautiful woman?" He led them into his office and closed the doors.

"This is Sangmouane Sayasithsena, who lives here in Vientiane. But her name is so hard to pronounce, she was given a nickname by my brother and sister-in-law who met her recently. We call her Faint Chance."

She bowed politely.

"Hah, hah." The Baron laughed out loud. "Faint Chance. What an outrageously lovely name. I love it!"

His office inside was considerably larger than it appeared from the reception area. His desk was huge and ornate, as was the furniture. The room was had an additional table, a round one, for meetings. He motioned for them to sit in front of his desk.

Seeing Cameron look about, the Baron said, "This is just a modest office I keep here for what little business I do in Lao. You might be pleased to know that I have incorporated your ideas into the new house in Chiang Rai and set the locals on making your changes. I told them they can put their little turned up tips on the roof wherever they want, so long as they incorporate your ideas. You are a genius! If I ever build anything again, I'll first call you."

"You are too kind," Cameron said. "I would be honored to have a chance to do something substantial for you one day. But I'm taking the liberty of calling on you for a favor."

"Certainly. You need only ask."

"Faint Chance has applied to immigrate to the United States. She had met my brother and his wife, both research doctors, last year, and they want her to come to the United States to live with them. They have offered to be her sponsors and set in motion the immigration application. It was thought, or at least they thought, that it would only take a few months to get things done. But that turns out not to be the case. In fact, it turns out that it may not even happen, or, if it does, it could take years. Now I'm here, and I want to bring her back to live with me before her papers come through for immigration. So, I tried to get her an entry visa. I confess I have a personal attraction for her."

It was the first time that he had announced in front of her his affection and his intentions. She looked at him, but said nothing, listening politely.

"I went to the American Embassy," he continued, "and I was told that now, since she has applied for immigration, she cannot get a tourist or other visa and will have to wait until her papers come through. Further, I was told that the papers might never come through. The US is tightening up on its immigration policies, especially with all the terrorist threats."

"My, oh my. This is a very popular girl." The Baron chuckled. "It seems everyone wants her." He looked at her, "What is your secret, my dear?"

She just smiled.

What a coincidence that he should ask such a question? Cameron thought. *If he only knew. She holds the secret to the next step in human evolution. And now, she has the most valuable secret in the world. What super rich man would not take her, if not for her charm, but to have the smartest child in the world? Yet, the Baron must bargain with people from all over the world, and must see that there is something special about Faint Chance. Can he really detect that she has a secret?*

"You travel so much," Cameron said. "I thought you might know someone who would be able to help. And, so here we are. Here is her correct name." He passed a paper to the Baron with her correct name on it and date of birth.

"Well now, I just might. Let's see." The Baron leaned over to an old fashioned, leather-bound personal phone directory on his desk. "Ah, yes, here." He picked up a phone and called a contact. "Hi. Baron Von Limbach here. How have you been?...I've been wonderful too. Say, I have a request. A very good friend of mine from America is trying to get a visa for a Lao girl. They're here now in my office. It seems that she has been turned down since she has already applied for immigration not too long ago. Can you fix that? Here's the spelling of her name and date of birth." He read it aloud.

The Baron looked at Faint Chance as he spoke. It was obvious that he was also taken by her, with her looks and emerald-green eyes, and that he was wondering just what other secrets or charms she possessed.

The Baron listened and, after only a minute or slightly more, he said, "Wonderful. I'm obliged. Yes, I'll tell her to go to the American Embassy tomorrow after lunch. Everything will be there, right? Good. I can't thank you enough."

Cameron was speechless. He had never experienced such influence. A person at the embassy said she wanted to help but could not do so as the Department of Immigration had to handle the matter, and that department was in the United States with no office in Lao. And months or years would pass at best. But one call from this powerful Baron fixed it all.

"So, all you have to do is to go to the American Embassy tomorrow after lunch," the Baron said, "and you will be given an unrestricted, multiple entry visa without limitation. Will that be satisfactory?"

Blown away, Cameron said in a squeamish voice, "I'm your architect for life at no charge."

"Now, now, what are friends for? It was nothing. Well now—" The Baron looked at his watch. "—you must excuse me. I'm preparing for a meeting with some Lao Government officials in just minutes. And, I'm afraid, I'm leaving the day after tomorrow, early, so I'll not have time to entertain you. Perhaps next trip? Or you might catch me at one of my other offices, on the card."

"Baron, I shall always be in your debt. And Faint Chance as well."

And with that, the Baron stood. Cameron and Faint Chance respected the Baron by standing.

Faint Chance bowed to him with her most humble, deep, bow, hands in prayer. "Mr. Baron," she said. "Sir, you have changed my life, and I'll always carry you each day in my prayers." Her eyes watered as she spoke.

She looked at Cameron, and he nodded, knowing what she wanted to do, which was decidedly non-Laotian. She went to the Baron and put her arms around him, squeezing him, completely out of place for Lao women, and kissed him on his cheek.

The Baron was startled at such display of affection from an Lao woman, but enjoyed it. He composed himself and said, "It was nothing, really. I'm pleased to be able to help my architect and such a beautiful girl who is in extremely high demand."

On the way out, an older Lao man in a gray suit, was waiting just outside his door. The Baron said hello to him in Lao.

Behind them was a younger man, an assistant to the older and, and then, in turn, two armed soldiers in uniform.

The Baron went toward the door, his older friend beside them, talking. The two soldiers fell in behind.

Outside were six additional solders, standing on either side of the entry. Waiting was an armored limousine, another military car behind it, and a dozen motorcyclist soldiers.

They got into the limousine and drove off, the additional car and the motorcycles following.

As Cameron and Faint Chance walked away from the building, Faint Chance said to Cameron, "He is not selling teak and teas. That older man is the Lao Minister of Defense."

"The Baron must be an arms merchant," Cameron said, only now beginning to grasp the incredible influence he just experienced.

ᘒᘓᘒ

They went to her friend at SilkAir and booked tickets all the way to the US. Cameron was so elated by the experience that he decided to pay for first class. And, she had never flown anywhere, so it had to be as good as he could possibly provide.

On the return to the hotel, he had her bring them to a shop that sold spices. Cameron said to Faint Chance while holding up a glass jar of dry spices, "One cannot bring plants or fruits into America. So, we must crush up the plant leaves, and put them in something like this. Let's take it to the hotel."

Outside the hotel, he dumped the spice in the jar in the gutter. Inside, he washed and dried it and then put the special leaves inside the jar. "Customs will think this is spice. If they knew it was a plant, they would confiscate it and destroy it. Can you imagine, after all the effort to get it to have it dumped out by cretins at customs?"

"Will they let me bring in my northern *Lao-Lao*?" she asked. "It's very important to me."

"Yes, we can bring in two bottles each of anything, but for the life of me I cannot imagine why you want to bring that bowel obstruction and liver bile mix to America. One would think you would want to use up your two bottle quota with XO brandy, Johnny Walker Blue Label, or something normally expensive that you can get without duty."

"It's very special to me."

Cameron wrote off trying to convince her that she should buy some fancy liquor with her two bottle quota and let her waste it on what she wanted.

"What is a cretin?" Faint Chance then asked.

"Another name for a government employee," Cameron answered.

ᘒᘓᘒ

In the dark of night, a man in dark clothes approached the Harrington home, walking low in a stooped position. He went around the house until he found the telephone utility box. From a satchel, he removed a small box, several inches square. It was painted white to match the color of the house, and unless someone knowledgeable looked closely, it looked like an additional utility box from the phone company. He fastened it with two-sided tape to the house, and secured it with a screw. He then connected the wires to the phone service. The sophisticated device monitored the two lines of household, and had a lithium battery charged from the line voltage which would continue to work uninterrupted if there was a power outage. It connected the residence phone service to an internal mobile phone, such that when anyone called in or out, the cell was activated to relay the number and monitor it over a mobile transmitter to a person working for the Oyabun.

In a nearby motel room, two Japanese men sat with a special receiver which heard everything on the Harrington phone line via the transmitter they hooked up to the Harrington phone line on the side of their house. A Japanese man phoned the Oyabun.

"Everything is in place, sir," he said in Japanese.

"I want to know anything said about a plant or the brother, Cameron Harrington, coming back to America as soon as it is said, and if important, at any hour."

"Yes, sir. Just as soon as we hear anything, we shall call you, day or night."

Chapter 42

This is south Indian food," the Tamil Indian, second adoptive father of Faint Chance, said to Cameron. "It's spicier than that of the north. How do you find it?"

Cameron sat at the farewell dinner in Faint Chance's family home. His mouth was burning from the spices. "Very tasty. With all this spice, you don't need to eat as much to be satisfied. Mrs. Dorasamy, what are these gastronomic delights?"

"I'm so glad you like them. Please call me Janu," her mother said, now sitting after serving the various curries. She wore a traditional Indian sari, a colorful outfit that left a portion between the lower part and the top part bare, and the end of the cloth flowing over the shoulder. "That is Meen curry, which is fish curry," she said, pointing. "This one is idli, which is rice cake to dip in the curry. This one is sambar, which is a south Indian vegetable lentil curry. This one is mutton dalcha, which is mutton ribs in coconut curry and lentils. This is chicken briyani, which is rice baked with chicken and spices. This one is murtabak, which is wheat flour bread stuffed with lamb and peas. Sangmouane made part of these and helped prepare the others. She will be able to make these in America, and make a husband very happy."

Cameron thought about that and looked at Faint Chance. They smiled at one another. She wore an Indian sari that evening, as opposed to her usual tubular *sinh* dress. Cameron could not help but fixate how utterly sexy she looked in the flowing form of the sari, her stomach bare. Her sari was dark blue, with magenta, orange, white and light blue flowers, and she wore it so well.

"Please call me Krishnan," her adoptive father said. "We are beyond sad to see our lovely Sangmouane leave us. But her happiness will be ours as well, as we want her so much to be able to migrate to America. We migrated here from south India, from Madras. We would have migrated to America, but it was impossible for us to consider. We could not get visas as we did not have the money,"

Cameron became aware of the magnitude of numbers of how many truly wonderful and deserving people wanted, and want, to come to the US, but could not. "She will be able to return to visit you," he said. "And, I invite you and your wife to come to America to visit her. The tickets will be my gift to you."

"Oh, my! We would be so honored to come," Krishnan said.

"Will you please take very good care of our only daughter?" Janu pleaded. "She is grown up now, but she will always be our little Sangmouane."

"You have my promise," Cameron assured them.

After dinner, Janu and Faint Chance cleared the table, and Krishnan gathered everyone in the family room. He produced a jewelry box about a foot long. Opening it, he took out an intricately designed woman's chain of twenty-four karat gold. Attached to it was a locket of two inches in diameter, made of intricately woven strands of tiny gold thread, woven in a pattern of loops and turns in several layers in an incredibly beautiful art taking hundreds of hours of work. It was obviously a very old piece from India. The necklace chain was equally interesting, consisting of little Indian swastikas, a quarter inch square each, laced in-between with elaborate designs of twenty-four karat gold as well. These were swastikas ages before Hitler discovered the figure.

Faint Chance took the locket from her father, and put it on her neck. She knew it was his only family heirloom, and the importance of his giving it to her overwhelmed her. She began to cry, went to him, and hugged him with tears in her eyes. "I will not need the locket to think of you." And then she went to her mother and hugged and kissed her. "Or you."

Then her mother's eyes teared as well. Their daughter was now fully mature and making her decision to leave the nest. It was her choice to go to the other side of the Earth for a better life, and they wondered if they would see her again.

"Now stop that, or you'll have us all crying," Krishnan said.

Cameron could see Krishnan's eyes watering also. It was such a scene that Cameron shed a tear himself.

Later, Faint Chance went to the bathroom to dry her tears. In the private way of Asians over personal matters, she took out the small bag of the *ton mai piiset* that the chief had given her for her wedding. The new locket was just right for holding those leaves, and she put them in it. She put the chain and locket around her neck, and looked at it in the mirror. Now she had combined her heirlooms from both of her adoptive parents into one, a perfect match. She would be able to remember them both and pray for them at the same time by holding the locket. She held the locket in her hand, squeezing it, and said a prayer for the slain chief before going back to the others.

൭൭൭

Faint Chance brought her things to the hotel as it had been agreed that they would leave from there, and her parents would meet them at the airport for the parting good-bye. She had only two bags of clothes and things, as that was all she owned.

Cameron held up the *ton mai piiset* in the spice jar. "I'll put this in my carry-on. If asked, remember that this is spice as it says on the label on the jar. Candice and Spencer said customs at the US will confiscate any plants. One cannot bring plants into America for fear of medflies and similar insects."

"What is medfly?"

"It's a nasty little insect that can ruin a whole fruit crop of a huge area."

"Is it as bad as those insects with the blue bump we killed at the bottom of the tree?"

"Well, the medfly kills crops, not people. Spices in containers don't have medflies, and customs will allow spices. Only plants and fresh fruits have medfies, so we should be okay with the plant in a spice jar."

The hotel room phone rang, and Cameron answered. "Spencer."

"Cameron. How is everything?"

"Wonderful. I was able to get Faint Chance a visa. She'll be coming with me tomorrow. We'll fly to Bangkok then to Tokyo for a layover and then home. Let me give you the flight numbers and information. But I have more great news. We were able to switch the plant leaves with the bandit and now have them back again. We put them in a spice jar."

ຕາຕາ

"Sir, I have just heard the schedule for the return of Cameron Harrington," the Japanese man in a private office across town from the Harrington home said over a radio phone connection to the Oyabun. He gave him the flight information. "He's traveling with the Laotian girl. They have the real plant leaves in a spice jar."

"Excellent," the Oyabun exclaimed. "They'll be in Tokyo at the Narita Airport for a two hour layover. Good
work. Continue to monitor for any changes."
"Yes, sir."

Chapter 43

Although the sun only shone through the clouds the next morning for a short while in a break in the rain, it was the saddest and yet at the same time the most exciting day for her ever. She had to say goodbye to her parents and friends but also entered the dream of her life to migrate to America where she understood was the land of so many wonderful things.

Her Indian parents and thirty of her friends all came to the airport. Teary, parting goodbyes were made as they headed for the jet that would take them to their first stop, Bangkok. Cameron had in his bag the spice jar containing the *ton mai piiset* disguised as a spice. Faint Chance had in hers two bottles of northern *Lao-Lao*. Cameron continued to be perplexed by her insistence at bringing to America such a potion, as she might have brought back some good stuff duty free instead of liver bile from a bladder of a cancer patient mixed with battery acid.

Faint Chance sat at the window and waved furiously at her friends as the jet rolled out down the taxiway.

After arriving at Bangkok, Cameron went to Thai Airlines ticket counter to check in. They were to fly to Tokyo, with a layover of two hours there, and then on to America.

When the big 747 was ready, they heard the announcement in the first class lounge. To the front of the plane they went, enjoying the royal treatment of boarding before the masses.

"Champagne?" the pretty Thai stewardess asked holding a tray of it already poured into tall champagne glasses.

They both said, "Yes."

Soon it took off, a little late, during which Faint Chance squeezed Cameron's hand tightly, as she was still afraid of the takeoff. Cameron went to the magazine section and looked for a paper in English. It had been some time since he had any news from the US, which was rather nice, considering the provincial nature of US news.

Cameron picked up the *Straits Times*, the Singapore newspaper, from the newspapers and magazines available to the first class passengers in the newspaper rack. Returning to his seat, he saw an interesting article on the second page.

"Let me read you something of interest. 'Yesterday at Court Twenty-Six of the District Mentions Court of the Subordinate Courts of Havelock Square, a Mr. Morio Uto, of Tokyo, Japan, was charged with trafficking diamorphine. Trafficking of more than fifteen grams of diamorphine is an offense of Section Five of the Misuse of Drugs Act, Chapter One-Eight-Five, and carries a mandatory death penalty. Mr. Uto was arrested at the Changi Airport, entering Singapore from Vientiane, Laos, on SilkAir last week. In his possession were point-seven kilograms of pure heroin. Trial is set in forty days at the High Court. The accused is held without bail. The trial is not expected to be a prolonged one. There has not been such a large quantity of heroin seized in Singapore for twenty-five years.' Revenge is sweet," he said.

They smiled at each other and kissed.

Chapter 44

Narita Airport at Tokyo was as busy as usual. International travelers in transit use the portion of the terminal that didn't require them to go through customs. First class passengers were entitled to go up the small elevator to the lounge that overlooked the airport while they waited in transit with free drinks and refreshments of the first class lounge. Cameron had his carryon bag with the special contents.

Neither of them noticed an unusually huge man who followed them into the lounge, using a first class club pass of the Oyabun for entry. He was six feet, resembling a very large Sumo Wrestler, and, most notably, without any discernable trace of neck.

They showed their tickets to the pretty girls behind the entry table and were invited in. A seating table near a window looked good, and Cameron put their carryon bag down in a vacant seat next to them. "Let's have a drink, what do you think?" he said with a smile.

"What are you going to have?"

"Vodka, rocks?" he said.

"Make it two," she said.

Cameron went over to the liquor table, and poured two. He looked over and saw Faint Chance standing, having moved over to the windows to watch pensively all the planes, coming from or going to places that she had no knowledge of, mesmerizing just to watch.

Cameron brought the drinks over and gave her one as she stood. She continued to look out the window at the jets. "Imagine, all those jets going all over the world to so many exciting places. I'll bet there are many places to go that I have not heard of."

Cameron looked back to the seat with his carryon bag and noticed the strangely-shaped, huge man hesitating near where his bag had been placed. He looked too big to sit in one of the waiting area seats, as those had armrests narrower than he. Cameron put the vodka bottle down and looked up again.

Kubi Nashi had picked up Cameron's carry-on bag with the plant inside.

He was heading for the toilet, holding Cameron's bag. Cameron darted quickly to go after him. Kubi Nashi went into the toilet that was part of and for the first class passengers who were in the club.

The door closed in front of Cameron. He pushed it open and went in to face Kubi Nashi, who was rifling through Cameron's carryon bag with the plant. He had found the spice jar and determined that was the plant. He put it in his suit coat pocket.

Cameron charged Kubi Nashi head on, hitting him with his head in the midsection. The charge drove the monster back against the wall, but did not so much as faze Kubi Nashi. He picked Cameron up by the waist and threw him to one side, where he hit a toilet stall door so hard the door broke. Cameron was knocked to the floor, barely conscious.

Kubi Nashi hurried out of the men's room at a fast walk down the hall to a security door and staircase to a restricted area on the first floor, where a previously well-bribed airport worker was waiting to open the door for him. He went down into the restricted, cargo loading area, and was escorted to a loading van for packages.

He got into the back of the van, the doors closed, and

they drove off. His escape had been well orchestrated and well-greased with bribes.

Cameron was awake, but hurting. A concerned looking Japanese business man was holding his head up from behind.

Then Cameron realized what had happened. He sat up and felt a sharp pain in his head and neck. He slowly looked around. Lying on the floor was his bag, open, and his things strewn all about.

He collected his things, but could not find the spice bottle. The monster knew what he wanted. He must be connected to Uto and the kidnapers.

Cameron laid back on the floor, still dizzy.

Someone went for a policeman. In the Japanese police tradition, the cop had on a white policemen's hat and white gloves. Faint Chance was looking for Cameron and came into the men's room as well. A few men were gathering about, looking. Soon a medical team of three people showed up and began to fuss over him, checking his pulse, looking in his eyes, observing.

Cameron declined any medical attention and stood up. The policeman requested that he follow him to a room, and Faint Chance followed. A policeman who spoke English appeared, and asked what happened.

Cameron recounted the event, making no reference to his special cargo. When asked what may have been stolen, he replied "Spice. That is all." He considered that saying that the bandit just took the plant that would alter man's future was probably not a good idea.

The policeman told the other two in the room in Japanese, and they all chuckled, as though it was no crime at all. They assumed that since no valuables were stolen, it was hardly a major crime. But they were concerned that the security of a passenger was threatened, and airport security breached. They took information, and let Cameron and Faint Chance leave.

There was still time to make the flight. "We might as

well go on back to the flight," he said to her. "I don't think we are ever going to see the plant leaves again. We could try to go back to Lao for more, but that would be another ordeal, that we would have to set it up again. I only saw one other plant growing on the cliff when I was there. And I don't think the new chief would welcome us coming for more plant after causing his father to be killed and us having to reveal that others already want the plant, and we were unable to so much as get it to the United States. He might just have us killed as he almost did before. You are en route to your new home in America. It's time to look ahead. Let's just go on home—that is, to your new home."

It was time to embark their flight, so they headed directly to the gate and got on the airplane.

천ల쇼

At the Oyabun's home, Kubi Nashi arrived with the bottle of *ton mai piiset*. The Oyabun had a big smile on his rough face. He had just successfully orchestrated a daring theft at Narita Airport and was proud of it.

Holding out the spice jar, Kubi Nashi proudly announced, "Here is what you wanted, sir."

The Oyabun said to them, "Excellent." The Oyabun held up the spice jar with the purple and orange leaves in it and carried it back to his study to call the scientist he had already lined up to get to work on immediately synthesizing the plant contents into a chemical that could be reproduced.

Sitting at his desk, with a gleam in his eyes, he looked up, imagining things, and said aloud, "I'm going to be the richest man in the world. And I will also have a special son by this plant to carry on my name."

Chapter 45

For the last leg of the trip to America, the loss of the plant leaves left Cameron very somber. The purpose of his mission had failed.

"Spencer and Candice the suffered the trauma of having their Devan kidnapped, and now will never realize their ultimate medical research goal. Perhaps worse, the wonderful chief has been murdered. My mission is a failure, except for making your acquaintance. Whoever has the plant leaves, probably someone in Japan, will race to make the formula to synthesize it. They will get the patent. There is a huge amount of wealth that will follow the patent, by the way, more than beyond your dreams."

Faint Chance sat quietly for a time, thinking pensively. "It's now time to tell you something. I have a secret."

"What's that?"

"To keep the powers of the plant from being taken by another, the chief left something out when he gave you the plant leaves."

"What are you talking about?"

"Do you remember when we were in the chief's home in the evening, and he wanted to speak to me alone, and you took a walk about the village without me?"

"Yes, of course."

"He predicted others would try to steal the plant leaves

and told me not to tell you about the additional ingredient needed to make it work until such time as I thought it was a proper time to do so. He was so wise to predict what would happen. And he did just that."

"He was the wisest and most interesting person I have ever met," Cameron freely admitted, in awe of the wisdom of the chief.

"Now it's time. My karma is now tied to you, and it is time for you to know. The plant leaves do not summon the spirits without an additional ingredient."

"What? We have Devan as proof that it does," Cameron retorted.

"I gave Spencer and Candice the plant leaves during the ceremony with *Lao-Lao* from the north. Do you remember visiting the lady who made the *Lao-Lao* near Ban Houei Sai?"

"Of course."

"Do you remember the special black mushroom that she used in the *Lao-Lao*?"

"Yes, I do. What about it?"

"The northern black mushroom is necessary to make the plant leaves summon the spirits. Unless it's mixed with the leaves, the leaves will do nothing. Following what I was taught to do by the chief, when I gave the plant leaves to Spencer and Candice, I gave them *Lao-Lao* from the north. It is always made with the special northern black mushroom. The black mushroom will not last long in the open, but it lasts in the alcohol of the liquor *Lao-Lao*. The chief told me to use northern *Lao-Lao* when no fresh mushroom was available."

"So all this time I have had only half the facts. That's why you wanted to use up your two bottle quota of imported liquor into the US by bringing in northern *Lao-Lao*."

She smiled. "I hope you will forgive me. But the chief made me promise not to tell as he knew others would want it dearly. Without my secret, it won't work. The chief said I could tell you at the right time. I think he knew much more about what was going to happen than us."

"So, whoever stole the plant from us will never figure out why they cannot synthesize it or make it work," Cameron said. "Whether it needs a catalyst that is a chemical, or one that is spiritual, or both, no matter. Both require the black mushroom. Whoever stole the plant will spend millions trying to figure it out and never get it. That's great justice."

She looked at him quietly. "I have an even better secret for you." She took off her gold chain with the locket on it that her Indian father had given her at the going away dinner which was a family heirloom. She put a cloth napkin on her lap, and held it carefully over it. She then opened the locket.

As she opened the gold locket, the contents revealed what was inside as though it was the Holy Grail.

Cameron's eyes opened impossibly wide as he stared in disbelief. It was filled with the purple and orange *ton mai piiset*!

He could not speak for a short while. Finally, he exclaimed, "My God!"

"Did you forget that the chief gave some to me separately for my wedding?"

"Of course. I completely forgot." Then he remembered. "But you specifically promised him that you would save these second leaves for your wedding. He might not allow you from the spiritual world to make use of these leaves except for your marriage."

"He asked the Spirits to follow the plant with us across the ocean," Faint Chance said. "The chief said to me that it only takes a little to summon the spirits. There is enough here for me and my husband as the father to be of my child, and the rest can go to Spencer and Candice to use to make more."

She closed the locket and put it back on her neck.

"The mission is saved," he exclaimed.

After a time, she looked at him sheepishly. "You don't want children, do you?"

Cameron sat back. He started to react as he normally did on the subject, with a sarcastic joke. But then he realized things had changed dramatically. Faint Chance would find a husband who wanted a child, and that would not be him. He hesitated for a time, and then said, "Well, I have always been repulsed by the thought of having to care for an infant. But I confess if I were to have a child like Devan, I might change. Would you consider marrying me if I agree to a child? We could use the gift from the chief. I would pay for your parents to fly over for the wedding. I don't want a huge wedding, as I would prefer to use the money many spend for a wedding to go toward a house or investment property."

Faint Chance became emotional, and her emerald-green eyes began to water. She bowed her head humbly, unable to speak. Too much was happening to her in her life at one time.

A young, East Indian, Singapore Airline Stewardess came by and paused when she saw Faint Chance weeping. "Is there anything the matter?"

Cameron wanted to take attention away from Faint Chance weeping. "We left Tokyo an hour late. My relatives are picking us up, and I hope they don't have to wait long. What are the latest, updated chances as to us arriving on time in the United States?"

"Sir, I don't know, but I will ask the captain." She went ahead to the captain's security door, knocked, and was admitted. She returned and leaned over the seat, "The captain says that strong, jet stream winds are blowing from behind us and will speed our arrival. As to your chances of arriving as you wish, you have *Faint Chance*."

About the Author

Brent Ayscough or Ace, as he is known to friends, retired from the practice of law and lives in a house overlooking the sea in Southern California. He has always loved machines, from airplanes to motorcycles, structural design, and other interests. He has enjoyed the acquaintance of diverse and interesting people, and is widely traveled. Bits and pieces of characters he has known, places he has been, seasoned with the spice of his imagination, help him create unusual stories and characters. Extensive collaboration with experts and sources, hopefully, make his stories credible and interesting.

www.ingramcontent.com/pod-product-compliance
Lightning Source LLC
Chambersburg PA
CBHW060943120726
47910CB00002B/468